WHAT WOULD
JANE AUSTEN
DO?

WHAT WOULD
JANE AUSTEN
DO?

LAURIE BROWN

SOURCEBOOKS CASABLANCA™
AN IMPRINT OF SOURCEBOOKS, INC.®
NAPERVILLE, ILLINOIS

Published by Sourcebooks Casablanca, an imprint of
Sourcebooks, Inc.
P.O. Box 4410, Naperville, Illinois 60567–4410
(630) 961–3900
FAX: (630) 961–2168
www.sourcebooks.com

Library of Congress Cataloging-in-Publication Data

Brown, Laurie.
  What would Jane Austen do? / Laurie Brown.
      p. cm.
  1. Women costume designers—Fiction. 2. Americans—
England—Fiction. 3. Haunted places—Fiction. 4. Ghosts—
Fiction. 5. Time travel—Fiction. 6. Aristocracy (Social
class)—England—Fiction. 7. Austen, Jane, 1775-1817—
Fiction. I. Title.
  PS3602.R72227W47 2009
  813'.6—dc22
                    2008043077

      Printed and bound in the United States of America.
         QW 10 9 8 7 6 5 4 3 2 1

To my husband Brit,
my real life hero.

One

"I sensed a strong presence of spirits at Twixton Manor Inn. Two distinct females... one who cannot leave and the other who won't."
—Crystal Darkhorse, psychic, in her newest travel book *Haunted Destinations II*

"WHAT DO YOU MEAN, NO RESERVATION?" ELEANOR fought to keep her tone pleasant despite physical and emotional exhaustion. "Please look again. P-O-T-T-I-N-G-E-R."

"Noooo," the little gray-haired woman said as she watched the names scroll across her computer screen. Her plastic name tag identified her as the manager, Mrs. Ruth Simms. She turned and peered over the counter. "I'm so sorry. The Jane Austen Society is holding a conference here, and it's Regency Week. We have no vacancies." She frowned. "Why does your name sound familiar?"

"I have a confirmation letter," Eleanor said. She stooped to dig in her carryon for the piece of paper.

"Now I remember," the woman said, her birdlike

voice floating over Eleanor's head. "We received several boxes marked: Hold for E. Pottinger."

"The costumes for my fashion seminar on Friday," Eleanor explained without stopping her search. Thankful the shipment had arrived on time, she mentally crossed one item off her list of things to worry about.

"I'll have Harry fetch your boxes."

"Got it!" Eleanor stood with the prized confirmation letter held high.

Unfortunately, the shutters had been drawn across the opening of the registration counter. She looked around for a bell or buzzer and noted the changes made since her last visit two years earlier. The service counter was newly built into the doorway that had previously led to a cozy room once known as the ladies' parlor.

The impressive entrance hall with its sweeping staircase, marble floor, and carved paneling looked a bit… well, less elegant than she remembered. A modern fixture replaced the original crystal chandelier, and the suit of armor standing guard near the front door could use a good polish. To the left of the entrance, double doors led to the main parlor where a number of guests milled around, most in Regency dress, all with those silly stick-on name tags.

A wave of exhaustion swept over Eleanor. She desperately needed sleep after fifteen hours of travel. She knocked on the shutter. A few moments later, she knocked again.

A young woman, much tattooed and pierced, opened one shutter and responded. "Gram has gone to fetch Harry. You might as well have a seat." She gestured toward a wooden bench that looked like it had once been a church pew. "It'll be a while. He's out having a smoke." She sucked air between her thumb and forefinger, indicating more than a plain cigarette. "Either that or he's fiddling with that old motorcycle some guy left here instead of paying his bill. Either way, Gram won't find him anytime soon, especially if he hears her coming."

"I have my reservation confirmation."

The girl took the paper with the same enthusiasm she might accept a traffic ticket. She tapped on the computer keyboard and looked in an old-fashioned ledger. "It says you cancelled your reservation. The bridal suite?" She looked up, obviously curious.

Eleanor was not about to share with a stranger that her fiancé had dumped her for a tall, bosomy blonde talent agent who'd promised to make him a movie star.

"Bummer," the girl said.

Yeah, it had been. But once the rose-colored blinders had been removed, Eleanor had realized Jason wasn't the man she'd thought he was. Painful as it had been, she'd emerged a stronger person and focused on her career. Since the plane reservations for the honeymoon in England were nonrefundable, she'd turned it into a business opportunity. And a chance to find out more about the necklace.

"As you will note on the confirmation letter, I changed the reservation from a double room to a single room six months ago."

"Here's something. Uh-oh. Gram's not going to like this."

"What? Did you find it?"

"She put you in the book, but forgot to enter you into the computer. Your reserved room is currently occupied by a Colonel Artemis Hoover. Uh… this is not good."

Eleanor had a sinking feeling in her stomach. What could be worse than Colonel Artemis Hoover in her room?

"Gram is going to kill me," the girl muttered.

"Pardon?"

"Not that it matters to you, but that's my writing in the book. And it's not my first f-up. Gram threatened to send me back to Pittsburgh if I wasn't more careful."

"I'm sorry," Eleanor said for lack of anything else.

"You would be if you had to live with Mr. and Mrs. Clean-Cut Doctor. No problem. I can fix this. I'll find you a room at one of the other inns." She twirled the one long lock of purple hair that sprang from her orange spikes as data scrolled across the computer screen. "Nada. Zilch. Not an empty room anywhere. Well, I'm not going back," she said under her breath before she plopped a big old-fashioned key on the counter. "Are you afraid of ghosts?"

"What?"

"Are you afraid of ghosts?"

"I don't believe in ghosts. Why do you ask?"

"We don't usually let the tower suite unless someone specifically asks for it. It's haunted."

Eleanor weighed her need for sleep against the possibility of sharing a room with Casper.

"It's the answer to both of our problems." the girl

said, her voice a mixture of desperation and hope. "If you tell Gram you wanted the tower suite all along, I'm off the hook and you get a place to stay. Win-win."

Eleanor had a sneaky feeling she'd gotten the short half of the candy bar. Before her sluggish brain could kick into gear, she'd signed the register, explained the airline would deliver her lost luggage as soon as it was located in Frankfurt or Vienna, and followed the girl up the stairs. "Uh, Miss…"

"Karen Simms. But you can call me Spike." She touched her stiff hair. "My mother hates it," she added with a self-satisfied grin. She pulled a cell phone from one of her many pockets. "I'll text Harry to bring up your boxes." A few lightning-quick taps later, she clicked it shut. "All set."

"About this tower suite—"

"You're gonna love it. You're a history buff, right? I mean, I assume you are because you're here for the conference. Well, this suite has been completely restored. Two bedrooms and a sitting room overlook the south lawn. Which, by the way, I gave you for the single room price at the conference discount."

"But if no one ever stays in it—"

"No problem. We keep it pristine clean so the ghosts don't get upset. At least that's what Gram always says."

"About those ghosts—"

"Deirdre Cracklebury and her younger sister Mina. They were born in the manor house and lived here around the time of the Regency. I'm not real sure about exact dates, but you could check with

Gram if you want to know the details. Everyone here just calls them 'the girls.' Several of the staff, and a few guests, have claimed they encountered paranormal stuff like cold spots and misty apparitions in the hallway—you know, weird junk like that. I've never seen anything myself."

Spike stepped aside to let two giggling women guests pass on the stairway. Eleanor's first impression was that two delicate porcelain dolls had come to life, but her attention was quickly caught by their exquisite costumes: one in dark rose and the other in deep blue silk. She noted the intricate handwork on the gowns with envy and foreboding. If this was the quality of the competition, was she wasting her time and money starting her own costume business?

She could still go back to her old job at the movie studio. Were Spartan togas and mummy rags her only future? She almost turned to ask the women about their clothes, but she noticed Spike had taken a right turn at the top of the stairs and had gotten quite far ahead. She hurried to catch up.

"You've missed supper," Spike said, trucking down the hall at a speed that made the chains on her oversized cutoff jeans jingle-jangle. "But if you're hungry, I could get you a sandwich or something from the kitchen."

"That's not necessary. I'm fine." She'd eaten a protein bar in the cab from the train station.

"The welcoming reception has already started. Costumes are optional, so if you don't have time to change, that's okay."

Eleanor didn't bother to look down at her

rumpled brown travel pantsuit before shaking her head. "All I want is a hot shower and a bed." Local time might be only seven-fifteen in the evening, but she'd had little sleep in the last twenty-four hours. Her eyes kept crossing from fatigue. She had to fight to refocus them.

"This suite has a bathing chamber with a huge old-fashioned claw-foot tub. No shower." Spike paused at the end of the hall where it turned left into the south wing. She used another of the large old keys on a big ring to unlock the door tucked at an angle in the corner.

Eleanor entered an elegant sitting room decorated in shades of green and gold and filled with antique furniture. Across from the door a round area with eight windows was the obvious reason why it was called the tower suite.

Spike scooted in behind her. "This is the last room in the oldest portion of the house. The wings were added in the mid-1700s, giving the manor its U-shape. I'd recommend the bedroom on the left. Newer construction, so to speak. Plus it has the bathroom."

"I think I stayed in the newer section last time I was here," Eleanor said. Her room had been quite ordinary. Nothing like this.

She headed straight for the room on her left. Inside, a four-poster bed with pristine white linens tempted her to kick off her shoes and climb the three-step riser to sink into the feather mattress, travel-mussed clothes and all. Although there was lots of dark wood, the delicate blue and white touches kept the room from being overpoweringly depressing.

Spike walked past the bed to an armoire placed against the far wall. "The *en-suite* was added decades ago, probably when indoor plumbing was first invented, but it's in good condition because it's rarely been used. The entrance is a bit tricky. This armoire is really the door, and the handle is on the side. See? Just lift this rosette to release the latch." She pulled the door to the bathroom open. Without missing a beat, she turned to her left. "And here's the closet." She slid open a section of paneling and then closed it.

A tap on the door signaled Harry's arrival. The skinny adolescent's face had not yet filled out enough to balance his oversized nose and ears, but he was obviously still growing because his pants were at least an inch too short. Unless that was the style for English boys his age. He awkwardly hustled two large boxes on a wheeled dolly into the room. Eleanor directed him to set them in the corner. After expressing her appreciation in generous tips, Eleanor was finally alone.

First, she called her father. His voice mail kicked in, meaning he was probably at lunch with his golfing buddies or one of his lady friends. His old-fashioned manners dictated that it was rude to answer the phone when one was in the middle of a conversation, so he always turned his cell phone off when he was in company. She left him a message to let him know she'd arrived safely and would call him as usual on Sunday night. She tucked her phone into a pocket on her carryon as she headed to the bathroom.

Because of increased airline restrictions, she'd packed her toiletries and cosmetic bag in her suitcase, which by now was probably in Istanbul. Fortunately, the airline had provided each passenger with a Ziploc bag that contained soft footies, an eye-mask, and best of all, a disposable toothbrush and tiny tube of toothpaste. She'd had the forethought to snag the extra one from the empty seat beside her and drop it in her carryon. She dug it out.

After a quick dip in the tub, she promised herself a long luxurious soak before she left the inn. For tonight, sleep took precedence.

Wrapped in a large fluffy towel, she unpacked the smaller box and put on a floor-length, granny-style nightgown. Even though it was part of her planned presentation on a Regency lady's wardrobe, it would serve until her suitcases were located.

Because she wasn't a morning person, Eleanor had developed the habit of setting out her clothes the night before. Knowing she would sleep better if she had everything organized, she checked the seminar schedule and laid out her outfit for the following morning: a day dress of white muslin embroidered with green leaves and tiny violets, period underclothes, white silk stockings, and flat shoes made of green fabric.

She added the matching beaded reticule, so small that it held only the absolute necessities: ID, credit card, registration confirmation letter, a handkerchief instead of tissues, breath mints, lip gloss, and the big old-fashioned key to her suite. Then she hung up the rest of the dresses from the larger box. Running out of steam, she climbed the riser and flopped into the bed with a sigh, asleep the second her head hit the pillow.

"Who is that in your bed?"

"I haven't the vaguest idea," Deirdre answered.

Mina peered closer. "She resembles our cousin Ellen. Same dark auburn curls, heart-shaped face, and green eyes."

"Her eyes are closed."

"I noticed the striking color earlier when we passed her on the stairs. And her smile. She has great teeth, straight and—"

"Our cousin Ellen died nearly two hundred years ago. This person is alive."

Mina leaned over the figure in the bed. "Who are you?" When she got no response, she poked the sleeping female's arm. "Why are you here?"

"Isn't it obvious?" Deirdre said. "She's one of the guests."

"They rarely put guests in our rooms. Are you sure she's not dead?"

"Of course I'm sure. Well, we had best wake her up and scare her off," Deirdre said.

Mina tipped her head to one side. "She has a gentle face. Couldn't we let her sleep a bit longer?"

"Easy for you to say. She's not in your bed."

"I wonder who she is. I still say she resembles Cousin Ellen."

Deirdre pulled the sleeping female's travel bag out of the bathroom and looked through her belongings.

"What are you doing?" Mina asked in a horrified voice.

"Finding out who she is."

"That was a rhetorical question. You should not—"

"Her name is Eleanor Pottinger and she's from—"

"... Where is she from?"

"Los Angeles, California. That's in America."

"I know that," Mina said. She glanced over her shoulder at the still sleeping figure. "She must be exhausted from her long journey."

"Airplane-legged," Deirdre said as she continued to dig in Eleanor's bag.

"Jet-lagged," Mina corrected. Although both ghosts attempted to keep up with current events, Mina had the greater interest in modern culture.

"She keeps a journal," Deirdre said as she sat back and opened the leather-bound book. She scanned the neat handwriting, starting from the last written page and working her way backwards through the book quickly.

"You shouldn't read that."

"Why not? People read historical journals all the time."

"That's different." Mina pursed her lips. "Historical journals contribute to knowledge of the period by placing events of the day in a personal context."

"If I'd known my words were going to be read by anyone else, I would not have included personal information. I'm glad we got in the habit of hiding our journals so Aunt Patience couldn't read them. And now no one ever will."

"Exactly my point," Mina said, nodding toward the book in her sister's hands.

Deirdre shut the cover, dropped it back into the carryon, and shoved the small suitcase back into the bathroom. "There was little of interest anyway. Dull business plans, mention of a failed love affair without any interesting details, and research she wanted to complete regarding Jane Austen."

"Aha!" Mina turned to look at Eleanor. "I knew she had some reason for traveling alone."

Deirdre dusted her fingertips together as if to dismiss the matter. "There is still the issue of her being ensconced in my bed."

"It's not as if you actually need to sleep," Mina countered.

"Why are you so concerned about a stranger?" Deirdre's eyes narrowed. "What is going through that conniving mind of yours?"

Mina wanted to consider all possibilities before revealing her thoughts. "Oh, look, she's waking. Quick, douse the lamp."

Eleanor blinked away her momentary confusion as she remembered where she'd fallen asleep. Her bleary eyes refused to focus. Watery moonlight seeping through the thick glass of the windows told her it was the middle of the night, but her internal clock and a full bladder insisted she get out of bed. She swung her legs over the edge and rolled to a sitting position.

As she slid forward, she remembered climbing onto the bed and managed to get one foot on the second step of the bed riser. Off balance, she nearly tumbled to the floor, saving herself by lunging sideways and wrapping her arm around the sturdy bedpost. Forward motion swung her around until she slammed into the footboard, stubbing her big toe in the process.

"Ouch." The pain brought tears to her eyes.

Blinking, she limped toward the bathroom door that was disguised as an armoire and fumbled for the handle without success.

"Damn," she muttered under her breath. "Where is that release… thingee?"

"A hand's-breadth higher," a voice whispered.

Eleanor found the catch that opened the door and rushed into the bathroom, thankful a motion-sensitive night-light had been provided. Once her physical discomfort had been relieved, logic resurfaced. Had that voice been her imagination, or had she really heard someone? She couldn't remember ever using the term "hand's-breadth," not even in her wildest flights of fancy. Did the night-light really have a sensor, or had someone turned it on?

Suddenly nervous, she put her ear to the door. Nothing. She felt a bit silly. If there were intruders, why would they help her find the door latch and turn on the light? Unless she wanted to sleep in the tub, she would have to leave the bathroom sooner or later. She blamed her imagination for her unease. Surely nothing out of the ordinary had happened. She looked around for a possible weapon. Just in case.

She took a deep breath and swung open the door. Her still sore toe caused her to cross the room in a hop-step-hop-step. "Ouch, damn, ouch, damn." She vaulted into the bed and pulled the covers over her head.

Her heart pounded and her breath came in gasps. Had she seen something? Over by the window… someone? The combination of fatigue, stress, and whatever was in that energy bar had obviously sent her imagination into overdrive. How could she sleep until she made sure no one was in the room? She scooted under the covers to the edge of the bed and snaked one hand out to turn on the bedside lamp. Then with one quick motion, she threw back the cover and lunged to her knees in the middle of the bed, arm raised and ready to throw the bar of soap at any intruder.

Across the room, two delicate women in Regency costume sat primly on the window seat of the tower alcove and stared at her as if she'd sprouted a second head.

After moment of shock, Eleanor recognized the women she'd passed on the stairway earlier. Sensing no threat, her breath left her in a whoosh and she relaxed in relief like a balloon losing air. "I'm afraid you have the wrong room," she said, tucking her erstwhile weapon out of sight beneath the covers. "And I admit you gave me quite a fright."

"I'm Mina Cracklebury, and this is my sister Deirdre," the woman in the rose-colored dress said. "We're sorry we disturbed your slumber."

Deirdre shot her sister an incredulous look. "Yes, of course we are, but in fact this is—"

"A perfect opportunity for us to become acquainted." Mina flashed a brilliant smile. Obviously sisters, both wore their blonde hair pulled back into chignons with a few wispy curls framing their faces. "You may have heard about us. We are the ghosts of the manor."

"I don't believe in ghosts." Suddenly, Eleanor understood. Spike must have recruited these two to scare her. If she left voluntarily, then the girl would be off the hook. "Nice try. You can tell your friend Spike that it almost worked, but I recognize you. I'm not leaving—you are. Fabulous costumes, by the way. Good joke. Ha, ha. Now, if you don't mind, I'd like to go back to sleep."

Deirdre jumped to her feet. "We are not friends of that... person," she said, stomping her foot. "We are fully materialized ghosts, and this is our suite of rooms. And that is my bed!"

"Please excuse my sister's manners," Mina said. "We don't entertain often."

Deirdre rounded on her sister. "I have never entertained in my bedroom, and I refuse to start now. Whatever mischief you are planning in that devious mind of yours, I will have no part of it." With a snap of her fingers, her figure disintegrated into specks of light, and then she disappeared.

"Oh dear," Mina said. "Not an auspicious beginning."

"Is this some sort of magic trick?" Eleanor asked, peering around the room. "Where'd she go?"

Mina shrugged. "Neither of us can leave the manor grounds. She's not in this room, which is in itself a measure of her upset. And that will make it much more difficult to convince her to help us."

Eleanor shook her head. She closed her eyes and pinched the bridge of her nose. "I cannot be talking to a ghost. There are no such things. When I open my eyes, no one will be there." She peeked with one eye. The ghost was still there. Smiling.

"You have to believe what you see."

"No, I don't. I know what it is. I'm dreaming.
That's it. Only a dream." Talking to a dream figment
was just like talking to yourself. Lots of people who
weren't crazy did that. Right? "How can I make you
go away like your... what do you mean, convince
her to help us? I don't want anything to do with you.
And for the record, I can think of a dozen dream
characters I would much rather talk to. Like Mr.
Darcy or Heathcliff."

"Perhaps I phrased that wrongly," Mina replied,
unperturbed. "I can help you, and you can help me."

"You don't even exist. How can I possible help
you?"

"I'm so glad you asked."

"I didn't mean—"

"Deirdre believes we're stuck here until we do
appropriate penance or learn a particular lesson or
some such thing. The problem is we can't figure out
what it is. My solution is to travel back in time and
prevent... change what happened. Thereby solving
the problem at the source. However, we can't talk to
ourselves when we go back, and even if we could, it's
doubtful we'd listen. Do you listen when you talk to
yourself? La... I am rambling on without mentioning
what I can do to help you."

"There's nothing—"

"Didn't you come here to do some research?"

Eleanor gave her a sharp look. "Can you read
minds?" She rolled her eyes. "Of course you can.
Since you're only a projection of my imagination, it
stands to reason—"

Mina's laugh sounded like a tinkling wind chime.

"No, I can't read your mind. Most guests who come during Regency Week have an interest in something related to Jane Austen. Don't you? Perhaps I can help with that."

Eleanor shot her hand to her throat, but relaxed once she felt her amber cross still in place. She hadn't told anyone about the necklace she'd inherited from her grandmother. If the family legend was true, it had belonged to Jane Austen, and Eleanor could sell it for enough money to put her business on solid footing. That is, if she could bear to part with it, a decision she hadn't tackled just yet.

"Miss Jane Austen was not a close friend of ours due to our age differences," Mina continued, "but we certainly were well acquainted. We attended many of the same functions, since she lived nearby. Just down the road. At Chawton Cottage."

"Yes, I know."

"Ah, I see you are familiar with her life. Are you a fan of her books? Would you like to meet her?"

Eleanor could see she wasn't getting rid of this figment easily. Maybe if she went along with the dream, it would get to the inevitable conclusion of waking up. Then she could take a couple of antacids and get some rest. "Fine. Yes, I'd like to meet Jane Austen. Who wouldn't? Are you going to make her ghost appear?"

"Don't be silly. We are going to travel back in time to when we were alive, and you will meet her there."

"But that's impossible."

Mina grinned. "Actually…"

Deirdre reappeared with a bright flash of rainbow-colored lights. "I heard what you said. I knew you had another crazy scheme stuck in your bonnet."

"I know it will work this time," Mina said with a pleading look at her sister.

"No, it won't," Eleanor interjected. "Time travel is a physical impossibility."

Deirdre faced her with a raised eyebrow. "Have you never heard of Einstein's theory?"

"Everyone has."

"Then you know his theory that gravity affects time has been proven."

"Yes, but—"

"And you know that gravity is simply another form of energy."

"Yes, but—"

"Therefore, it logically follows that energy affects time."

"We pool our energy," Mina interjected in an excited voice, "and use it to create a powerful vortex that will take us all—"

"We can take you back in time, but we are not going to do it." Deirdre turned to her sister and whispered, "Must I remind you of what happened last time? We only made matters worse, and that's why our Teddy was killed."

"Who's Teddy?" Eleanor asked.

"Our dear brother," the ghosts said in unison.

"And this time Eleanor here is going to save his life," Mina continued. "It's a perfect plan. We take her back. She prevents Shermont from seducing… us, thus preventing the necessity of Teddy defending our honor and hence dying in the duel."

Deirdre shook her head. "It'll never work."

"Of course it will," Mina argued. "We can help her with everything she needs to know."

"There's too much to learn. Dancing, proper address, conversation, deportment, and manners. We studied from the time we were little girls. She has no chance of success."

"All she has to do is keep us out of Lord Shermont's way," Mina argued.

"We had a chaperone for that—to little avail."

"Ha! Aunt Patience's only concern was Teddy's welfare. She couldn't have cared less about us."

"That's not true."

They volleyed reasons back and forth like tennis players until Eleanor put her hands over her ears. "Stop!" When the sisters looked at her with surprised expressions, she folded her hands in her lap. "Please stop arguing," she said in a moderated tone. "My head is already pounding."

"We were only—"

"Whatever," Eleanor said. "The discussion is now over. Time travel is impossible. Therefore the question of whether I can do the job is moot. Now, I would like to wake up or go back to sleep—whatever it takes to end this dream and make the two of you go back to wherever you came from." She stretched out on the bed and put the pillow over her head.

"But you did say you would like to meet Jane Austen?" Mina asked.

"Yes. Now, good-night."

"And you agree to help us if we can introduce you to her?"

"If it means you'll go away and let me get some sleep, I agree to whatever you want. I'll fly to the moon. I'll dance on a flying carpet of gold. I'll—"

"Good. Deirdre and I will take care of everything."

"No we won't."

"Listen to…"

And then there was silence.

After what seemed like several long minutes, Eleanor sat up and looked around. The room appeared normal and best of all empty. She let out a deep sigh of relief. "What a crazy dream," she mumbled as she snuggled back under the covers.

She regretted it had just been a dream. Wouldn't it have been cool if it had been true?

When she sat up once more to turn out the lamp, the room began to spin. Bolts of rainbow-colored electricity zoomed around the walls. The bed seemed to rise and float.

Eleanor was usually a woman who confronted her problems head on, but this was too weird, outside the realm of anything she'd experienced before. The spinning room made her dizzy. The flashing lights hurt her eyes with their laser intensity, and her head throbbed with what she could only describe as unheard sound. She dove under the pillow, covered her ears, and closed her eyes tightly.

Two

ELEANOR WOKE AND HAD NO IDEA WHAT TIME IT WAS. She fumbled for the watch that she'd left on the bedside table. At least she thought she'd left it there. Had she put it in her carryon? She sat up and blinked in the pale light.

Mina and Deirdre were seated by the window.

Eleanor pinched herself. "Ouch!"

"Good morning, slug-a-bed," Mina said with a bright smile. "It is half past ten on Wednesday the twenty-third day of June in the year 1814."

"Oh no," Eleanor said, shaking her head. If she wasn't dreaming, that meant the ghosts were real. "Why are you still here? Why are you haunting me?"

"We promised we would be here to help you with the nuances of Regency life," Mina said.

"Even though there is much you cannot possibly understand, especially in the short time available," Deirdre added.

Eleanor held up her hand. She needed a minute to deal with this... whatever this was. What was it they always said to ghosts on TV? "You should go toward the light. Move on to whatever—"

"We explained that we can't leave this property."

"Right. I remember. Look, I'm only going to be here for a week. There is no other room where I can stay, so why don't we come to an agreement? I'll try to not bother you if you'll try to not bother me. Sound reasonable?"

"But we can help you—"

"I don't want your help. In fact, I don't want to see you anymore, or hear you, or... or sense your presence. Is that clear?"

Mina nodded, her expression sad.

Deirdre crossed her arms and narrowed her eyes. "You are not properly prepared to manage—"

"Whatever happens this week, I'll figure it out. Now, I want you both to promise you'll leave me alone."

"Perhaps you should listen to her," Mina said with a nod toward her sister.

"Arrrgh!" Eleanor flopped back on the bed and pulled the pillow and blanket over her head. "Go away!"

After a few minutes, Eleanor realized she might as well get up because she wasn't going back to sleep. Yet she hesitated. What if the ghosts were still there?

She heard the door open and someone moving around. In one quick move, she whipped off the cover and sat up. "Why are you—"

A scream stopped her mid-sentence. A maid stood in the center of the room, her hands to her mouth, her eyes as wide as if she'd seen a ghost.

Eleanor apologized for startling the girl, who didn't look much over the age of fourteen. At the same time, she was impressed that even the maid was dressed in an appropriate period costume for

Regency Week. She wore a white mobcap and a simple gray ankle-length dress covered by a long white apron.

"I weren't expecting no one to be here," the maid said as she picked up the dropped linens and draped them over her arm.

"Understandable." Eleanor gave the young girl a sympathetic smile. "I arrived late last night, and Karen Simms put me in here."

"I don't be knowing no one by that name, but they made a terrible blunder. This be the mistresses' suite. Miss Deirdre won't like a stranger sleeping in her bed."

Eleanor didn't want to hear more about the ghosts. "I'm sure everything will be fine." She got up and put on the robe she'd left on the foot of the bed. "My luggage should be arriving from the airport, if it hasn't already. I'd appreciate it if you would keep a look out for my suitcases. Two, both black. My name is Eleanor Pottinger. I'm from America, but I'm sure you already deduced that from my accent." The girl still seemed nervous. "What's your name?" Eleanor asked to put her at ease.

"I be Twilla." The maid curtseyed, maintaining her role, but she had a confused expression. "Miss Eleanor from America. Two black cases arriving from the port." She repeated the information as if memorizing foreign language phrases. Suddenly her face lit with comprehension. "Aye, you must be the cousin they been expecting for over a fortnight."

"Actually, I'm—"

"I'll be right back with a pitcher of hot water."

Now Eleanor was confused. But she had no time to question the maid before the girl scurried out. Eleanor looked around the bedside table for her watch. She got down on her hands and knees to look under the bed.

"Miss?"

Eleanor sat back in surprise. She breathed a sigh of relief when she realized it was the maid, not the ghosts. Perhaps it really had been no more than a dream.

"I forgot to ask if you want a breakfast tray. Cocoa? Toast?"

"Coffee would be great." Eleanor stood and brushed off her hands, even though there was no dust on the floor she could have picked up. "Thank you."

"If you was looking for the chamber pot, it's in the corner," Twilla said. "Behind the screen."

Eleanor turned in the direction the maid indicated. She didn't remember seeing the three-panel Chinese screen before. A chamber pot! She was all for realism in attire for the conference, like not using zippers or polyester fabrics. It was fun to imitate the manners and activities of the Regency, but expecting the attendees to sacrifice use of a modern toilet was too much to expect. She turned to say something, but the girl was gone.

The respite gave her time to realize the maid was not the appropriate person to speak to about sanitation arrangements. When Eleanor went downstairs, she planned to have a talk with the inn manager, Mrs. Ruth Simms. Until then, she would play along with the program.

Twilla returned, a pitcher of steaming hot water in one hand and a bundle in the other. She deposited both behind the screen. An even younger girl followed her into the room carrying a tray with a silver coffee service, delicate china cup and saucer, plate of toast, and a large snowy napkin. The child set the tray on the table near the window and then curtseyed on the run as she scurried out.

"I've brought everything I expect you'll need for your morning ablutions. Be there anything else, Miss?" Twilla asked. "Simply ring when you are ready, and I will return to help you dress." She indicated the bellpull that hung next to the painting over the fireplace.

Eleanor hadn't had anyone help her dress since she'd learned to tie her own shoes. "Thank you. That won't be necessary."

The maid quickly masked her surprise and nodded. "As you will, Miss. Nuncheon is served for the ladies at eleven o'clock. The dancing master is in attendance today."

"Thank you."

"Just ring when you are ready, and I will take you downstairs."

Eleanor was sure she could find her way without a guide, but she nodded rather than argue. As soon as the maid left, Eleanor headed straight for the bathroom. The rosette latch on the armoire wouldn't budge. She tried every bit of decorative carving, in case she had remembered the location of the latch wrong. Nothing moved.

"Damn it."

Locking the bathroom door was taking matters too far. Mrs. Simms was in for an earful.

In desperation, Eleanor was forced to use the chamber pot. Without her suitcases, she had to make do with the materials provided by the inn. She added the skimpy linen washcloth and hand towel to her list of complaints. On the plus side, the tiny square of handmade soap that smelled of honeysuckle was an unexpected pleasure.

She examined the wide-toothed comb that appeared to be tortoise shell. Since that was illegal, like ivory, it must be plastic. Good imitation. She pulled the comb through her hair, glad she'd recently cut it short and allowed it to curl naturally.

Then she examined the wood-handled toothbrush with strange brown bristles. She set it aside with a shiver of revulsion. A small round can labeled "tooth powder" contained a white substance that tasted like baking powder with a touch of mint. Since her disposable toothbrush was locked in the bathroom, she used her finger to rub a bit of it over her teeth.

As she dressed, she thought about Twilla's earlier announcement of the day's activities. The schedule change was a bit of a worry. What if they'd changed the time she was to speak? She'd better get downstairs and register for the conference so she could check the handouts for other revisions.

At least she didn't need to change the outfit she'd planned to wear. The sprigged muslin was appropriate for luncheon, or nuncheon as it was called during the Regency, and a dancing lesson. Although Eleanor was mostly interested in the fashions of the Regency, she'd planned to attend as many seminars as possible in order to make contacts and check out the costumes the competition had produced.

She decided not to spare more time looking for her watch, which she would have stuffed in her reticule anyway, so as not to spoil the illusion of the period dress. A gauzy shawl of sunny yellow and a Japanese fan completed her outfit.

In the hall, a faint feeling of unease niggled at the back of her brain and slowed her purposeful stride. Nothing seemed familiar. True, she'd been exhausted last night, but apparently she'd totally spaced out. The colorful Turkish rug beneath her feet was at odds with her vague memory of generic neutral carpeting. And a plethora of portraits and landscapes hanging on the walls replaced the tastefully framed photos of the manor's architectural features that she remembered.

When she reached the landing halfway down the grand stairway, she came to a complete stop. She blinked. "Omigod," she whispered.

Either a crew had renovated the entrance hall overnight, or she was in a different place. Gone was the shuttered monstrosity of a registration desk. A round table topped with a large Oriental vase of flowers sat directly below an ornate crystal chandelier. The tarnished suit of armor was gone. As Eleanor descended the last steps, a footman dressed in blue and gold livery and a white pony-tailed wig opened the ten-foot-tall double front doors and stood at attention to one side.

Eleanor was treated to a scene from a movie version of a Jane Austen novel. Two men dismounted their horses and handed the reins to a stableboy. In a classic macho moment, the taller one thumped the other on the back. She didn't hear what was said, but male laughter rumbled ahead of them as they strode up the front steps. As they entered, the first man removed his tan leather gloves. His high stiff collar, snowy cravat, buff breeches, and knee-high Hessian boots were accurate in every detail, fitting his physique as if they had been glued on his body. His dark hair was casually windblown and a bit on the long side. He handed his high-crowned hat, gloves, and riding quirt to the footman with an air of entitled nonchalance not many men could pull off. His intense gaze drew her attention to his stormy gray eyes, but his frown caused her to quickly look away.

The other gentleman, also wearing an impeccable riding costume, had blond curls à la Byron, boyish good looks, and laughing blue eyes. Standing side by side, it appeared as if an angel and one of Satan's own had declared a temporary truce. The angelic one noticed Eleanor standing on the stairway and said, "Ho, now, what have we here?"

A butler, who seemed to appear out of thin air, proffered a folded message on a silver salver and whispered something into the blond man's ear.

"Thank you, Tuttle," he said, dismissing the servant with a wave before stepping toward her. "My dear cousin, please allow me to welcome you. A bit belated, but no less sincere."

She descended the stairs in a state of confusion. Did the festival have an official host? If so, they'd chosen well. He must be a politician or used car salesman in his real life. Unlike the taller dark-haired man who stood glowering, this man was open and friendly.

"I'm so pleased you are arrived in time for the house party," the host said. Her puzzlement must have shown on her face. "Come now. I can't have changed that much." When she didn't respond, he continued, "But maybe I have. I'm Lord Digby in case you haven't guessed." He made a low elegant bow, one leg forward. "But I insist you call me Teddy, as you did when we were children. After all, you are a member of our family." He looked at her expectantly, waiting for her to say something.

Eleanor tipped her head slightly to the side, trying to make the circumstances fit into a logical framework. Had some attendees of the festival assumed a persona like reenactors sometimes did? Nothing in the conference literature had mentioned role-playing. Maybe they had hired actors to play the residents of the manor who lived during the Regency.

"I'm overwhelmed," she said. And that was the truth.

"My sisters will be pleasantly surprised you have finally arrived. We passed their carriage on the road, so Deirdre and Mina should be here shortly." Digby turned and motioned his companion forward. "Lord Shermont, allow me to present my cousin from America—"

The rest of the introduction was lost to her. Shermont's presence was the undeniable last straw. Eleanor could no longer rationalize everything that had seemed out of place. As she was descending the last stair, the unbelievable truth hit her mid-step.

Omigod. The ghosts had actually done it. She'd really traveled back in time.

The enormity of the realization caused the earth to drop from under her feet by at least two inches. Or so it seemed as she stumbled forward. Shermont steadied her by supporting her elbow. Even so, she nearly fell into his arms.

"Sorry," she mumbled, regaining her balance and pulling free. She crossed her arms and surreptitiously rubbed her elbow, still tingling with the warmth of his touch.

"Meeting you is a… unique pleasure," Shermont said with a wicked, teasing smile that sent her blood racing.

"Here now," her erstwhile cousin said. "I'd heard of females throwing themselves at you, Shermont, but I never thought to witness it myself."

"Mind your manners, Digby," Shermont said in a low, just-short-of-threatening voice.

The younger blond man only laughed at the reprimand. "This is the Age of Sensibility, and man must follow his penchant. It is my nature to be too honest and forthcoming."

"Also known as rudeness."

Digby frowned. "If that comment had come from anyone other than you, Shermont, I might be obligated to defend my honor."

Surely Regency men wouldn't duel over such a silly reason. Eleanor felt she should say something, but she had no idea how to diffuse the situation she'd inadvertently caused. Quick, quick, what would Jane

Austen do? The scene that came to mind was when Knightley criticized Emma after the picnic where she had treated Miss Bates so badly.

"Gentlemen, isn't the essence of good manners to make sure no one is uncomfortable?" Eleanor asked.

Shermont quirked an eyebrow in recognition of her riposte.

She continued, refusing to acknowledge the heat his tacit approval ignited. "Please don't compound my embarrassment by turning my clumsiness into an *affaire d'honneur*."

Both men were immediately contrite, verbally stumbling over each other in attempts to absolve her of any responsibility and to assure her their sparring was only good-natured jibes between friends and of no consequence. The impromptu competition of flowery apologies was thankfully cut short by the arrival of Deirdre and Mina. The sisters looked exactly like their ghostly counterparts, only the live ones were more vibrant in coloring and manner— more... alive.

Lord Digby interrupted the girls' enthusiastic greeting of Eleanor to present his sisters to Lord Shermont.

"Haven't I had the pleasure previously? You both seem quite familiar," Shermont said. He rubbed the spot where a faint one-inch scar marked his forehead.

"I don't think so," Deirdre said. She made a slight pout with her lips as if trying to remember.

"No doubt we would—"

"Highly unlikely that we have met," Deirdre said, interrupting her excited sister. "Neither of us has been presented at court as yet, and therefore we have not been in attendance at any functions of London society."

Mina rocked forward on her toes. "Our brother promised next spring we—"

"Perhaps you have been a guest at another country house in the area?" Teddy offered. "Perhaps last summer?"

"Unfortunately, my affairs usually keep me in London year-round," Shermont said.

"Then I insist there will be no discussion of business this entire week." As Teddy spoke the footman closed the front door. "Where is Uncle Huxley?" Teddy turned to his sister. "Didn't you delay your homecoming so he could accompany you?"

"He went with the coach to the stables," Deirdre said as she removed her bonnet. "He brought his new filly along and wanted to see her settled properly."

"I dare say he thinks more of horses than people," Mina said as she handed her bonnet to the maid who waited nearby.

"Then we shall go to the stables to welcome him," Teddy said.

"And perhaps take advantage of the opportunity to show off your new stallion," Shermont said.

"I have been caught out," Teddy admitted with a laugh. He turned to his sisters. "I'm told the fairest of our guests are in the parlor, and I'm sure you would prefer their company. If you will excuse us?"

"You are excused, but only because you are not properly dressed to be considered desirable company,"

Deirdre replied to her brother. She turned to Shermont. "A dancing master has been engaged to demonstrate the latest steps. I do hope you will join us later this morning, even though you probably know all the new dances from London."

Shermont gave a slight bow. "One can never be too well-versed in the pleasures of the dance."

Though his answer was noncommittal, Deirdre smiled and preened under his direct attention. Eleanor easily decided Deirdre must be the sister who was seduced.

When the gentlemen were gone, Deirdre turned to Eleanor. "Dear Cousin Ellen," she said. "We are so pleased you have arrived safely. I can hardly believe it's been eleven years since your father took you off to the Colonies."

"You look just the same," Mina said. "Well, maybe a little older, but your teeth are still good. That's an advantage in the marriage mart, believe me."

"I'm not—"

"We won't talk about marriage just yet," Deirdre said. "Ellen just arrived."

"Such a long time-consuming journey," Mina said.

She didn't know how right she was. "Actually, my name is Eleanor Pottinger, and I must tell you—"

"And we want to hear everything, absolutely everything. You've had such a terrible time these past three years, losing your father, your house, your fortune, and your husband to the war. May God rest Captain... what was his name again? Oh, yes, I remember. May God rest Captain Pottinger's soul."

Eleanor blinked at the list of woes. Poor Ellen.

"But you must consider this your home now and stay as long as you want." Deirdre hooked her arm through Eleanor's. "You'll share our suite until after the ball because we have so many houseguests expected. We will have a long cozy chat later. Just now I am parched and cannot bear another moment without a cup of tea."

Mina took Eleanor's other arm. "Dear Cousin Eleanor, you are not to worry. Deirdre and I will take care of everything."

Her words had a familiar echo. Inside the parlor, Eleanor was presented to their aunt, Patience Aubin, whom she was supposed to recognize, but, of course, didn't.

Patience was in her mid-forties, at least, and dressed in the fashion of a woman half her age. Her neckline was cut too low and her corset laced too tight, resulting in the danger of her ample breasts popping out of her bodice. A few stray wisps of unnaturally orange hair escaped her old-fashioned turban headdress.

The older woman gave her an assessing glance. "Welcome back to Twixton," she said.

Although the words were correct and polite, Eleanor detected no warmth or sincerity in her tone.

Deirdre introduced Eleanor to the other guests present, starting with Mrs. Holcum and her daughter Beatrix. The mother was elegantly attired with not a hair out of place. She gave Eleanor a condescending nod and immediately turned back to her previous conversation. The daughter was a walking advertisement for aristocratic breeding: flawless complexion, small straight nose, rosebud lips, flaxen hair, and an attitude of entitlement.

"Always a pleasure to meet Teddy's, I mean Lord Digby's, relatives," Beatrix said, although the sentiment didn't reach her icy blue eyes. "I've heard so much about you from his dear sisters."

"All good, I'm sure," Eleanor said with a smile.

Beatrix blinked, apparently unable to think of an appropriate put down. She turned and flounced away.

Deirdre pulled on Eleanor's elbow, directed her to the woman sitting on the sofa next to Aunt Patience, and introduced her to Mrs. Maxwell, who was in attendance with two daughters. Fiona and Hazel, still in their teens, stood by the large bay window. Both willowy girls had dark hair, lively brown eyes, delicate features, and sweet smiles, obviously taking after their paternal lineage. After curtseying gracefully, they returned their attention to whatever was outside the window.

Deirdre took an empty seat next to the table with the tea service. Mina dodged a pacing Beatrix and joined the others by the window.

Eleanor grabbed the arm of a chair in the corner and eased herself down. As chitchat regarding various journeys and the weather swirled past her, she tried to wrap her mind around what had happened. Even though she knew time travel was impossible, she now had no choice but to believe. If the ghosts brought her here, could they send her back? She intended to ask them—no, demand that they...

Suddenly she realized someone stood directly in front of her, blocking her view of the rest of the room.

"I know why your cousins invited you to live with them," Beatrix Holcum said softly, her voice a sneer. "You can forget any notion of marrying Teddy, because he and I have an understanding."

"I hadn't—"

"Shhh. Don't play the innocent with me," she whispered, crossing her arms. "I know your sad little story, but I am not responsible for your troubles. You and your cousins may expect their brother to marry you, but Teddy is already promised to me. You will have to look further afield for the rich husband you so desperately need."

Even though Eleanor didn't have any designs on Teddy, she didn't particularly like the way Beatrix was attacking her. "An understanding? What exactly does that mean?" she whispered back. Tipping her head to one side and putting her finger on her chin, she added, "Oh, yes. That's the same as not engaged, isn't it?"

Beatrix dropped her arms to her sides and curled her hands into fists. "We are engaged. We are only waiting to make the formal announcement until after his sisters are presented this fall during the Little Season. We will be married in January."

"Really?" Teddy hadn't told his supposed fiancée that he wasn't going to take his sisters to London until spring. Not only did the beloved Teddy sink in her estimation, she suddenly felt a kinship to poor Beatrix, another woman who would get cruelly jilted. Of course, even if she told Beatrix, she probably wouldn't believe her. "My grandmother always said, don't give the milk away for free if you want to sell the cow."

Beatrix looked confused. "Your grandmother was a dairymaid?"

"Of course not." Before Eleanor could explain her advice, they were distracted by the commotion near the window.

"It's him. It's him," Fiona cried out. She leaned forward, nearly knocking the vase of flowers off the table. "They're coming back from the stable."

"Let me see," Hazel said, squeezing in next to her sister to get a better viewing angle. "He's so handsome."

The girls reacted as if a rock star was walking up the drive. Their whispering and sighing prompted their mother to ask, "Whom are you talking about?"

"Lord Shermont, of course," Fiona said. After a lingering look out the window, she turned and flounced across the room to join the other women. "I do hope he asks me to dance."

"I think I'd faint if he asked me," Hazel said, arriving on her sister's heels.

"I'm disappointed we didn't get a look at Huxley's filly," Shermont said as they reentered the manor.

"Believe you me, you're not missing much," Digby responded, again handing his hat to the footman. "She's not much to look at."

"Appearances can be deceiving." Shermont considered himself a good judge of horseflesh and knew from experience speed and stamina did not always come in a pretty package.

Digby waved off the words of wisdom. "Bit rude of Huxley to put the exercise of his mount over greeting his host, don't you think?"

"Not necessarily. Owning an animal carries responsibilities as well as joys." If the horse had been kept tied to the back of the carriage the whole way over, the animal probably needed and deserved a good run.

"That's why we have grooms," Digby said.

Shermont understood not wanting a stranger on his favorite horse. "I don't allow anyone else to ride my stallion. A heavy-handed groom would ruin his sensitive mouth."

Digby could not deny that, so he changed the subject. "I'd much rather spend time with the ladies. I intend to change and join them." He started up the stairs.

Shermont followed with a similar plan. He entered his room and threw off his coat. "Carl?"

His valet appeared with a basin of hot water and fresh towels. "Yes, milord," he answered in his somber tone. Dressed in his usual black, his demeanor was funereal except for his one vanity: an elaborate and ugly wig to hide his baldness and protruding ears.

Born in the mews of London to an abusive father, Carl had left home at the age of eight after his mother died of consumption. Admitting only to being fifty years old, he'd had various careers: pickpocket, sailor, acrobat, jockey, cat burglar, to name a few. The previous Lord Shermont had recruited him straight out of Newgate to steal an incriminating document from a third-story bedroom. A patriot despite all, Carl had stayed on to help find and neutralize foreign agents who were selling information to the enemies of the crown. He could now add valet to his colorful resume. The bandy-legged little man had proven himself a worthy partner.

"I wish to change and get back downstairs as quickly as possible," Shermont said, stripping off his clothes.

"Some men take as much as two or three hours to complete their toilettes," Carl said with a hint of disapproval. "A gentleman is often judged by the care he takes with his appearance."

"Attention to detail is fine. Wasting time is not. We have another suspect. There is a new guest. A female."

Something about her—the way she talked, the way she acted—seemed familiar. Was it a memory from the past he couldn't remember? As usual, thinking about his life before what he called the "accident" gave him an instant headache over his right eye, a stabbing pain that blurred his vision. He applied pressure on the scar and cleared his mind. The throbbing lessened to a manageable level.

"The cousin from America," Carl said with a nod. "She could well be a Napoleon supporter."

"Digby wasn't acting very cousinly toward her." Shermont dismissed the niggling jealousy, calling it excitement that their hunt for a foreign agent in the area was finally achieving results. He hoped that by changing clothes in record time he could get downstairs to question her before Digby arrived.

"A distant cousin," Carl clarified. "According to the servants, she's a childhood friend of the sisters. Their uncle Huxley was married to a Roberta Donaldson, and her brother is Mrs. Pottinger's father."

"Married to…"

"Widowed eighteen months ago."

Shermont released a breath he wasn't sure why he'd been holding. "The husband?"

"No one seems to remember him. Only reference was to the Captain. They did say her husband was killed in battle," Carl continued. "Another reason she would have no love for the English despite being born here."

"Send a message to our contact at the diplomatic corps, and see if they have any information on a Captain Pottinger. He could have been military or even a private ship's captain. Did you find out why she's here? Seems a dangerous time to make such a hazardous journey simply to visit old friends."

"According to Twilla, the ladies' maid, the sisters hope to foster a marital alliance with their brother. It would be an advantageous match for the American, as she has no fortune and no prospects. Other servants are quite sure Digby will marry Miss Holcum."

"What does his valet say?" Shermont asked, knowing a man could keep few secrets from his manservant.

"His valet is closemouthed, as is proper."

Shermont had finished dressing and turned to the mirror to check his cravat. "Excellent." He patted the elaborate knot Carl had tied. "Keep your ears open," he encouraged as he headed for the door with a light step.

"Yes, milord."

Three

Interested in the topic of their conversation, Eleanor left her seat by the window in the parlor and joined the other women around the coffee table. She accepted a cup of tea from Deirdre.

"Shermont will not ask either of you to dance if he has a lick of sense," Mrs. Maxwell said to her daughters. "Your father would—"

"It's just a dance, Mother," Fiona said.

"No. It's your reputation."

"What is it about that man young girls find so fascinating?" Mrs. Holcum asked. "Oh, I know he's handsome, and titled, and—"

"Now he has a title," Mrs. Matthews interrupted. "But I heard…" She paused for effect, and the other chaperones leaned forward. "Five years ago, the elder Shermont found him on the roadside beaten near to death by brigands, as the story goes. He survived, but he has no memory of how he got there or any events before being found. He does not even remember his real name. Since the elderly Shermont's sons had both been killed fighting Napoleon, he later named this stranger his heir."

"Can someone adopt a grown man?" Eleanor blurted out.

"Not adopt," Deirdre explained. "Named as his heir. Not unusual for a man without a son to name a nephew or cousin or distant relative—"

"But a stranger?" Aunt Patience shook her head. "Who would have thought it possible?"

"And most surprising, Prinny approved," Mrs. Holcum said. "He missed an opportunity to have the sizable estate revert to the crown. Not that I would say anything bad about the Regent, but to elevate a man of uncertain breeding…"

"I met Shermont several years ago," Mrs. Matthews said. "He had an accent I couldn't place, definitely unrefined. Perhaps he is a Colonial, like your cousin," she added to Deirdre.

Eleanor bristled and would have made a scathing comment about intentional rudeness, but Mina quickly remarked, "I find her accent charming."

"We are at war with the United States," Mrs. Holcum said with a sniff.

"I understand your concern for your brother serving in the Navy, but England is not at war with our cousin," Deirdre said, putting deliberate emphasis on the last two words.

Mrs. Holcum pressed her lips into a hard white line, saying no more along the ugly American theme. Eleanor decided to cut the woman some slack. She'd forgotten about the War of 1812, as it was known in America. Although the presence of men in uniform was mentioned several times in Jane Austen's work, Eleanor had always assumed they were destined to fight Napoleon.

"The Americans. The French. Is there anyone we're not fighting?" Fiona sighed. "These wars have created a dearth of available young men, and any still in England speak of nothing else." She propped her elbow on the arm of the chair and rested her chin in her hand. Her mother tutted her disapproval, so Fiona sat up as straight as a yardstick and folded her hands in her lap.

"The Spanish are our allies," Mrs. Holcum pointed out.

"And if a Spaniard appears on our doorstep, we will offer him our hospitality," Deirdre said. "Currently, Lord Shermont is our guest and as such can expect nothing less than appropriate civility."

"He seems quite proper," Aunt Patience said. "He's been here for several days, and his manners have been above reproach."

"Well, he has spent time in polite society," Mrs. Matthews admitted. "Perhaps one should not be too hasty to judge a person solely by his antecedents. Other factors should be taken into account."

"Other assets aside, I hear he has a large... um... fortune," Aunt Patience said.

Mina and Hazel giggled and whispered and giggled more. Eleanor fought to keep from rolling her eyes.

"Good heavens, Patience, don't say such things in the presence of impressionable ears." Mrs. Holcum gave her daughter a stern look. "My daughter will not dance with that man. For all we know he could be the son of a... a..."

"Highwayman or pirate," Mina supplied with a wistful smile.

Eleanor shivered, but her reaction was not fear.

"A rather fanciful notion," a deep voice responded.

Lord Shermont sauntered into the parlor, with Lord Digby on his heels.

Deirdre jumped up and greeted the newcomers. She put her arm through Teddy's and said, "Brother dear, do say something in defense of our guest."

"I might point out that ne'er-do-wells rarely speak several languages, quote classical literature, or understand scientific and mathematic principles," Teddy said, almost hiding his reluctance at singing the other man's praises.

Mina stuck out her bottom lip. "There could be an educated pirate."

"Obviously my sister has been reading too many romantic novels," Teddy said as he shook his head and spread his hands.

Shermont stepped forward to execute a gallant bow in front of Mina. He raised her hand to the barest brush of his lips. "While I'm flattered to be compared to the hero of one of your books, I expect when the truth of my previous circumstances is known, my heritage will prove quite ordinary."

"I think not," the entranced girl whispered.

Eleanor changed her mind and decided Mina must be the one who was seduced. Shermont moved away from Mina and stood by the fireplace with one elbow on the mantle. Even though he appeared to ignore her, he was close enough for Eleanor to detect the spicy scent of his cologne.

Teddy cleared his throat. "So where is the dancing master? You have here two gallantly agreeable partners.

That is, at least in my case, if you're willing to risk your toes in the pursuit of learning the latest fashionable steps."

"My dear, you are a marvelous dancer," Aunt Patience said. "But poor Mr. Foucalt was so distressed by his arduous journey from town that I told him we would wait until tomorrow for our lesson. We can have the footman fetch him if you would prefer today."

"Not necessary," Teddy said. "It is too nice to remain indoors anyway."

"Let's go on an outing," Mina suggested, clapping her hands. "To the ruins."

"Capital!" Teddy agreed. "Cook will pack a picnic, and you won't have to return until late afternoon." He yanked on the bellpull, and the butler appeared almost instantly. "The party will need transportation to the ruins. Both the carriage and the landau, I should think."

Tuttle bowed. "Yes, milord."

"I noticed you didn't call for your horses. Won't you gentlemen accompany us?" Mrs. Holcum asked Teddy.

He laid his hand over his heart. "Unfortunately, duty takes precedence over pleasure. I must remain behind to welcome the other guests expected to arrive today."

Shermont wasn't given a chance to reply before Mrs. Holcum spoke up.

"Perhaps we should delay the picnic until tomorrow," she suggested. "It looks as though it might rain this afternoon, and I'm sure your other guests will enjoy such an outing."

Eleanor deduced Beatrix's mother didn't want to wander too far away from the fish she thought her daughter had caught.

"I agree," Deirdre said. "I have had enough of the inside of a carriage for one day. We could play croquet."

"Excellent idea," Aunt Patience said. "We will meet you gentlemen on the south lawn in half an hour. That should be time enough to fetch our bonnets and parasols. With your leave."

She stood and led the ladies from the room.

A fraction of a second late in understanding she should tag along, Eleanor jumped up. Because she wasn't used to wearing a long dress, she stepped on the hem of her skirt and lurched forward to catch her balance. Shermont caught her arm, preventing her from taking a header.

"Once again, I've had the pleasure of rescuing you," he said.

Eleanor pulled free and avoided rubbing the tingling spot where he had touched her. "Thank you. I appreciate your saving my dignity again. I'm not usually so clumsy."

"That's good. I believe it's a rule that after three rescues you would be formally obligated to dance with me at the ball."

"And that's bad?"

"Absolutely." He leaned forward as if to confide a secret. "I am a terrible dancer. I tread on my partners' feet and make wrong turns. I can't make small talk because I'm counting the steps out loud. Deplorable."

His rakish smile told her his self-depreciation

was charming nonsense. Teddy's snort of disbelief reinforced her intuition.

She pasted an innocent look on her face and batted her eyelashes a little. "In that case, should the possibility arise, I will be sure to wear my steel-toed dancing slippers."

He raised an eyebrow. "Then I hope you won't step on my feet."

The tone of his teasing contained an unspoken challenge she found stimulating. "I would hate to make a promise so easily broken."

"Then maybe we should substitute another activity for the obligatory dance. May I suggest a walk in the garden?" His deep blue eyes suggested she'd discover more than scented pathways.

His charm was made all the more dangerous by her physical reaction to his nearness. She forced herself to remember what had happened to Deirdre and Mina. "Perhaps next time you should just let me fall on my face."

He gave her a wounded look that was plainly a sham. "As a gentleman, I could never stand by and allow such a catastrophe to happen."

"Nor would I," Teddy said, stepping between them. "My duty is to look after you, and with that in mind, I shall endeavor to be by your side the next time you need rescuing."

Eleanor tipped her head in what she hoped was a gracious nod. "I'll try to remain solidly on my feet in the future."

"Then I shall have to find some other means to be of service to you. For the nonce, may I escort you to

your room to fetch your bonnet and shawl before we
go outside?"

Teddy offered his arm, his expression smug, almost
as if he expected her to respond to his mild flattery with fawning adoration. Despite his angelic
looks and charming manner, his attentions made
her uncomfortable.

"Thank you, but I'm sure you should be making
arrangements for the croquet game. I can find my
way upstairs without assistance." She sidled out of his
reach and left the room as quickly as she could without
breaking into a run.

Shermont's knowing chuckle followed her up
the stairs.

Was he laughing at her hasty flight or the fact
that Teddy's offer had been refused? Either way, she
would be in trouble. Good thing she planned on
going home as soon as she could find those pesky
ghosts and convince them to send her back. And
the best place for that would be the bedroom where
they'd met.

She pushed aside a tiny bubble of regret. It could
have been interesting to... no, she wouldn't think
about that.

Eleanor ran to the room where her adventure had
started. She called out to the ghosts as soon as she
entered the sitting room.

Deirdre came out of Mina's bedroom. "I'm surprised
to see you so quickly."

Within a heartbeat, Eleanor realized the speaker was
the live girl and not one of the ghosts she was hoping
to see.

Mina stuck her head around the doorjamb. "For heaven's sake, Ellen—"

"Eleanor," she responded absently. How could she get rid of the live girls so she could talk to the ghosts?

"As you wish, Eleanor." Mina marched into the room and stood with her hands on her hips. "Although you needn't put on airs with us."

"We left you downstairs so you could speak to Teddy alone," Deirdre said.

"Did you flatter him?" Mina asked. "Let him know how happy you are to be back at the source of so many happy memories? You know, set the plan in motion?"

Eleanor was confused. What plan was she talking about? "Uh… not exactly. I guess I'm still a bit overwhelmed."

Mina raised her hands in exasperation.

"Never mind her theatrics," Deirdre said. "We'll have time to talk about your marriage later. Hurry and put on your bonnet. We don't want to keep Shermont… I mean, our brother waiting."

Now Eleanor understood why the girls had invited poor Ellen to visit. If their friend married Teddy, they would have an ally in the matter of getting to London for the Season. But that subject would have to wait. Eleanor still needed to talk to the ghosts about sending her home. "Why don't you two go on ahead? I… I think I need a few minutes alone to gather my thoughts. Everything is happening so fast."

"Fast? You were on the boat for six weeks," Mina said.

"I guess the fact that I am really here is still so unbelievable. I never expected to—"

"See, that premonition of the ship sinking that you mentioned in your last letter was only your imagination. You were merely worried about the drastic changes you're making," Deirdre said. "Just remember, it's all for the better."

"We'll give your regrets to the other guests," Mina said with a sympathetic expression that quickly morphed into a grin. "With you resting, I'm more likely to catch Lord Shermont's eye because he won't be paying so much attention to you."

"Me?" Eleanor asked. Had he been paying special attention to her? He'd made her feel as if he were intrigued by her presence, but she'd thought that was because of her reaction to him.

"I intend to ask Shermont to teach me to play croquet," Deirdre said.

"Hah! You have been playing since you were six and can beat everyone in the—"

"He doesn't know that. And a true sister never divulges family secrets."

Eleanor ignored the continued bickering and paced to the window. Her body warmed just thinking about his exhilarating touch. She recalled their all too brief encounters and judged that he hadn't paid her more attentions than any other woman present. She turned to face the others and interrupted their chatter. "Back up a step. What makes you think Shermont even knows I'm alive?"

Mina snorted in a very unladylike manner. "As if you didn't notice him staring at you."

"Teddy certainly noticed," Deirdre said. "If you're trying to make him jealous, it is already working."

"Why would I want to make Teddy jealous?"

"So he will propose marriage sooner." Mina's exasperated expression was the Regency version of a twenty-first century "Duh!"

"I…" Eleanor tried to think of a reason that Ellen would not want to rush into marrying Teddy. "We hardly know each other anymore. To be truthful, I'm not in a hurry to get married."

"You're not getting any younger," Deirdre pointed out as she plopped her bonnet on her head and tied a bow under her left ear. "Twenty-six is not completely on the shelf, but it's getting uncomfortably close to old maid status, or in your case, old matron."

Eleanor hid a smile. What would the girls say if they knew she was actually twenty-eight? True, her biological clock was ticking, but she could ignore it a little while longer.

"And we're not getting any younger either," Mina added. "You remember Letticia Wilson who was a year ahead of Deirdre at Miss Southerland's Academy? No? Well, she was six years behind you, so that's to be expected. The point is Letticia has already been presented, married, and produced an heir. We are still waiting for our Season. Once you and Teddy are married, you can sponsor us—I hope before we are both on the shelf, too."

"He said he planned to take you to London in the spring."

"Teddy promises that every year, but something

more important always comes up and prevents us from going," Deirdre said.

"We're counting on you to make certain that doesn't happen again," Mina said.

"I'm not sure I—"

"We'll have to discuss this later," Deirdre said. "Right now, we have guests waiting."

"Oh my, yes." Mina wrapped a light shawl around her shoulders and let it fall to her elbows.

"I'll come down in a few minutes," Eleanor promised.

"Take whatever time you need. In fact, why don't you take a nice long nap, so you'll be well rested for dinner?" Mina added as they exited.

Eleanor waited until she heard their voices trail down the hall, then she slipped into her bedroom and closed the door.

"All right, you two mischievous ghosts, we need to talk." The low volume of her voice did not lessen its commanding tone. "Time for you to make an appearance."

No response.

She pulled the desk chair to the middle of the room, sat down, and folded her arms. "I'm not leaving until you show yourself."

"Do you think we should let her know we're here?" Mina said so that only her sister could hear.

"She doesn't appear to need our help," Deirdre said. "At least not yet. We did promise we'd leave her alone."

"Come on, you guys." Eleanor had to force her voice to remain strong. "I know you're here." Purely a bluff, but she sensed their presence. A feeling like when a word is beyond your grasp, but you know it's there somewhere. "Energize. Manifest. Whatever it is you do to appear, do it now."

What would she do if they weren't there? How would she get back to her own time? "Mina? Deirdre?"

"Maybe we should tell her—"

"No. Our word is our bond."

Eleanor stood and paced the room. "I said I'd like to go back in time, but that was when I didn't think it was possible." She turned and headed back toward the window. Her steps slowed. "Okay, okay, we made a deal. And you've done your part—or at least the first step. I remember what I said I would do for you, but surely you can't expect to hold me to a promise based on wishful thinking. Let's just call the whole thing off. I'd really like to go back now."

She stopped and closed her eyes, waiting for the room to spin. On second thought she sat in the chair. "I'm ready."

Nothing happened.

Maybe she needed to be in the bed. She jumped up, climbed onto the feather mattress, and plopped into a prone position. "There's no place like home," she whispered and clicked her heels together three times for good measure. Nothing happened. "Beam me up? Abracadabra? Please?"

Still nothing.

Apparently, there were no magic words.

Four

"FINE." ELEANOR ROSE FROM THE BED AND STOMPED back to a post by the window. Her mind awhirl, she absently watched the servants set up the croquet course on the south lawn. So the ghosts were sticklers to the conditions of the deal. Apparently, the only way home was to complete her task.

She reached up and held the necklace as she often did in times of stress. The amber cross was a connection to her grandmother who had believed anything was possible as long as you followed your dream and worked hard.

"Okay, I will try to keep the two of you out of Shermont's way—I mean, the live versions of you," she clarified, since she was talking to the ghosts. At least she hoped she was talking to them.

She'd committed herself without the slightest idea of how she would make it happen. She took a deep breath and exhaled. What would Jane Austen do? Probably something proactive, even though she wouldn't have used that word.

The fastest way to accomplish her task was to confront Shermont directly. As Eleanor changed into walking boots, she wondered what she would say. Should she threaten him with something drastic if either girl's reputation was ruined?

That tactic hadn't been successful previously. Even the possibility of a deadly duel had not deterred him. Perhaps she could find something interesting in the paper to induce him to return to London. Worth a try, but since she'd just met the man, she had no idea what he would find fascinating. She'd have to wing it.

Eleanor picked up her bonnet and shawl. She paused at the door. "In return, I expect you to keep the second part of the bargain. Jane Austen had better be at this ball, and I had better get an introduction. And just so you know, I don't think it's fair not to tell me which one of you I need to protect."

She didn't bother to wait for a response she knew wasn't coming. Instead she headed downstairs, planning to stop in the library for a peek at the latest newspaper. After that, she intended to confront Lord Shermont.

Eleanor rushed down the stairs and grabbed the ornate newel post for balance as she made a sharp left turn toward the library. She nearly ran into Teddy as he exited carrying a sheaf of papers.

He flashed an angelic grin. "May I hope your eagerness is for my company?"

"I'm looking for a newspaper," she blurted out.

He raised an eyebrow.

"Ah… I've been away so long I was hoping to catch up on current events."

Not exactly a lie.

"Uncle Huxley requested the newspaper, but I'm

sure we can locate a *Godey's* or *Home Companion* for you to read. I am at your service."

As much as she would enjoy reading either and would especially love to look at the latest fashions, that indulgence would have to wait. A woman's magazine was unlikely to help in her quest for an item to entice Shermont to return to London. She shook her head. "Perhaps later. Have you seen Lord Shermont?"

"What is it about him? Five years ago no one had even heard of him, and now every female under the age of eighty has set her cap for him."

"I have not set my cap for him."

"See there, Digby. Your theory has been disproved."

Eleanor whirled around to see Shermont lounging against the doorjamb of the entrance to the library. Speak of the devil.

"Either that or Mrs. Pottinger is older than she looks." Shermont eyed her from head to toe. When his gaze returned to her face, he grinned and winked.

Judging by her body's response, his blatant perusal might as well have been accompanied by the touch of his hands. The warmth of her reaction seemed to draw all the blood from her brain, and his use of the unfamiliar title flustered her until she remembered she was supposed to be Cousin Ellen, a widow. Although she was sure her cheeks were flaming, she returned his bold stare. "The year of my birth would indeed surprise you, but it shall remain a well-kept secret."

Shermont bowed. "As it should be with all ladies."

Teddy held out his arm to Eleanor. "I'm so pleased we have some time together. I want to hear all about your life in America. I've read of wild Indians, ferocious bears, fierce feral pigs, and other dangerous animals. How do you cope?"

Eleanor remained where she stood. "Actually, there's not—"

Tuttle, the butler, entered with a wax-sealed message on a tray. Teddy excused himself and stepped away. After a muttered conversation, of which Eleanor heard only "office" and "urgent," he instructed the servant to fetch a maid to act as Eleanor's chaperone. Shermont raised an eyebrow.

Eleanor interpreted the gesture as either an unspoken comment on the fact that Shermont had interrupted Teddy and Eleanor alone together or an acknowledgement that Teddy didn't trust him.

To cut the tension, Eleanor said, "A chaperone is hardly necessary. After all, if I can fend off wild Indians and ferocious bears, I should be able to handle Lord Shermont." It was a lie, of course, but she was beginning to do that quite easily.

Teddy bristled at her refusal of his suggestion, and Shermont hid his surprise with a nod of appreciation for her riposte.

"As a widow you are exempt from certain strict observances," Teddy said with a sniff. "However, a reputation is rather fragile and should never be put at risk."

The butler returned with a timid maid in tow, and Teddy reluctantly left to see to his business.

"You're not like other females." Shermont said.

"But I am. One head, two arms, two feet. Quite the same. Quite ordinary."

He shook his head. "There is a subtle difference I can't quite put my finger on." He rubbed the scar on his forehead.

"Perhaps because I am an American?"

"I don't think so." He stepped closer and picked up her hand that still rested on the newel post.

Again, his touch sent a tingling feeling straight to her core.

Ignoring the presence of the maid, he drew Eleanor toward him and leaned forward. "If this were any other hand, I would not desire to do this." He placed his warm lips on the back of her hand and then turned it over to kiss the palm.

Her breath caught in her throat. Such a simple action, not one she'd ever thought of as erotic, caused her knees to weaken and her toes to curl.

He looked up at her face from under his long eyelashes. His eyes deepened to dark gray, telling her he felt the same electric current.

"And that makes you different," he said, his voice husky.

Before she could form a response, the bickering of Mina and Deirdre announced their imminent arrival. Shermont quickly pulled away. After hesitating for a heartbeat, he mumbled an excuse, bowed, and disappeared into the library.

Of the same mind to avoid the sisters, Eleanor took advantage of the maid's open-mouthed attention on Shermont to duck through another doorway. Although safe from the girls for the moment, she was soon hopelessly lost in the maze of parlors and sitting rooms. She wandered from room to room until she found an exit. The French doors led to a flagstone patio that had several paths leading past walls of greenery. Assuming she would eventually run into the south lawn and the others, she headed to her right to walk around the house.

A decision she soon regretted. The paths were designed for people to stroll leisurely through the gardens. There were alcoves with Greek statues, nooks with stone and iron benches, and stunning, colorful displays of myriad flowers she couldn't name. Not a straight get-from-here-to-there stretch among them. An army of gardeners must be needed to keep everything in such pristine order, but she didn't encounter a single servant she could ask for directions.

She'd read somewhere if you were lost, you should sit and wait for someone to find you. If you kept moving you might wander into areas already searched and not to be revisited. She was ready to sit on one of the benches when the path widened onto another flagstone patio. Shermont sat in a cast-iron chair. A book lay open on his knee and he appeared to be concentrating intently. He didn't look up until she was quite near. Upon seeing her, he jumped up and greeted her.

"I'm sorry to disturb you," she said, even though it was a lie. He was just the person she wanted to see. Although she knew which topic she wanted to discuss, she decided it would be better to open the conversation on a general note. "What are you reading?"

"Oh." He bent over to retrieve the slim volume that had fallen to the ground and looked at it as if it had suddenly appeared in his hands. "I... ah... just picked up this copy of Sheridan's *School For Scandal* to pass the time."

Fortunately, her high school drama class had staged the classic play, so she was familiar with it. "Although the play lacks the cohesion of his earlier work *The Rivals*, I thought the auction scene quite clever."

He appeared taken aback for a moment. "Ah yes, as an American you would be familiar with Sheridan, since he sided with the Colonials in Parliament. Quite surprisingly, he was never challenged to a duel, despite using his wit in defense of such controversial topics."

She hadn't known that about the playwright, but it gave her a perfect opening. "Speaking of duels…" Over his shoulder she noticed Teddy exiting the house with a man in working clothes. As the other man left, Teddy turned and obviously spied them. From the glower on his face, she wouldn't have another chance to speak to Shermont alone.

She rushed to say her piece, while trying to ignore Teddy stomping in their direction.

"Lord Shermont, if your intentions toward Mina or Deirdre are anything less than honorable, I beg you to stay away and not lead either impressionable young girl astray."

He reared back in what appeared to be genuine shock. "I have no interest in either girl, honorable or otherwise. Good heavens, madam, they're mere children, barely out of the schoolroom. I am insulted."

"But your reputation—"

"Despite what some may say, I assure you I am not in the habit of seducing virgins."

"Surely you're aware of their interest in you?"

He dismissed any anxiety with a casual flick of his hand. "A schoolgirl crush. They will recover soon enough without encouragement. I'm more concerned with what interests you. Lord Digby seems to have laid claim to you."

"I'm not a piece of property. I'm a person," she said. Knowing Teddy was within earshot, she continued, "I have no intention of anyone claiming me."

"It appears I have arrived just in time to forestall an argument," Teddy said with a pleased smile as he offered his arm to her. "Come, my dear cousin. My sisters await us."

He obviously hadn't realized her words were for his edification, too.

She laid her hand on his forearm. "No argument," she said in a pleasant voice. "Just stating a fact."

"Please don't tell me you have become one of those dreadful bluestockings?" Teddy asked as they strolled out of the garden and along a terrace. He gave a slight shudder.

"I'm rather in favor of the bluestockings," Shermont said as he followed several paces behind. "An educated, literate female is a more interesting… companion."

Somehow she knew he'd almost said lover. Eleanor peeked over her shoulder at him. He grinned in response.

"A lady who verbalizes her desires is more likely to get exactly what she wants," Shermont said. His statement had the ring of a promise in disguise.

"And is likely never to be quiet," Teddy added.

"That's not very flattering," Eleanor said, her tone chastising.

"I'm not referring to you, my dear. My sisters are always demanding the latest gewgaw or trinket."

"Fashions change rapidly," she said. "We all like to remain *au courant* with the latest trends."

Teddy sighed. "So I am learning. A guardian's responsibility is a heavy burden when one carries it alone." He looked at her with sad, puppy eyes in a blatant bid for sympathy.

She patted his arm. "You're lucky to have Aunt Patience, Uncle Huxley, and a bevy of servants to share your affliction."

"Affliction. Yes, that's a good term for my situation."

The dig had apparently gone over Teddy's head, but Shermont's cough sounded suspiciously as though it covered a chuckle.

The promenade ended at a wide expanse of lawn. The chaperones were seated to the left of the field under a majestic elm. The girls in their pastel dresses practiced their swings with wooden mallets. The pastoral scene brought to mind Georges Seurat's *A Sunday Afternoon on the Island of La Grand Jatte*. She had first seen the pointillism masterpiece as a child, while visiting the Art Institute of Chicago with her grandmother. The large painting, nearly seven by eleven feet, made a grand impression and remained one of her favorites for its sense of harmony. No untidiness, nothing disordered. The bucolic vista before her evoked the same poetic peacefulness.

Eleanor enjoyed the elegant scene for only a moment before Mina spotted them and shrieked her welcome. Although Mina and Deirdre called Eleanor's name, she was astute enough to know the real object of their enthusiastic greeting was Shermont, who stood directly behind her. Even without touching him, she was aware of his presence, his warmth. Aware that if she took a mere two steps back, she would run up against his body.

The girls came running like a pair of joyful puppies, only to pull up short upon catching sight of Teddy's disapproving frown. They walked the last twenty feet in sedate propriety.

"We have been awaiting your arrival to start the game," Mina said with a curtsey.

The entire group strolled toward the wire rack that held the rest of the mallets and colorful striped croquet balls.

"As the guest who has come the longest distance, I think Cousin Eleanor should choose her color first," Teddy said. His tone implied that he was used to his suggestions being taken for law.

"Excellent idea," Deirdre agreed. She turned to Eleanor. "Of course, Teddy always plays blue, like his beautiful eyes."

"And Deirdre always plays green," Mina said. "I'm yellow."

Beatrix piped in her claim for white striped ball. And Hazel and Fiona spoke up for brown and orange.

"Then it's a good thing my favorite color is red," Eleanor said with a smile.

"And black for me," Shermont said. "I'm glad the one left isn't pink."

As play began, Eleanor realized the countryfolk took their croquet seriously. She hadn't played since she was a child and concentrated on watching the others so she wouldn't make a fool of herself. Even so, she could tell Shermont's head wasn't in the game.

Shermont mentally kicked himself for allowing a female to distract him. He'd hoped to learn something incriminating by listening at the estate office window, but Eleanor's arrival had caused him to lose focus. Instead of narrowing his list of suspects or finding out where the foreign agents met to pass on military information to Napoleon's agents, he'd been discussing a play with Eleanor.

Something about that female made him forget everything else. He rubbed the scar on his forehead.

Despite the girls surrounding him and clamoring for his attention, he rededicated himself to his mission. He would not let Eleanor distract him again. From the corner of his eye he noted Digby helping Eleanor apply a proper grip to her mallet. Shermont turned away. To maintain his persona of carefree lord, he busied himself with the girls. He was careful not to show particular attention to anyone.

Beatrix moped at the edge of the circle of friends, and he wasn't surprised at the venomous looks she shot in Eleanor's direction. Digby seemed determined to send everyone else back to the beginning to clear a path for Eleanor to win. Shermont felt more than a bit uncharitable toward the man himself.

Eleanor was not overly pleased with Teddy's behavior either. When it came her turn to play, Eleanor set herself to take a long shot toward the next wicket in the prescribed pattern, which happened to be guarded by Shermont. Teddy interrupted her, wrapping his arms around her to correct her hand position. His intimacy didn't do anything for her, surprising in view of his good looks and the similarity in coloring to her former fiancé, or maybe because of it. She thanked him for his help, but insisted on making her own shots. The ball traveled the distance, missing the wicket. While the others took their turns, she strolled along the path her ball had taken.

On his turn Shermont gave his ball a gentle nudge, lining it up to follow hers. He barely missed touching her ball and having a chance to send her back to the beginning.

"Tough luck," she commiserated.

"I'm right where I want to be," he said in a low voice.

His nearness made her a bit nervous. After one rotation of play, her chance came to get away from him. She overswung, missed her shot completely, and caught the wire wicket, pulling it out of the ground. Embarrassed, she made a grab for it. Shermont reached for the wicket at the same time.

Their hands brushed. That intense sparks of desire could be generated by such a simple action took them both by surprise. A long look passed between them, but the thwack of one heavy ball hitting another caused her to jump back.

Teddy sauntered up. "Sorry about that, old sod," he said with an insincere mope. "Guess I have to send you away." Unable to hide a triumphant grin any longer, he positioned his ball next to Shermont's, held it in place with his foot, and swung his mallet with precise acrimony. The black striped ball took off like cannon shot and traveled deep into the wooded area bordering the lawn.

Shermont saluted Teddy and with a rueful expression headed into the woods after his ball.

Eleanor spent the next half hour trying to stay as far from Teddy as she could. Deirdre declared that anyone not on the course must miss a turn rather than hold up the game. Eleanor was just thinking Shermont had been gone an inordinately long time when he came out of the woods, dirty and disheveled, his empty arms stretched wide.

"I can't find my ball," he called. "I am therefore forced to concede the match." He shrugged his shoulders and looked appropriately heartbroken. "If you will excuse me, I must attend to my torn coat."

Despite his woebegone expression, Eleanor noticed an incongruent sparkle in his eyes.

The party fell flat after he left and broke up as soon as Deirdre won the match. As the guests straggled into the house, Eleanor couldn't help but look back at the woods and wonder. Just what, or who, had Shermont encountered in the woods?

Five

As SHERMONT ENTERED HIS SUITE OF ROOMS, RELIEF warred with excitement. Finally, he'd found a clue.

"I fear you've ruined your coat, milord," Carl the valet said in the same tone as if he were announcing a beloved pet had passed. But that was how he always sounded.

"Where is that folio of maps?" Shermont asked as he slipped out of the garment. He walked to the desk and searched through a pile of books and papers.

Carl extended the coat to arm's length. "I had not realized croquet was so… pugilistic."

"I chased my ball into the woods," Shermont said absently as he opened drawers and pawed through the contents.

"Dirt. Mud. I'll never get these grass stains out."

"I'm sure I brought a detailed map of the local area." Shermont turned to face the shorter man. He crossed his arms. "Have you been straightening my work again?"

"If I were allowed to keep your papers organized, you would be able to find what you're looking for." Carl held up the ruined coat with two fingers poking through rips in the fabric.

"Thornbushes."

Carl shook his head and made tutting, clucking noises like an old crone eyeing her broken rocking chair.

"Forget the damn coat. Help me find that map."

The valet took one last affectionate look at the coat and then tossed it over his shoulder. He walked to the desk and withdrew the map from a stack of papers.

"Carl, you're a magician."

"Yes, milord."

Shermont sat at the desk and spread out the map. He tried to ignore his valet's fussing about, moving objects that didn't need straightening. Finally, he turned and asked, "Is there something you wanted to say?"

"Nothing in particular," Carl said with a shrug.

"Come on. Out with whatever is bothering you."

"It's that female."

Shermont didn't need to ask which female he was talking about. Carl's consistent doom and gloom attitude could get a bit annoying at times, but he'd proven perceptive in their activities for the crown.

"Something about her doesn't ring true." Once started, Carl didn't pull any punches. "I'm concerned your attraction to her will distract you from your mission—"

"Our mission."

"And may blind you to the chance she could be involved."

Despite the fact he'd already learned Eleanor was dangerous to his equilibrium, he denied the possibility. "Nothing I can't handle."

"You will by necessity be much in her company. There is the ball and a picnic tomorrow."

"You worry too much."

Carl heaved a sigh. "It is my nature, my job, my curse, and my reason for being."

"And it has saved our lives a time or two. Just try to keep it to a minimum until there is really something to worry about."

"Yes, milord."

"Now, have a look at this." Shermont smoothed out the heavy paper and pointed. "This is where I entered the wood. About here I found a path… but it's not marked on the map."

"Probably just an animal trail. Deer in those woods, I hear. And wolves, if gossip is to be believed."

"I found a heel print and other signs of human usage. The trail widened at an ancient oak tree. I followed it to a point just this side of that bald, flat-topped hill where the path joined the road to town. I think the French agent is using the tree as a drop point for messages. A courier takes the information to Napoleon and brings back the payment. By necessity, that person would have to move about and cross the Channel without being noticed, probably a sailor or fisherman. Therefore he couldn't frequent the house without causing comment. Using the large bole in the trunk of the tree as a drop point leaves everyone else none the wiser."

"Or it could be a lover's trysting place."

Shermont shook his head. "I think we're onto something."

"I will notify our agent in town to watch the road and pick up anyone leaving the woods."

"No. The courier is small potatoes. We can pick

him up anytime. Our quarry is the man who leaves messages in the tree."

"Or the woman."

Which, of course, brought Eleanor to mind. Shermont rubbed the scar on his forehead.

"Another headache? I'll prepare one of my herbal remedies for you," Carl said.

Shermont nodded his thanks while he stared at the map. What route would someone from the house take to remain out of sight? Even at night the light coming from the many windows would illuminate large sections of lawn.

Carl served the tea.

"Thank you. I want to explore the area after dark. Please arrange for a tray to be brought up for dinner. Make whatever excuse you think appropriate. And let Lord Digby know not to expect me at the card table before midnight."

After the croquet game broke up, the rest of the party drifted into the house talking about the plans for the picnic on the following day. In the grand entrance hall, two maids and a footman waited to take hats, bonnets, parasols, and shawls.

"Won't you join us in the parlor?" Aunt Patience asked Teddy.

"As much as I would enjoy being the only thorn among so many lovely roses, estate business tears me away. If you will excuse me?" he asked with a bow.

Patience nodded, and he left. "Well, my friends.

Shall I have Cook serve us tea now, or would you prefer later?" she asked the other chaperones.

"I think we will take tea in our room," Mrs. Holcum said for herself and her daughter. "A bit of rest is always called for after exercise."

"Excellent idea," Mrs. Matthews agreed. "The sun gave me a smidgen of a headache. A lie-down before dressing for dinner would be just the remedy." She turned toward the stairs. "Come along girls."

Fiona and Hazel followed with no enthusiasm. "Naps are for babies," one muttered, only to be hushed by her mother.

Aunt Patience and Mrs. Holcum ascended the stairway chatting, and Beatrix trailed meekly behind.

"This is a perfect time for us to get reacquainted," Mina said, linking her arm through Eleanor's.

Deirdre took her free arm and they followed the others upstairs. "Yes, we want to hear everything. Tell us all about life in the Colonies. Have you seen any wild Indians?"

"Well…" Eleanor didn't want to lie more than necessary. "I saw the Atlanta Braves… battle the Cincinnati Reds once." The only pro baseball game she'd ever attended.

"What about Colonial men?" Mina asked. "Do they all have big bushy beards and wear bearskin clothes?"

"Don't be silly. Americans dress like everyone else."

Deirdre opened the door to their suite of rooms. "I had wondered if your wardrobe would be up to snuff, but at least the dress you're wearing is reasonably up to date." She plopped down on the green and gold settee and put her feet on the gold-tasseled hassock. "Waists are moving lower every year."

"I've never seen a design like that," Mina said, taking the place next to her sister.

"Do you like it?" Eleanor asked. She twirled in a circle, proud of her handiwork. "I designed it myself. The crisscross bodice and side pleats hide hooks, so I can dress without assistance."

Both girls stared at her as if she'd spoken in tongues.

"Why would you want to dress yourself?" Deirdre asked.

"You made your own clothes?" Mina exclaimed. "Are there no dressmakers in the Colonies?"

"I'm sure there are. I just enjoy sewing. Don't you?"

"Well, we embroider handkerchiefs and the like. And we help Aunt Patience with the mending, and she sews Teddy's linens."

"We make shirts and baby clothes for charity. Every gentlewoman does needlework. Idle hands and all that." Mina tipped her head to the side. "Where do you get patterns?"

"I look in fashion magazines for ideas and then make my own."

Mina jumped up and headed for Eleanor's room. "I want to see the rest of your wardrobe."

Deirdre and Eleanor followed. They spent the next hour happily trying on one another's clothes, matching accessories, and sharing fashion tips.

"Are you wearing this to the ball? I have a lovely string of amber beads that would go perfectly with this gold-washed silk," Mina said.

Eleanor touched her talisman. "I designed the dress

specifically to wear with my favorite necklace. The trim echoes the filigree on the sides of the cross."

The sisters admired the amber cross. "I think I've seen something similar," Deirdre said, frowning. "But I can't remember where."

Mina looked closely at the embroidered hem. "Look at this. Have you ever seen stitches so even?" She held out the dress to show her sister.

"Ah…" Eleanor didn't know when the first sewing machine had been invented, but she was sure the kind with cams to embroider designs was very modern. "I had help. Singer did most of the actual work." Time to divert their attention. She grabbed the leather case that held her Regency jewelry, flipped it open, and pulled out a necklace. "These dark blue glass beads would complement the dress you're wearing," she said to Deirdre.

"You're right. I hadn't thought to wear dark blue with this pale yellow muslin. You have a good eye for color."

Mina arched her neck to see what else was in the box. Hiding a grin, Eleanor set it out on the table and invited the girls to look at her jewelry. She admitted that most of the stones were worthless imitations.

"All our jewels are paste, too," Mina said as she held up a peacock-shaped brooch.

"Mina!" Deirdre said in a low warning tone.

"Well, they are."

"Teddy told us never to discuss our jewels."

"She's family." Mina turned to face Eleanor. "Come. I'll show you mine, even if Deirdre wants to be secretive with hers." As she led the way into the other bedroom, she continued, "Teddy had replicas made of all the jewelry we inherited from mother so we wouldn't have to worry about having it stolen. He keeps the real jewels locked up somewhere safe."

Mina used a small key to unlock the wide top drawer of a massive dresser. Inside was an amazing collection of nearly every gem and type of jewelry imaginable, so many pieces that the velvet lining was hardly visible. "Of course, most of these we won't wear until we go to London and are presented at court. Can you see me decked out in these to play croquet?" She held up a fabulous necklace of diamonds linked together by star sapphires. The pendent on the end was as large as a quarter. A matching bracelet, ring, and tiara completed the set.

"This parure is my favorite," Mina said, displaying a comparable set made with large square-cut emeralds. "Family legend says Queen Elizabeth gave them to our ancestor, the first Lord Digby, for unspecified services." Mina wiggled her eyebrows and giggled.

"I hope all this is insured," Eleanor said.

Mina shrugged. "Teddy handles those matters."

"You really should take an interest in your business affairs."

"I don't understand why. We don't know anything about investments. Teddy does a fine job managing our funds, and when we marry our husbands will control everything."

"You could have control of your own money built into the marriage contract. Then, if a husband turned to drink and gambling, he wouldn't leave you destitute."

"Oh, poor Eleanor. Is that what happened to you? Is that why you're so poor that you have to make your own clothes?"

"Absolutely not. I... I'm not poor. I just think a woman should have control of her own destiny, that's all."

Mina and Deirdre looked at each other. "Bluestocking," they said together.

"If that's what you call an independent woman, I'll wear the sobriquet proudly."

"Well, don't embroider it on your bodice," Deirdre said. "It won't secure you any dances at the ball."

"We shall keep your secret," Mina promised.

"Dancing partners are the least of my worries." Eleanor would have to turn down any offers because she didn't know the steps. She still had to make it to that point and keep Shermont away from the sisters.

"Well, our Teddy is sure to ask you to dance," Deirdre said with a satisfied smile.

"He was very attentive to you while playing croquet," Mina said.

Perhaps too attentive. "Please do nothing to promote an alliance with your brother. I don't..." Would they even believe she didn't find him attractive? "I'm not ready for a new relationship yet."

"You're out of mourning."

"It's not as simple as that. Please understand, and bear with me."

"Perhaps we should give you a few weeks to adjust to being here," Mina suggested.

"I think that might be sufficient," Eleanor said with a sigh of relief. Now if she could only convince Teddy of the same. That burden added to her task of watching the sisters, as well as dealing with her unexpected attraction to Shermont, made the coming evening loom ahead like a dentist appointment for a root canal.

A knock sounded on the outer door. "Girls?" Aunt Patience trilled from the sitting room. "Where are you?"

Mina grabbed the tiara from her head, swept all the jewelry into the top drawer, then closed and locked it before Patience entered, making Eleanor wonder about the relationship between the girl and her aunt.

"There you are, my dears." The older woman plopped into the chair by the window and fanned herself. "I know you are the official hostess this evening, Deirdre, but I truly had to act quickly when I heard the terrible news."

"What's wrong?" Deirdre asked.

"What isn't? First, Mrs. Matthews arrives a day earlier than expected with both daughters instead of just the eldest. That makes nine females for dinner. Now, one of Teddy's military friends can't come until tomorrow—some silly excuse about being on duty. I mean, what could he possibly be guarding against in the middle of the English countryside? Marauding cows? Pillaging pigs? Thank goodness Miss Austen sent word she and Miss Jane are not coming today."

"I did not get that note," Deirdre said through tight lips.

"You were not here yesterday," Patience explained. "As acting hostess I felt it necessary to open the note to be informed. For Lord Digby's sake."

"But they are coming?" Eleanor could not help asking.

"Yes, yes," Aunt Patience said. "They will arrive late tomorrow afternoon with their brother, Mr. Edward Knight. And I've already sent a note to the vicar saying we need him and the rector to fill out the table tonight."

Deirdre stiffened. "You seem to have coped with everything... in my absence. Need I remind you I am now here?"

"Then you can handle the latest problem. Lord Shermont has asked for a tray in his room."

"I hope he's not ill," Deirdre said.

"We should offer to nurse him," Mina suggested hopefully.

Aunt Patience shot her a quelling look. "Not necessary. His valet mentioned a headache as the reason. Rude man. He has absolutely no consideration for the inconvenience he's causing me... I mean you, Deirdre."

"I'm sure the valet did not mean to be inconsiderate."

"Not him. Shermont."

"But you said—"

"Never mind. What are you going to do about the uneven numbers? We don't know any more presentable gentlemen who can fill in at this short notice."

"I'll gladly take a tray in my room," Eleanor volunteered. She hadn't completely adjusted to the change in time zones, and jet lag was catching up with her. "I'm still rather tired after my journey."

"And have everyone speculate on the absence of two guests?" Aunt Patience appeared horrified. "Especially after his marked attentions to you? Absolutely not."

"Everything will be fine," Deirdre said, remaining calm in the face of terrible disaster—uneven numbers at the table. "We will not be judged by London standards out here in the country. This is a simple family dinner with a few close friends in attendance."

Aunt Patience sniffed. "Well, I intend to give Lord Shermont a piece of my mind if he joins the party later in the evening as that odious little man intimated he would."

"Lord Shermont is our guest," Deirdre said, issuing an unspoken restraining order that did not sit well with her aunt. She held the door open. "And it's time to dress for dinner."

Aunt Patience huffed her way out.

"You don't seem to have a... loving relationship with your aunt," Eleanor commented.

Deirdre folded her arms and set her mouth into a straight line. "Aunt Patience refuses to admit I'm grown up and perfectly capable of running this household."

"She's not really our aunt," Mina explained. "Patience simply arrived with Teddy, her sister's bastard..."

"Mina!"

"Well, it's the truth. We eventually pieced together the story. Father met Teddy's mother, Victorine, at Versailles while on his Grand Tour. She was beautiful and angelic. He was already engaged."

"The proverbial star-crossed lovers."

"Before he could make arrangements to break his commitment and marry Victorine, he was recalled to England because Grandfather was dying. Father sent word to her, but none of his letters were answered.

Then, during the French Revolution, he lost hope and did as his father had wished. He married the girl he'd been engaged to—our mother."

"I'm sure he must have cared for her, too," Eleanor said.

"They were not an... emotional couple," Deirdre said in a matter-of-fact voice. "But they were well-suited nonetheless. An arranged marriage."

Eleanor told herself such was the custom of the day, but it seemed so calculated and cold.

"Father did finally hear from Victorine," Mina said. "She'd had a child and feared for his life. He sent money for her to bring his son to safety in England. Even though he couldn't marry her, he intended to acknowledge little four-year-old Teddy.

"Victorine died on the journey," Deirdre said. "Her sister Patience brought Teddy the rest of the way here. Mother refused to receive either one, and it created an irreparable rift between our parents. She died several months later. I was three years old, and Mina was still an infant."

"I wouldn't know anything of Mother if it weren't for the stories the older servants told us. She was sweet and kind and loved us very much." Mina sniffled. "Father named Teddy his heir, and he was the proverbial apple of his eye."

"We might as well have been invisible," Deirdre added, sounding more candid than bitter.

"But your father took care of you in his will. The jewels. Your dowries. That must mean he loved you."

"He probably did, in his own way. But as far as the inheritance went, he didn't have a choice," Deirdre said. "As heir, Teddy received the entailed property, but the bulk of the estate came from Mother's family and was already designated for her offspring in the marriage contracts."

"Much of the artwork, silver, household goods, and the money in the funds belonged to our mother, and she left detailed documents specifying how everything is to be divided between us. She didn't want us to squabble over who got what and become estranged as had happened in her family."

So Teddy got the title, the land, and the manor house, but the girls got the bulk of the money and almost all the stuff. "You should take a clue from your mother and be involved with your finances."

Mina shook her head. "He may be in truth only a half-brother, but he has always taken good care of us. Why, after Father died, Teddy could have set us out of our very home if he'd wanted. Where would we have gone?"

"We trust Teddy," Deirdre said. "On the other hand, we are a bit wary of Aunt Patience."

"She takes things," Mina said. "Like a magpie. Shiny baubles find their way into her room. We saw Mother's dresser set in there, but she denied taking it. After that she started locking her door."

"She has always placed Teddy's interest over ours," Deirdre said. "And he treats her like the mother he never knew. We have learned to be careful around her."

Eleanor already knew Aunt Patience hadn't done a good job chaperoning the girls, or one wouldn't have gotten into trouble and precipitated a duel. Now that she knew she couldn't depend on any backup, her job got more difficult.

Fortunately, she wouldn't have to deal with Shermont at dinner. She refused to name her disappointment as anything other than relief.

Six

AS THEY WALKED DOWN THE STAIRS TO MEET THE REST of the party, Deirdre hooked her arm with Eleanor's. "I'm sorry you will be paired with the rector as a dinner partner, but I really have no other option since you are the lowest ranking female guest."

Walking behind them, Mina giggled. Deirdre shot a frown over her shoulder.

"I'm just happy it isn't me," the younger sister replied.

"I'll make it up to you, I promise," Deirdre said to Eleanor.

"I hope I don't make a fool of myself by using the wrong fork or something."

"Copy what Deirdre does," Mina said. "That's what I always do. And when in doubt, talk about the weather."

Pausing at the parlor entrance, Deirdre turned to the butler standing at attention nearby. "You may ring the assembly gong, Tuttle."

He bowed, and with an air of solemn ceremony he opened a tall case of darkest wood to the left of the front door, exposing a large brass circular plate with exotic engravings. He removed a batonlike device from a high shelf and struck the gong.

Eleanor resisted the urge to cover her ears.

"An ancestor of our mother's brought it back on his return from the Second Crusade," Deirdre said. "Come. Our guests will be arriving shortly." The sound of the front door knocker followed their entry into the parlor. "Ah, that would the vicar and his rector. Always punctual."

"Especially if it involves a free meal," Mina whispered to Eleanor as she took her place beside her sister. "If I were you, I'd find an out of the way corner until other guests arrive, or you'll be stuck talking to the rector all evening."

Eleanor took Mina's advice and sat in one of two chairs that faced the window. If she peeked around the high wingback, she could see nearly the entire room, but she was out of the traffic pattern.

As the first guest to arrive, the vicar positioned himself near the fireplace and watched the entrance with a welcoming smile. The rector took a post next to a table that held a bowl of sugar-coated nuts that Eleanor knew as Jordan almonds, her favorite movie theater treat. She'd once read on the back of the box that a honey-coated version of the confection dated back to the ancient Romans and that the sweet had been around in recognizable sugar-coated form since the fifteenth century. The rector put one candy in his mouth and another in his pocket. He repeated the process every time the vicar looked the other way.

Although the girls had not set up a formal receiving line, over the next fifteen minutes Deirdre greeted each newcomer, took the person by the arm, introduced the guest to someone, and provided a topic of conversation of mutual interest before moving back to the door to start the process over again. If Deirdre was busy, Mina smoothly took her place. They made it look easy. Eleanor was left in awe.

"Why are you hiding in the corner?"

Eleanor started. She hadn't noticed Teddy's approach. Bent over, his face was inches from hers. She leaned back. "I... uh..."

"Shall I fetch you something to relax your nerves? I could smuggle in a brandy."

"I'm not nervous," she lied.

"Hey ho, Digby," a handsome young man in uniform said as he approached. "Not sporting of you to keep the most attractive lady in the room all to yourself."

Teddy visibly fought for composure. "Cousin Eleanor, may I present Major Alanbrooke of the Forty-Second Hussars, temporarily bivouacked near here while on maneuvers. Alanbrooke, Mrs. Pottinger, recently arrived from the Colonies."

"Ah, so you are the widow Digby's sister told us about."

Eleanor glanced over her shoulder and caught Deirdre's eye. The girl grinned and winked before turning back to the vicar with a solemnly attentive face.

"I'm compelled to warn you," Teddy said. "Alanbrooke here runs with a rather fast set."

"No help for it," Alanbrooke said. "My family motto is: Ride fast, shoot straight, and love well. Have to live up to the family dictum, don't you know?" His serious tone was tempered by the twinkle in his eye.

Something else was there too. Sadness? She sensed

the man had given his heart totally and irrevocably elsewhere. The woman was unavailable, or his love was unrequited. His teasing banter held no motive other than a bit of pleasantry to pass the time. Intuition told her she'd found a friend, so she felt comfortable returning the conversational lob with her own bit of innuendo.

"My family motto is: Beware of charming horsemen who are armed," Eleanor responded.

Alanbrooke grinned and spread his hands wide. "You have disarmed me with your beauty and wit."

"No man…" she said as she dropped her gaze momentarily to his waist, "with a sword is ever completely disarmed."

"As you see, I left my saber at the door with my hat."

"You have a saber?" she asked with an innocent smile.

His hoot of laughter caused a moment of silence in the room. He offered his arm. "With your permission, there are two pompous young lieutenants yonder who need to be put in their place, and I have the notion you are just the person to do it."

Alanbrooke escorted her to the other side of the parlor and introduced two fresh-faced officers resplendent in scarlet uniforms. Parker, tall and thin with red hair and freckles, stammered his pleasure at meeting her. Whitby, stocky with a head of riotous curls the same shade as his laughing brown eyes, kissed her hand and made a gallant bow.

That was how Eleanor became the center of attention of the military contingent, much to Teddy's obvious frustration. He tried unsuccessfully to shift the conversation to a familiar subject. Eleanor didn't help him out.

"The problem with being attracted to an officer in uniform is that eventually it comes off." She stated the innuendo with a straight face and sweet smile to make it more effective. The lieutenants attempted to hide embarrassed laughter behind feigned choking. "You two are horrible." She stomped her foot as if she had been misunderstood. "You know I meant when the gentleman retires."

The lieutenants' faces got redder and redder.

"I believe the term you are looking for is 'cashes out,'" Alanbrooke supplied after taking pity on his men. "When an officer leaves military service he sells his commission, thereby cashing out."

"Did Alanbrooke tell you we were in the same form at Eton?" Teddy asked her.

"No, he didn't. Is that how you two met?" she asked her new friend.

"Yes. Rockingham also. You'll meet him tomorrow. Parker and Whitby here are a few years our junior."

"We were so flattered to be included with upper classmen we didn't even mind having to wear dresses," Parker said in a rush, as if he seldom got to say a complete sentence. Whitby punched him in the arm.

Eleanor let her surprise show in her expression.

"Completely innocent, I assure you," Teddy said.

"I think we must explain," Alanbrooke said. "We needed to raise funds for... ah... extracurricular activities. Digby had a crazy idea to put on a play and charge admission. He wrote it and then recruited underclassmen to play the female roles."

"I was much shorter then," Parker said.

"I should think so," Eleanor said, straining her neck to look up at him. He was now the tallest man in the room, a gangly youth with a prominent Adam's apple.

"It was successful beyond our wildest expectations. So we did several a year," Teddy said.

"I neither drink nor gamble," Parker said. "So I saved all, well, most of my share to finance my summers in Italy studying painting."

"I bought two brood mares and stud service to start a racing stable," Whitby said.

She turned to Alanbrooke.

"I drank and gambled to excess and graduated without a ha'penny to my name."

She turned to Teddy.

"We should put on another play," he said, avoiding her unasked question regarding his activities with slick ease. "Tomorrow night. Just like old times."

"I can't," Parker said with a long face. "My father made me swear on my great-grandfather's sword never to put on a dress again."

"How did he find out?" Teddy asked. "We were so careful to keep your identity a secret."

"You probably shouldn't have kept the costume," Eleanor said. She'd meant it as a joke, but from the shocked look on Parker's face she realized she'd hit a bull's-eye.

"Only the silk stockings," he whispered.

She put a sympathetic hand on his arm. "And your father found them?"

Parker nodded. "Apparently, when I fired my valet

he went straight to Father to exact his revenge. It's the only way the old man could have known exactly where I kept them."

"You should have told him they belonged to a doxie," Whitby said. "At least that wouldn't have been so bad."

"Well, you won't have to wear a dress this time," Eleanor said. She patted the young man's arm. "There are plenty of us who would be willing to act the female roles."

"You would do that? You would be in our play?" Parker asked.

"Why not? And I'm sure Mina and Deirdre will agree too."

"I do not think that is a good idea," Teddy said. "My sisters on stage?" He shook his head.

"It's only a bit of entertainment for friends and family," Alanbrooke said. "Hardly scandalous."

"I suppose…"

Teddy did not seem convinced.

"With you in charge," Eleanor said to him, "I'm sure everything will be above reproach."

"Of course it will," Alanbrooke agreed.

"Very well," Teddy said. "They can participate."

"Bravo. It will be so much better with real females," Whitby said with a boyish grin.

"You're telling me?" Alanbrooke said, and everyone laughed.

"Will I have a part?" Parker asked.

"All the young people will have a role," Teddy promised. "I'll write plenty of small parts so no one will have many lines to memorize."

"I don't know how you're going to do all that by tomorrow," Eleanor said.

"Never question a master," Teddy said.

Mindful of her task—at least she told herself that was the reason she spoke for him—Eleanor said, "Don't forget a part for Shermont."

"Is he here?" Whitby asked.

"Yes. He'll join us at the gaming table later, if you have a mind to play a few hands," Teddy said.

While the others discussed that possibility, Alanbrooke turned to Eleanor with a raised eyebrow. "Shermont?" he mouthed silently.

She shook her head as a blush rose in her cheeks. Alanbrooke must be intuitive. Or was she that transparent?

Thankfully, Deirdre wormed her way into the circle. "I hate to take Eleanor away, but she has yet to meet her dinner partner." At the groans and offers to take his place, Deirdre shook her finger at them. "And you gentlemen have been shamefully neglecting your own designated partners. Dinner will be served in a few minutes, so I suggest you make amends before you're doomed to endure a silent meal." She took Eleanor's arm and led her away.

"I take it you enjoyed yourself," Deirdre said with a smug smile. "Unfortunately, it's now time to pay the piper." Moments later, she introduced Eleanor to the candy-eating rector, Mr. Fleckart, who by now had a bulging pocket full of Jordan almonds.

He took her hand and bowed. While he waxed eloquent over the honor Miss Cracklebury bestowed upon him by inviting him to partake of what he was sure would be an exemplary meal, Eleanor pulled her hand back and surreptitiously tried to wipe off the sticky residue he'd left. Deirdre gave her an apologetic look.

A sudden hush caused her to turn toward the door. Lord Shermont had entered.

"Good evening," he said loud enough for all to hear. "I do hope my appearance is not the cause of any inconvenience."

Of course, he would have to know the opposite was true, but all would forgive the ranking male. If Eleanor could judge by Mina's welcoming smile, she'd already done so.

Aunt Patience scowled and made a "harrumph" noise.

Deirdre excused herself and rushed to her sister's side. "We are relieved you are no longer unwell," she said to him. "And pleased you decided to join us."

"There I was eating my solitary meal when I realized I was missing the opportunity of spending time with the loveliest females in England."

Mina giggled, and Deirdre grinned as he bent over her hand. Eleanor understood their reaction and felt a similar welcoming elation. In the course of making his bow, he glanced at her and smiled as if he'd read her mind. Warmth spread through her veins like melted honey.

Shermont made the rounds to greet the guests he already knew, including Major Alanbrooke, and to meet the lieutenants. Despite Carl's insinuation that the decision to dine downstairs came suspiciously soon after he'd relayed the servants' gossip regarding Eleanor's interest in the military men, Shermont's assessment of the situation proved he'd made the right choice. The younger officers were garrulous, and, in their eagerness to impress, they could inadvertently reveal information valuable to the enemy.

Shermont positioned himself near the fireplace where he could overhear the voluble officers and watch Eleanor, thereby mixing duty with pleasure. On the other hand, it put him in proximity to Patience Aubin, who was not happy to see him, even though she didn't have the nerve to give him the cut direct.

Patience wore a heavy coating of powder on her face that did little to hide the deep pits that marked her as a smallpox survivor. But it did provide a clue to her vanity—and show him a path he could use to charm himself back into her good graces.

First, he tried a bit of flattery regarding her hideous headgear, an old-fashioned, shiny white turban with an ostrich feather that looked as if it had sprouted from her forehead. Then he added a deferential bow to her judgment on the unnecessary education of girls, even though he had to bite the inside of his cheek to keep from voicing his true opinion, and he managed his goal with ease, if not comfort.

"As I fast approach the status of elder," he said with a gesture that included the young Maxwell girls and the two brash lieutenants by the window, "I find myself championing the value of experience over the exuberance of youth."

"One would hardly call you old," Patience responded, flipping open her fan and covering the lower half of her face as if she were still a shy girl. "You are still a youngster to us. Don't we agree—Lord

Shermont is in his prime?" she asked the other chaperones seated nearby.

"Then I must bow to your opinion. If I had a glass
in my hand, I would raise it to experience."

The older ladies responded with girlish titters.

Within a short time Deirdre had realigned certain
members of the group with new dinner partners. Her
deft handling of the emergency impressed Eleanor,
even if the changes did not reach as far down the
ladder as herself and the rector.

Fortunately, Fleckart's incessant chatter on the
trials and tribulations of his position needed little
input beyond an occasional nod or monosyllabic
response. When the gong sounded again, they lined
up with the others for the promenade to the dining
room. The table was impressively packed with
elaborate dishes and candelabra. As soon as they
were seated, the footmen served a greenish soup
from a large turtle shell. Since she found no peas
in the thick broth, she simply pushed the grayish
lumps she did find around with her spoon until they
removed the bowls.

Fleckart's single-minded application to the task of
stuffing his mouth freed her to watch the sisters for
clues to the proper etiquette of the intricate dining
rituals. When Deirdre, seated at the foot of the
long table, spoke to Shermont, seated on her right,
all the women conversed with the person to their
right. When the hostess turned and conversed with
Major Alanbrooke to her left, all the women turned
to their left. Because of the extra female guests at
the table, Fiona was seated to Eleanor's left, and

the young girl was more interested in making eyes at Lieutenants Whitby and Parker across the table than talking.

"Psst," Eleanor whispered to get Fiona's attention. "This style of dining is... ah... foreign to me. Any help you could give me would be appreciated."

The girl readily agreed without taking her eyes off Whitby.

Eleanor ate very little. And not just because neither Deirdre nor Mina nor any other woman except the chaperones tasted more than a few tidbits. Eleanor sat equidistant from the ends of the table, and a whole roasted pig had been placed smack dab in the center. His porcine eye stared directly at her, ruining her appetite.

She stole a glance at Shermont. He lounged back in his chair, looking straight at her. He raised his wineglass in a silent toast. His intense regard promised more, and it gave her a fluttery feeling in the pit of her stomach. She had to look away.

The dishes were not served or passed, but everyone simply partook of what was in front of them. Since the table was packed with serving pieces, there was a wide assortment within reach, but she recognized almost nothing. Eleanor had never considered herself a picky eater, but she quickly learned she wasn't adventurous. Cook apparently wasn't big on plain food and served almost every sort of meat disguised as something else. The few vegetables presented had been boiled to near mush before being drowned in assorted sauces.

Mr. Fleckart offered her a serving from a bowl in front of him. "Creamed pickled eel?"

Eleanor shook her head, looking away from what resembled slugs floating in clotted milk. She reached for one of the tomatoes placed among the unidentified greens around the pork centerpiece. Fiona, seated next to her, gasped and looked at her with wide-eyed shock.

"Those are poison."

"Tomatoes?"

"Love apples. They're only for decoration."

Eleanor wanted to argue and even prove the conviction false, but she doubted anyone would believe her. She decided the disturbance that proving her point would cause was not worth the trouble. Instead she reached for a plate of assorted cheeses.

The girl made a negative noise.

"No?" Eleanor asked. "Decoration?"

Fiona ducked her head and whispered from behind her napkin. "We do not eat cheese in mixed company because it is properly eaten with one's fingers. Most men find the aroma that lingers on a girl's hands and breath unattractive."

"Oh." But apparently men with smelly breath and stinky fingers were tolerated—that good old double standard. Again, Eleanor decided against challenging the cultural conventions. As much as she'd always admired the Regency period, she was beginning to miss modern times.

Mr. Fleckart cleared his throat. When she glanced back toward him he held another dish out to her. She must have missed whatever he'd said, but it appeared to be a smoked white fish devoid of unidentifiable sauce. She smiled and took a small piece.

She nearly choked on the heavily salted bite and drained her glass of wine in order to get it down. One of the footmen standing against the wall immediately refilled her goblet. Thankfully, Deirdre rang the tiny bell near her plate and all the gentlemen stood to pull out their partner's chair. Mr. Fleckart followed suit after stuffing an entire boiled egg into his mouth.

Eleanor breathed a sigh of relief that the women would be excused to the parlor, but she soon learned she was mistaken. The people, still paired with their dinner partners, milled around the table making conversation, all the time pretending not to notice the servants, while at the same time trying to stay out of their way. The table was cleared completely, covered with a fresh damask cloth, and then set with another bewildering assortment of dishes. If anything, this course was more elaborate than the first. The centerpiece was a peacock complete with feathers.

When Deirdre resumed her seat, everyone else did the same. Eleanor found several small carrots used as a garnish that Fiona didn't stop her from eating. A footman approached her with a dish in his gloved hand.

She stared at him, uncomprehending.

"Lord Shermont sends his regards," Fiona said with a sly smile.

"What is it?" Eleanor asked the footman.

He looked startled as he lowered the oval bowl to reveal green beans with almond slivers. "The beans are parboiled and glazed with lemon juice and clarified butter. His Lordship requested Cook prepare this specific dish for your enjoyment."

"Consider before you partake," Fiona warned in a whisper. "Sending choice tidbits is a sign of a man's favor. If you accept… well…"

Eleanor hesitated. What would Jane Austen do? Then Eleanor realized she was too hungry to care about the consequences. How bad could it be? She smiled her thanks to Shermont before taking a generous portion. Then she thanked the footman.

"For future reference," Fiona said, her voice dripping with scorn, "one does not talk to the servants during dinner."

"Isn't that rather silly? What if one needs something?"

Fiona shrugged. "Good service anticipates a guest's needs. Bad service means you're stuck. You can always ask your dinner partner to serve you something."

Eleanor glanced over her shoulder at Fleckart, still cramming food into his mouth as fast as he could chew.

"You will be glad to know," Fiona whispered, "no hostess worth her crystal salt cellars would repeat partners within a fortnight of dinners."

While the servants removed dishes for the second time, Teddy practically dragged Beatrix to where Eleanor stood with Fleckart. Mrs. Holcum followed her daughter by mere steps, and Uncle Huxley, the dutiful dinner partner, trailed along in her wake.

"I hope you are enjoying the evening," Teddy said to Eleanor.

"Of course, I am," she said, stretching the truth just a little.

Fleckart launched into an ingratiatingly appreciative speech that commanded Teddy's sole attention.

"So… educational to dine in the society of your betters," Beatrix said in a low, meant-to-be-overheard voice.

Mrs. Holcum supported her daughter with a nod and a smug smile.

"True. Many of your customs are dissimilar to mine," Eleanor admitted. The majority of her recent dinners had come from the freezer and had been heated in the microwave. "But different is not automatically superior." She pasted a sweet smile on her face.

Beatrix opened and closed her mouth like a surprised fish. Apparently, she was not used to those she considered beneath her status standing up to her.

Mrs. Holcum, however, did not let the comment pass. "Are you disparaging your host's excellent repast?"

Eleanor forced a questioning look and blinked a few times. "What an odd leap of illogical reasoning. I thought we were discussing cultural differences." She allowed her smile to show a hint of condescension. "Aren't new experiences one of the joys of travel?"

"Bravo! When in Rome, eh?" Huxley said as he slapped Mrs. Holcum on the back.

Eleanor could almost see the steam coming from Mrs. Holcum's nostrils as she rounded on Huxley. He grinned, and she visibly struggled to get herself under control. The exchange told Eleanor two things: Huxley outranked Mrs. Holcum's husband, and he was a bit of an eccentric, which was, of course, tolerated if one's rank was sufficient.

"Fortunately, I have not had to endure the deprivations of travel beyond this country's borders," Mrs. Holcum said. "But if the necessity to do so should ever arise, I'm certain I would uphold the high standards of an English gentlewoman, regardless of native customs."

"I'm sure you would," Huxley said.

Mrs. Holcum nodded, pacified by what she deemed a compliment. Although by the twinkle in Huxley's eyes, Eleanor doubted he meant it as such.

The older woman turned her attack back to Eleanor. "I've heard Colonials have adopted many customs of foreign immigrants as well as the native Indians."

"We are the great melting pot," Eleanor answered proudly.

"I developed a fondness for the American sensibility after making the acquaintance of Benjamin Franklin some years ago. We had good times when he lived in London. That man loved to sing." Huxley chuckled at his memories, leaned forward, and whispered, "Especially bawdy tavern ditties. I still miss him."

"Consorting with the enemy," Mrs. Holcum said with a disdainful sniff.

"Who's consorting?" Teddy asked after extricating himself from Fleckart's clutches. He rejoined the group, bringing Shermont and Deirdre with him.

"We were just discussing an American friend of mine," Huxley said. "Franklin taught me to take an air bath every day for my health." The elderly gentleman thumped his chest Tarzan style. "Solid as a strapping youth."

"What's an air bath?" Eleanor asked.

Mrs. Holcum grabbed her daughter's elbow and dragged her to the other end of the room.

Deirdre leaned close to whisper in Eleanor's ear.

"Uncle Huxley is infamous for sitting on the balcony of his bedchamber without a stitch of clothes on. Avoid the north lawn from two until three o'clock."

"Thank you for the warning."

"I believe it's time to resume our seats," Deirdre said in a normal voice. She shook a warning finger at her uncle and whispered, "No controversial talk."

Everyone followed Deirdre's lead and drifted toward their designated places at the table. Shermont had not needed the reminder that England was at war with the United States. And America was an ally of the French. Huxley went onto Shermont's list of suspects with the same reluctance that he'd added Eleanor's name.

By the third remove, Teddy, Alanbrooke, and the lieutenants had each sent Eleanor something from their area of the table. In order not to show favoritism, she accepted all the tidbits with gracious smiles, but she ate none of the sautéed gizzards, plovers' eggs in aspic, calf's foot jelly, or marrow pâté.

Finally, dessert was served. The table was cleared to the bare wood, and an assortment of fruit, cakes, tortes, pastries, and sugar candies was laid out. Footmen served champagne under the watchful eye of Tuttle the butler. Fiona pointed out the special silver fruit knife and fork. Eleanor chose a poached pear and enjoyed it nearly as much as Fleckart delighted in his apple turnover, chocolate mousse, berry tart, sugared walnuts, and gingerbread with lemon sauce.

Before she'd finished half her pear, Eleanor had to stifle a yawn. The time difference was catching up with her.

Deirdre nodded to Shermont, and he stood to hold her chair as she rose. The rest of the gentlemen scrambled to their feet.

"We will leave you gentlemen to your port and cigars," Deirdre announced. All the women stood. After thanking their dinner partners, they followed the hostess into the parlor where coffee and tea were served.

Mina, Fiona, and Hazel headed straight for the pianoforte.

"Play something soothing, my dears," Aunt Patience said as she settled on the settee and pulled out a bit of fancy needlework. The other chaperones clustered around her. They drew Deirdre into their circle to make plans for the picnic the following day, which left Beatrix and Eleanor to chat with each other. In a blatant ploy to avoid that inevitability, Beatrix retreated to the chair by the empty fireplace and picked up a book from the nearby table.

Eleanor recognized the cut, yet felt as if she'd received a reprieve. She wandered toward the window and sat in the chair she'd occupied earlier to listen to the music. The girls took turns playing. Eleanor recognized Beethoven's *Fur Elise* and the folk song *Greensleeves* among several unknown pieces. As she fought to keep her eyes open, she heard the melody from Neil Diamond's *Song Sung Blue*, and the thought made her smile.

"I could wish that sweet expression was for me rather than Mozart."

Eleanor opened her eyes and blinked at Teddy who had seated himself on a footstool near her. "What?"

"Piano Concerto No. Twenty-One? Mozart?"

"Oh. Is that what they were playing?"

"You know, it's quite depressing when my attempts to display my wit fail so miserably."

"Sorry. My fault. My mind was... elsewhere."

"I appreciate your wit," Beatrix said as she arrived to stand at his side. While Teddy stood, she shot her rival a venomous glare that disappeared as soon as he was in a position to see her face. "Mama wishes to speak to you about a letter she received from Father."

Teddy bowed and offered Beatrix his arm. As they left, Eleanor realized that if Teddy was no longer in the dining room, the rest of the gentlemen were probably not there either. She sat forward and peeked around the wingback of the chair—to locate Fleckart and avoid him, she told herself. She didn't see Shermont. She tried to ignore her disappointment. When she leaned back, she spied him lounging on the window seat nearly hidden by heavy brocade drapes. He raised his snifter of brandy in salute.

"How long have you been there?" she asked.

"I confess I've been watching you listen to the music. I was content to enjoy the music vicariously," he said. "I've not much of an ear. Do you play?"

"Not at all."

"Perhaps another instrument? Harp? Flute?"

"No."

"I thought every gentlewoman was required to have some musical ability on her list of accomplishments she displays in company."

Eleanor leaned forward and whispered in a conspiratorial manner. "I have no musical talent. I can't draw a tree in winter. I sing like a stuck pig. And I have two left feet. I have absolutely nothing to recommend my company."

"If that is a ploy to elicit a compliment, I must admit I am flummoxed by the unexpectedness of the content."

"I'm only being honest."

"Then I am completely discombobulated and yet spellbound by your atypical candor."

"I'm beginning to doubt we speak the same language."

"You appear by all indications to understand me."

She studied him for a moment. "Possibly better than you guess. I think your polysyllabic emoting is an attempt to distance yourself, for whatever reason, from the person to whom you are speaking."

"Or simply to appear wittier than I actually am," he said, even though he knew she'd hit the nail on the head. The annoying habit occurred when he was confused, which fortunately didn't happen often. Why now? He recalled the strong feelings of protectiveness aroused by seeing her with her eyes closed. And yet, he'd recently added her to his list of suspects. If she were one of the foreign agents, how could he protect her and fulfill his mission?

"Just when I thought it was safe to draw near, Shermont starts scowling again," Alanbrooke said as he approached. "The lieutenants have goaded me into this insanely brave act." He bowed, took her gloved hand, and brushed his lips against her fingers.

"I'm honored you risked the frightful and dangerous hazards of crossing twenty feet of carpet," she said.

"Scowl away, Shermont," Alanbrooke said without breaking eye contact with her. "But face yourself in the direction of those two young pups to keep them at bay."

Shermont made a low noise deep in his throat.

"He growls," she said. "But I don't think he bites."

"He doesn't have to," Alanbrooke said. "I expect I shall pay for my audacity later at the gaming table. However, I will consider it worthwhile if you will but promise me two dances at the ball."

"Then I'm afraid your travails are for naught. I can't promise what isn't within my power to deliver. As much as I'd love to dance, unless the poor dancing master recovers, I won't have the slightest notion of the steps."

"I assure you Mr. Foucalt will be recuperated by tomorrow morning," Shermont said.

She had no idea how he could make such a statement without having been a consulting doctor on the ill man's case, but she had no doubt Shermont could accomplish anything he set his mind to do. When she looked up at him, she saw only his profile as he turned and stomped away.

Major Alanbrooke chuckled. "That man is walking on quicksand and doesn't even know it."

"What is that supposed to mean?"

"Both of you?" Alanbrooke shook his head as he moved aside to make room for the lieutenants.

"I think you've had too much to drink," she said.

His only response was to laugh.

Seven

ELEANOR CRAWLED INTO BED AND IMMEDIATELY FELL into a deep, exhausted sleep without figuring out what Alanbrooke meant. She woke in the middle of the night, the echo of his laughter all she could remember of her fading, uneasy dreams. She had no idea what time it was, but it was inky dark in the bedroom. She turned the pillow to put the cool side against her cheek and tried to go back to sleep.

With her eyes closed, the uninterrupted silence pressed in on her. Her apartment back in L.A. was in a residential area, but a certain amount of ambient noise was normal. The soft whir of the air conditioner, the faint ticking of her alarm clock, the cars and trucks on the not so distant highway, the infrequent sound of her neighbor's stereo when the pilot was in town and entertaining, even the occasional siren or car alarm. None of those noises had bothered her after the first week in her new place. She pulled another pillow close and hugged it to her breast. Getting used to sleeping alone had taken a little longer.

The middle of the night was no time to think of the past. She tossed the pillow aside and sat up. Since she couldn't watch TV, maybe reading something boring might make her sleepy. Unfortunately, she couldn't see her hand in front of her face. If she opened the window drapes, could she find a candle and a match? She found her way across the room only to discover the drapes weren't closed. If there was a moon, thick clouds hid it and any stars.

Now totally awake, she wished she had a glass of warm milk, her grandmother's dependable remedy for sleeplessness. Her stomach growled, reminding her that Gram always gave her a few Oreos with her milk. And that she hadn't eaten much at dinner.

Without a kitchen handy, how could she go about getting some milk? If she could find the bellpull in the dark, Twilla would probably come to see what she wanted, but Eleanor didn't want to rob the hard-working servant of much needed sleep. Surely in a house this size somebody had to be awake, tending the fires or some such chore.

She made her way back, located her robe on the foot of the bed, and found her slippers next to the bed steps where she'd left them. Arms outstretched, she made her way to the door. If possible, the sitting room was even darker than the bedroom. She almost changed her mind and turned around, but spending sleepless hours until dawn loomed scarier than crossing the room. Moving slowly, she finally found the door. In the hall the dim light from a few widely spaced sconces seemed blindingly bright at first. Her eyes adjusted as she went downstairs.

She spotted a servant right away, a footman seated on a stool by the front entrance with a shuttered lantern handy by his feet in case a carriage pulled up to the door. Not only did she recognize him as one of the wine servers at dinner, but she realized he was slumped back against the wall and snoring gently. She didn't have the heart to wake him. When the clock chimed three times, he stirred and mumbled, "Come on, Alice. Give us a kiss."

Eleanor covered her mouth to stifle a giggle and turned away. Then she noticed light shining under the library door. Were the gentlemen still playing cards? She tiptoed closer and put her ear against the wood, listening for a clue to who was inside. Either the door was too thick, or they were silent card players. She eased the door open a crack.

To her surprise, the empty room was brightly lit and a small cheery fire crackled in the fireplace.

She stepped inside. "Hello?" she whispered.

Shermont had sensed her presence before she spoke. What was Eleanor doing up and about at this hour? He hesitated before rising from his prone position on the couch facing the fireplace. "Good evening. Or rather, good morning."

Eleanor whipped around in surprise, her hand clutching the lapels of her brocade robe. She looked adorable with her stubborn chin framed by the high lace collar of her granny nightgown, but her bed-tousled hair sent his thoughts in a decidedly wicked direction. "This is an unexpected pleasure," he added.

"You scared me half to death," she said. "I didn't see you there."

"Then I must, unfortunately, assume you weren't looking for me. Shall I leave? Are you expecting to meet someone else?" *Like another foreign agent?*

"No! No, I... ah..." Her stomach growled loudly. "Do you know where the kitchen is?"

"You shouldn't wander around without a chaperone. Why didn't you call for a maid?"

"I can take care of myself. If you'll point me in the right direction, I'll find the kitchen on my own."

"I don't know where it is either," he lied, wanting to extend their time together.

"Then I'll just get a book and leave you to your... whatever." She marched to the nearest bookcase and ran her finger across the leather spines. She found a slim volume and pulled it out. Finding *Pride and Prejudice* was like a surprise visit from an old friend. She tucked it in the crook of her arm and turned to leave.

"I may not know where the kitchen is, but I can call for assistance."

"No! I didn't want to wake anyone. It's all right. I'll go back to my room now."

"Then you don't want this ham sandwich."

"What? You must be joking."

"They're served at the Cocoa-Tree Club at Pall Mall and St. James. Lord Montague, not the current Earl, but the Fourth Earl of Sandwich, didn't want to stop gambling in order to dine, so he requested a piece of meat between two slices of—"

"I know what a sandwich is. I'm just surprised you have one."

Shermont turned, picked up a tray, and carried it to the library table. He took the cover off the plate with the flair of a Las Vegas magician and held out the chair for her. "Tuttle brought this in just half an hour ago."

"I can't take your sandwich," she said, even as she walked forward trancelike, unable to resist the lure.

"I'm not hungry." He had requested it to have on hand for Carl, who had spent the evening in the cold rain watching the oak tree for activity. Shermont expected him to return at any moment and had been waiting since the card game broke up at two-thirty. He wanted to let him in and discuss his findings.

"You wouldn't have asked for it if you weren't hungry." She eyed the thinly sliced pink ham, and her stomach growled again.

"I'll share it with you. For the price of a kiss," he offered on a whim.

Eleanor hesitated. "Deal," she said, to his surprise. She stood straight with arms stiffly at her side, tipped her chin up, pursed her lips, and closed her eyes.

Shermont had no intention of giving her the chaste kiss she obviously expected. He moved in close and gently cupped her cheeks in his hands. He explored her lips, tasting, teasing, and demanding a response. She wrapped her arms around his waist and leaned into him. He took her in his arms and pulled her closer... closer.

Her stomach growled again, vibrating against his gut. He chided himself for selfishly denying her sustenance while he fed his own hunger. Gently, he set her away from him, steadying her with his hands on her shoulders. "I think you've earned that entire sandwich," he said, forcing a chuckle into his voice.

He turned her toward the table and held the chair.

"Half is enough," she said as she sat down.

He picked up the book she'd dropped and laid it on the table. Then he took the chair opposite her. After looking at him and receiving a nod of encouragement, she picked up half the sandwich and took a healthy bite.

"I noticed you prefer your food without sauces. There's mustard on that."

"Mmm-mmm."

She closed her eyes in pleasure, revealing a sensuality he'd guessed was there but hadn't seen so blatantly displayed. His body responded and he rose, fetching his nearly empty brandy snifter as an excuse to put some distance between them.

"It's wonderful," she said.

He dawdled as long as he could. By the time he returned to his seat, she'd finished a quarter of the large sandwich.

"Is that beer?" she asked with a gesture toward the tall glass on the tray.

"Ale. Help yourself. I have my brandy."

She took a tentative sip and made a face. "It's a bit stronger and warmer than I'm used to." But she took another drink. A few bites later, she stopped and licked a dab of mustard off her lip. "Are you going to eat that pickle?"

He shook his head.

She picked up the large whole pickle and put the end in her mouth, her lips forming a pink O. She closed her eyes and sucked.

Reminding him of... he shifted in his chair. Then winced when she took a sharp bite.

"Not a fan of dill?" she asked with an innocent expression. And amusement in her eyes.

Shermont, endurance tested to his limit, looked around for a distraction and spotted the chessboard on the other end of the table. He occupied his mind envisioning moves and countermoves.

"Thank you. That was perfect." She wiped her fingers on the napkin, pushed the tray aside, and folded her hands on the narrow table within easy reach of his.

He slid the chessboard between them. "Do you play?"

"Not very well," she answered. She stared at him for a long moment before moving her pawn in a classic opening.

He'd suggested the distraction to keep his hands occupied, but quickly realized the game revealed much about his opponent. He played conservatively to judge her style. She was aggressive, but her defenses were weak. They concentrated on the game and soon half the pieces had been removed from the board. Surprising him, she'd held her own.

"I don't believe I've ever played with a lady," he said.

"From what I hear, you've played with a great number of ladies," she said, moving her knight to threaten his queen. "Oh, were you speaking of chess?" She grinned. "I'm honored to be your first and, I'm sure, not your last. Now you know we can play as well as men."

"That's debatable. I fear men will always have the advantage."

She bristled. "Why would you say that? Are you inferring our brains are inferior?"

Her challenge struck a familiar chord. Someone in the past he couldn't remember, a sister, a mother, maybe an aunt, had also believed women were equal to men—different, but equal. He rubbed his forehead out of habit, but the expected stabbing pain did not appear.

"Not at all," he said. "I acknowledge females have fine brains, and I know a number who are intelligent, literate, and clever. I also know several men who have not a thought in their heads beyond what coat to wear to the next social affair or which style to use in tying their cravat."

She nodded her grudging acceptance of his defense.

"My assertion that men will always have an advantage is based on the fact that chess is basically a war game, probably first played in ancient Mesopotamia to teach combat strategy. Great battles and tactics of distinguished generals are part of the normal curriculum of every boy's education." He shrugged. "Girls study needlework and how to manage a household."

She glared at him.

"Chess is supposed to be a contemplative activity," he said.

"Does that mean you don't want to talk anymore?"

"Only that it is a distraction."

"The entire education system will change when we get the vote," she muttered.

He dropped the castle he'd been in the process of moving.

"Did I shock you?" She seemed pleased to have disrupted his game.

"I cannot deny you have." He grabbed the piece and then stared at the board, unsure as to where he'd meant to put it.

"It will happen, you know. Woman's suffrage."

"One part of me is aghast and horror-struck at the possibility, and yet somehow there is an inevitable logic to the concept. A small part of me believes the world will not end. England will not fall, and females will not start wearing pantaloons just because they can vote."

Eleanor held her tongue.

He finished his move and then turned away to think about what he'd just said. Where had that belief come from? He didn't remember ever having formed an opinion on females voting.

Carl waving at him from the other side of the French doors interrupted his reverie. How long had he been out there? Shermont realized he'd allowed Eleanor to distract him from his duty again. He concentrated on ending the game quickly, lured her into a foolish attack, and swooped in for checkmate.

"I suggest you try to get some sleep," he said as he returned the chessboard to its former position and reset the pieces for the next players. "Tomorrow will be a busy day and will start early."

"Will you be attending the picnic?"

He ignored the question. "Shall I ring for a maid to escort you back to your room?"

She picked up her book, turned on her heel, and rushed out of the room. But not before he saw the look on her face. Her confused and wounded expression caused feelings he couldn't name and didn't want to examine. Instead he opened the French doors and let Carl into the room. The man was soaked and shivering.

"It's about bloody time," he said through chattering teeth as he rushed to hold his hands to the small fire.

Shermont apologized as he ascertained the footman was still asleep. "Let's go upstairs. You need dry clothes."

While the valet changed, Shermont built a fire in the sitting room grate and poured two fresh brandies. Carl returned and took the seat nearest the hearth.

"Anything?" Shermont asked, handing him one snifter.

"I hid in the bushes for hours, and no one came to the tree for any reason."

"Weather may have been a factor. We'll have to try again."

Carl groaned. "This might change your mind." He pulled a scrap of paper from his dressing gown pocket and handed it over. "I found that at dusk before it started to rain."

Shermont examined the scrap about an inch square. "Rough edges, obviously torn." He rubbed it between his fingers. "Good quality paper. The ink is a bit smudged, but the writer is educated." The word "midnight" was clearly visible as was a partial word below it. "Damn cocksure. Didn't even bother to use a code."

"The delicate writing and curly endings to the letters indicate a lady's hand. I told you it was a trysting place. Probably said 'Meet me at midnight.'"

"This second partial word 'oordina' probably was 'coordinate.' Not a word I would expect used in a lover's note."

"Coordinate meeting times. Coordinate stories. Maybe coordinate elopement plans."

Shermont sniffed the paper. "This smells like your soap."

"I had it tucked in my shirt. What? I was trying to keep it dry."

"Did you check it for perfume residue before you stashed it against your heart?"

"No," Carl admitted sheepishly.

"Too bad. An identifiable scent might have pointed us directly to the female writer."

"Then you agree it was a lady?"

"Yes, but that doesn't change anything. I'm more certain than ever the oak is being used as a drop point." Shermont sat back in his chair and tapped his chin with two fingers. His recent chess game had reminded him of the value of an oblique offense. He rose and went to the desk to write a note. "I want you to get this message to our contact at Court. Planting a news article in the *Times* should scare up activity among our quarries." He handed over the note.

Carl read it. "The *Times* is going to want confirmation before they run an unbelievable story like this."

"Who says it's not true? Don't worry. They'll run it in the morning edition."

"You want me to go now?" Carl asked with an unbelieving expression. "It's four o'clock in the morning."

"Well, I can't go. I'd never get back in time for the picnic."

Carl narrowed his eyes. "Too bad you don't have a sample of that female's handwriting."

They both knew to whom he referred.

"If there is nothing else, I will prepare for my journey," Carl said.

He wished Carl Godspeed, and the valet left him alone with his unsettled thoughts. Other than social obligations, Shermont had spent little time alone with a female that had not been a prelude to bedding her. And yet he had enjoyed the hour he'd spent with Eleanor—not that he didn't want to bed her—but that had not been his main goal. He wanted to get to know her. He tried, unsuccessfully, to convince himself that he found her fascinating due to the possibility she was involved in the selling of secrets to the French. Foreign agent or not, she was not like any other female he could remember.

❧

"Hurry up," Deirdre called from inside the open landau. "Everyone's waiting for you."

Eleanor took one last look at the picturesque scene. Two carriages, women in their colorful summer dresses and bonnets, men of the party on horseback, all lined up for the parade to the picnic site. Down the drive, a wagon with supplies and servants went ahead to set up for their arrival. She ran down the front stairs, and a footman offered an arm to steady her climb up the steps into the second conveyance. The carriage lurched forward as soon as she'd settled next to Mina on the seat facing backward. Deirdre and Beatrix sat across from them.

The other ladies of the party were in the larger, more comfortable closed carriage, much to Fiona and Hazel's disappointment. Mrs. Holcum had allowed her daughter to ride without a chaperone, but warned she would keep a sharp eye. She'd threatened the coachman. If anything untoward happened, runaway horses or any such nonsense, she'd have his job. She also promised him a half-crown bonus if he maintained a close distance from the leading carriage and all arrived safely.

The gentlemen, including spry Uncle Huxley, were mounted and rode alongside the carriages when the road width permitted.

"You girls resemble a lovely summer garden," Huxley said, referring to the various hues of their dresses.

Eleanor wore her sunny yellow muslin with a sprig of green leaves embroidered on the length of the skirt, ending in a border of tangled vines and tiny purple flowers. She'd debated whether to wear the yellow. Back in L.A., the color had accented her marginal tan beautifully, but when paler was considered better, the dress did nothing for her. She finally opted to wear it because she had a limited number of dresses, and it seemed absolutely necessary to change clothes several times a day. She covered her arms with long gloves and a white muslin shawl with embroidered tambour work that she borrowed from Mina.

Mina was in pink with rose accents, Deirdre in blue with orange accents, and Beatrix in white with red embroidery and ribbons. Each carried a parasol for shade, Eleanor having borrowed an old one from Deirdre. Small talk passed the time as the lead coach kept the pace to a crawl.

The horses, kept to the same pace by their riders, appeared to resent the slow walk.

Shermont pulled his mount, a beautiful black Arabian thoroughbred, next to Teddy's horse. "Dabir is restless. I'm going to give him a run to settle him down."

"Dabir seems a strange name for a horse," Deirdre said before Teddy had a chance to speak.

"It's Arabic for teacher." The horse danced a few steps sideways, and Shermont reined him in. "So named because he does his best to teach me patience." He smiled at Deirdre before turning back to Teddy. "We're racing out to that promontory. I call it a mile and a half. Five quid each to the winner. Are you in?"

"No, thank you. Messenger seems content to keep gentler company, as am I."

The lieutenants maneuvered their horses forward and begged the women for a favor to carry for luck. Mina giggled and gave Parker a small pink feather from the decoration on her straw bonnet. He tucked it in his hatband.

"I like your gray," Deirdre said as she tied a blue ribbon around Whitby's wrist.

They all looked to Beatrix who shook her head. Obviously, she didn't want to give her red ribbons to anyone other than Teddy, and he wasn't racing.

"Come on. It's just for fun. It doesn't mean anything."

Beatrix shook her head again. Mina and Deirdre frowned at her unsporting attitude.

"What about you," Mina said to Eleanor. "Are you going to participate in the spirit of the race?"

Not wanting to be a spoilsport like Beatrix, Eleanor removed a yellow daisy from her bonnet.

"Will she give it to Alanbrooke or Shermont? Or will the handsome newcomer Major Rockingham swoop in to take the honors?" Mina said in a hushed, excited tone to enhance the suspense.

"Don't be silly," Deirdre said. "She just met Rockingham this morning."

Everyone's attention was riveted on Eleanor. She hesitated. What would Jane Austen do? Eleanor smiled and passed her token to Huxley, wishing him good luck.

With a wink and a cocky grin at the younger men, he stuck the flower in the buttonhole on the lapel of his bottle-green coat. "The filly and I will endeavor to do you proud."

The men lined up alongside the road. Huxley threw his hat in the air, and when it hit the ground, they all took off. The women cheered their favorites. Mina begged the driver to stop the carriage so they could see the entire race. John Coachman was having no part of any foolishness and kept the horses to a steady, sedate pace. Too soon a turn in the road blocked their view.

Mina sat back against the squabs with a pout.

"I can't believe you passed up a chance to race your pride and joy," Deirdre said to her brother. "Thirty pounds sterling to the winner. Isn't that what you call easy money?"

"I could take the military horses with ease, but if Shermont's stallion decided to make a race, it might be another story. And Huxley is right keen on his filly. She's not much to look at, but he swears she's fast. He's thinking about taking her on the racing circuit."

"I can't believe Messenger is so calm," Mina said. "Is he ill?"

Teddy shook his head. "I had the grooms exercise him hard early this morning so he would behave in front of our guests."

Eleanor looked off into the distance. Not having been born to privilege, she couldn't help but wonder what time the servants had gotten up to prepare everything for this carefree party.

"Ha'penny for your thoughts," Teddy said.

She doubted he would understand. "The view is beautiful."

"Yes, it is," he agreed.

But when she glanced back, he wasn't looking at the countryside. She turned away. "What's that?" she asked, pointing to a tumble of rocks on top of the highest hill in the neighborhood.

"That's where we're going—the ruins of an abbey dating back to the twelfth century. It's part of the estate, but to get there by road we have to go around the long way."

"Is that a cottage in the woods?" she asked, squinting.

"Yes. An old gypsy woman lives there. The lord of the manor granted her use of the cottage for as long as she lived in payment for saving his child's life with a magic potion. That child was my great-great-grandfather."

"Impossible."

"If we had time, we could stop. I'd introduce you."

Eleanor shook her head, but she had to smile.

The carriages traveled across a bridge over a wide and swift stream. Several hundred yards upstream a mill wheel sloshed and creaked as it turned the huge stones inside.

Eleanor had never seen such a sight other than in books. Entranced, she said, "The sound of the water is almost musical."

"For good reason," Teddy said. "You, of course, have heard of the famous opera singer Carmelita Cadenza. No? Well, I suppose it was before our time. Apparently, Grandfather was besotted by the beautiful Carmelita. She was the toast of London, but she was terribly homesick. So she decided to return to her native Italy and the humble millhouse where she'd been born. Grandfather could not bear to see her go, so he built this for her. She retired from the stage and lived here happily for several years."

"How romantic," Beatrix said with a sigh.

"Carmelita loved her little mill. She tended her garden and did all the tasks a mill owner does, but she never gave up singing. She would sing as she went about her chores. Even the peasants would stop on the bridge to listen to her arias. Then suddenly, one day the wheel was still and the air silent. Poor Carmelita was dead. Unbeknownst to all but her maid, the opera singer had suffered from a rare and fatal disease.

"Grandfather was beside himself with grief, and after the funeral he returned here with an ax to take the mill apart piece by piece. The music of the water stopped him. It was as if he heard her singing. He let the mill stand, though he could never bring himself to come back again. They say she still haunts the mill she loved, waiting for Grandfather to return. Several have reported seeing her ghost in the old garden, and countless people have heard her singing."

All four women pulled handkerchiefs out of reticules and sleeves to dab at their eyes. After much sniffling, Deirdre demanded, "No more sad stories."

Teddy twisted around in his saddle and pointed to a group of buildings on another hill. "That farm once belonged to our family, but it was lost by the third Lord Digby to the current owner's ancestor in a card game. The story goes that Farmer Hasselrood coveted that particular piece of land so much he put up his beautiful eldest daughter against the deed. While the gamblers argued over exact terms and boundaries, word of the unusual bet traveled through the household staff like a greased pig on fair day and reached the ears of the third Lady Digby. She stormed into the card room as play was about to resume. With her staring daggers at him, Digby folded an ace-king combo, a surefire winning hand in vingt-et-un. The farm belongs to the Hasselroods to this day."

"I thought that was the Smith's dairy?" Mina said.

Teddy hesitated only a moment before he

laid one hand over his heart. "I cannot believe Hasselrood sold the family farm. I am shocked, astounded, and... and..."

"Lying," Eleanor supplied.

Beatrix sucked in her breath. "How dare you call him a liar?"

Deirdre and Mina only laughed.

"You are caught fair and square," Deirdre said to Teddy. She turned to Beatrix and Eleanor. "It's a game we used to play as children to pass the time on long carriage rides and keep Mina entertained. Of course, Teddy was always the best at it."

"It took me years to figure it out," Mina said, sticking out her bottom lip.

"Well, I think the stories were wonderful," Beatrix said. She spared Eleanor a superior glance before turning an ingratiating smile to Teddy. "I would never question your veracity."

"How did you know I was lying?" Teddy asked Eleanor. "Too far-fetched?"

For some reason, she didn't want to reveal his hesitation had tipped her off. "I'm not sure what it was. Just a feeling."

"My favorite story involved great-grandmother and the Sultan of Arabee." But Deirdre didn't have time to elaborate because the other gentlemen of the party rode up.

"Did you win? Did you win?" Mina asked Parker. She practically bounced out of her seat with excitement.

Sadly, the lieutenant shook his head. Whitby and Rockingham also indicated the negative. Huxley grinned and held up a purple velvet pouch that clanked when he shook it.

"Yeah, Uncle Huxley!" Deirdre started the applause, but everyone joined in.

Huxley gave a nod to Shermont and his horse, several yards distant. "That high-strung brute of his got spooked by a rabbit, or else Baby here would have been a close second." Huxley patted his horse's neck. "Nice race," he called to Shermont.

"Did you ask the girls about the play?" Whitby asked Teddy.

Mina turned her attention to her brother. "What play?"

"We're all going to put on a play," Parker jumped in excitedly. "Just like when we were in school, except with real girls to play the female parts." His voice trailed off at the end.

Blushing, he steered his horse to the outside of the pack as the carriage halted.

"We're here," Aunt Patience trilled as she alighted from the lead coach.

"What's the play about?" Deirdre asked.

"There's a princess in distress, a witch, a pirate, an enchanted frog, dastardly deeds, and a happy ending," Teddy said.

"Can I be in the play," Mina asked. "Please, please, can I?"

"All the young people will have a role," he promised.

"Unless they don't want one," Shermont said as he rode by.

Eleanor watched as he dismounted. He said something

to the stableboy as he handed over the reins that made the youngster grin while he led the horse away. She couldn't reconcile the man who'd callously hurt her feelings the previous night with the one she observed. He helped Mrs. Maxwell across the field to where several tables had been set up. Minutes later, his deft grab saved a footman from taking a header with a large tray. Shermont was helpful and courteous to everyone without making a big deal. To everyone except her.

Which didn't really matter, because in the dark sleepless hours before dawn, she'd decided to pay no attention to him. Not that she intended to cut him directly. That would be noticeably rude, and then she would have to explain her actions to Deirdre or Mina or Teddy. No. She would pretend he didn't exist unless circumstances necessitated speaking to him. And then she would be excruciatingly polite. Much the way Anne Eliot behaved toward Fredrick Wentworth when they met again after eight years in Jane Austen's *Persuasion*. Except Anne was still in love with Fredrick, and, of course, Eleanor wasn't in love with Shermont.

She didn't believe in love at first sight. Lust, perhaps. But pheromones and hormones were not love. And lust could be controlled.

Unfortunately, a campaign of indifference was far less satisfying when it wasn't even noticed by the target of her premeditated lack of interest. Shermont seemed to be ignoring her.

"Are you going to sit in the carriage all day?" Mina asked.

Eleanor started out of her reverie and realized everyone else was gone, already broken into small groups according to activity. The chaperones sat around a table sipping lemonade. Uncle Huxley, far enough away not to be included in their conversation, read the newspaper. Fiona and Hazel had climbed the stones of the ruins to the lookout point and postured in what they thought were provocative poses. Teddy and the military men had gathered off to one side. From their gestures and the occasional word carried on the breeze, she could tell they were discussing the war. Shermont was over by the horses, chatting with the groom and pointing to his stallion's hoof.

"Come on. Out, out," Deirdre insisted, motioning for Eleanor to get down. "Stretch your legs before we eat."

Mina spread her arms. "Welcome to our picnic area. Teddy wanted to build a folly over there, but we insisted he keep it natural. Isn't it gorgeous?"

"Yes, indeed." The top of the hill had been sliced off, leaving a broad, smooth, grassy field ringed by woods. A few trees had invaded two or three strides into the clear area as if on purpose to provide shade.

"We're going to pick wildflowers for the tables. Would you like to come with us?"

"No... ah... thank you, no."

"Are you ill?" Deirdre asked. "You are a bit pale."

"I'm fine. You go ahead." The sight of Huxley reading the paper had reminded her of an earlier idea to check for news items that might entice Shermont to return to London. "I'm going to have some lemonade."

"Are you sure?" Mina eyed the table full of chaperones with a grimace.

"Go on. Pick lots of flowers."

"If you're determined to go over there, be warned. Don't let them draw you into a game of whist, not even for pennies. You might win the first hand or two, but before you know it, you'll owe them three months pin money."

"Mina! You didn't!" Deirdre said. "No wonder you didn't buy those beautiful pink ribbons we saw last week."

"I promise I won't play cards with them," Eleanor said. *Especially since I have no idea how to play whist.* She excused herself and left Deirdre scolding Mina, while the younger girl defended her right to spend her allowance as she chose.

As Eleanor passed the group of men, Major Alanbrooke caught her eye. He raised an eyebrow as if questioning whether she wanted to join the conversation. She shook her head and continued walking toward the tables.

"Ah, here's our fourth," Patience called as Eleanor approached. "Won't you join us for a few hands of whist?"

"Thank you, but no. I don't know how to play."

"Then now's the time to learn. We would be glad to teach you how to play," Patience said with a smile intended to be sweet, but it failed to hide the avaricious gleam in her eyes.

Mrs. Maxwell stifled a giggle with her hand, and Mrs. Holcum took a quick sip of lemonade.

Eleanor declined the invitation and approached Huxley. "May I join you?"

He jumped up and reached to tip his hat, which

wasn't on his head. He looked around as if wondering where it could have gotten to and then chuckled. "The boy has not returned with my hat."

With his bald head, green coat, plaid vest, and well-worn brown leather breeches, he reminded her of an overgrown leprechaun. She liked his unpretentious air.

"Please, have a seat," he said. "I'm honored." He folded the paper and took his seat next to her. "May I take this opportunity to thank you for the good luck charm?"

"I'm sure your horse didn't need it. I heard you won by several lengths."

Huxley laughed. "Indeed I did. Still, I should have sought you out earlier to thank you." He looked at his clasped hands. "I regret we weren't closer before you moved so far away, but you always preferred the company of your younger cousins."

His statement seemed to question why she was there. "I saw you reading the paper and wondered what interesting events were happening in London. I've been away so long I feel like a stranger in a foreign land."

He nodded as if he understood. "Just the typical news. A new statue was dedicated in Hyde Park. As if we need another statue there. The usual war news from Spain and Portugal. Some good. Some not so good." He tapped the paper with his finger. "Oh, a clerk high up in the Ministry has been arrested as a French agent. Tut, tut. What is the world coming to?" He turned the paper over. "Ah, this should interest you. The Zoological Society has acquired a new animal—an American buffalo."

"Oh." Eleanor tried to hide her disappointment. She doubted those items would entice Shermont back to London. She would need another plan.

"I have been planning a trip to America myself. It's one of the places I must see before I die. I am a lepidopterist, you know," Huxley added in a conspiratorial tone.

Eleanor had no idea what he was talking about, but it sounded suspiciously like a contagious disease. She scooted her chair further away. She put her left elbow on the arm of the chair and slanted her body in that direction. She rested her cheek against her fingers, trying to assume a casual pose. "Really?"

He leaned closer. She retreated until she was afraid she would tip the chair on its side and land sprawled in the grass.

"I have over five hundred specimens." He waggled his eyebrows.

"Oh?" she squeaked.

"Yessiree. I've been a butterfly collector since I was just a boy," he said with a grin. "Insects and moths, too, but butterflies are my favorite."

Eleanor realized he'd been teasing her. She sat up straight and slapped at his arm. "You're a wicked old man. Making fun of my ignorance like that."

"And enjoying every minute. One of the few advantages of getting old is that one is allowed, nay, expected to be eccentric."

Eleanor shook her head but smiled.

"I'm serious about the trip to America. It's to be the first leg of my world collection tour. Been planning it ever since I acquired an emerald swallowtail,

Papillio palinurus. Not personally acquired, mind you. I bought it from a man who had been to Borneo. Fabulous specimen. Green and blue with a unique wing shape. Did you know there are more than ten thousand species of butterfly, and new ones are found every day?"

"No, I didn't know that."

"I can't wait to collect my own specimens." He leaned back in his chair and stared into the distance. "To witness the migration of the monarchs, *Danaus plexippus*, with my own eyes. I've heard so many butterflies head south to winter in Mexico that they block the sun. And to see a sixteen-centimeter tiger swallowtail, *Papillio glaucus*." He held up his hands six inches apart.

"Wow. That's one big butterfly."

"The *Attacus atlas* from India has been observed up to thirty centimeters." He widened the space between his hands to twelve inches. "Actually a moth and therefore active at night rather than during the day like a butterfly, it is beautifully shaped and multi-colored."

Eleanor was glad she would never see one of those moths hanging around the porch light on the balcony of her apartment.

"I'm looking forward to observing the brilliant *Priamis caelestis* in its natural habitat in New Guinea. And *Morpho peleides* in the West Indies. Can you tell I'm partial to blue ones?"

"Who isn't?" she said as if she knew a *Priamis* whatever from a *Morpho* whatsis. "Maybe you'll discover a new species."

"Wouldn't that be the achievement of a lifetime, eh?" He sighed. "One can only wish for such luck."

"When do you leave?"

"Hopefully soon. I have my own ship, you know. The *Swallowtail*. Outfitted with the latest in everything I might need. It will only take a few weeks to provision her, and then I'm off. I intend to travel the world until I die, and then I've made arrangements to have a glorious Viking funeral at sea. I'm just waiting for my nieces to marry. Got to keep an eye on them, you know, but I'm not getting any younger."

"Isn't Teddy their guardian?"

"Ah, there's the rub."

"What do you mean by that?"

"Nothing. Forget I said anything. You should never pay attention to an eccentric old man's rambling." Huxley picked up the paper from his knee and stood. He cocked his head to one side and gave her a strange look.

"Is something wrong?"

"No. It's just that you've changed since you were a child. You used to be such a... a morose little girl. Always predicting dire consequences if Deirdre ate too much custard or Mina climbed on the terrace railing."

Eleanor didn't know what to say.

"Of course, you were usually right. That time Deirdre did get sick, and Mina did break her arm. But you're much more pleasant company now."

"People grow up. Change is inevitable."

He shook his head as if to clear his thoughts. "Of

course, you're right. I'm going to fetch a glass of lemonade. May I bring you one?"

She declined. After he left, she looked around. The lieutenants had succumbed to Fiona and Hazel's lures and joined them on the ruins. Deirdre and Mina were nowhere in sight. Eleanor jumped up and went to search for them. She quietly asked Patience, but she answered without even glancing up from her hand of cards that she'd last seen them picking flowers on the far side of the clearing. She assured Eleanor they were fine as long as they were together.

Eleanor pulled Teddy away from his conversation, but he didn't know where they were either. He seemed unconcerned about their welfare. "How far can they get on foot? They'll return momentarily," he assured her before going back to his conversation with Rockingham.

Eleanor stood in the middle of the picnic area and turned slowly in a full circle. Shermont was also missing. Not that she was keeping track of him or anything, but suddenly she was worried. She'd assumed the seduction happened the night of the ball, but since the ghosts refused to give her details, it could have happened earlier. Had she already failed to protect them? Would the ghosts keep their end of the bargain if she didn't prevent the seduction and the duel that would inevitably follow?

Refusing to acknowledge the stab of jealousy she felt, Eleanor set off, determined to find Deirdre and Mina. She made a circuit of the clearing, peering into the woods for a clue to which way they went. She cautioned herself not to run or appear frantic. If she alarmed the other guests and a full-scale search were mounted, someone might find one—or both—sisters with Shermont. The two were rarely separated. Eleanor worried that's why neither would say who was actually seduced.

Something on the ground caught her eye.

⚜

"Shermont?"

Before responding he finished his business, buttoned his trousers, and rounded the screen the servants had set up near the tethered horses for the gentlemen to use as a privy. "Alanbrooke."

"Forgive me for seeking you out, but this is the first chance I've had to speak to you in private," he said as he fell in beside Shermont on the walk back to the picnic area.

"You have my ear."

Alanbrooke removed his hat and scratched his head. "It's all rather mysterious. Day before yesterday, a stranger approached me at my tailor's of all places and told me to give you a message in private. Somehow he knew I'd accepted the invitation to be here, although in truth it's nothing I concealed. The weird part is that he said you would also attend. Since you despise provincial parties, I dismissed his claim and counted him one of the loonies society tries to ignore, like the crazy men who accost you on the street and spout their 'end of the world' nonsense. But then I arrive, and here you are."

"Is there a point to this story? If you're asking my advice, find a new tailor. One who doesn't let in riff-raff off the street."

"Bear with me. The stranger—not my tailor—said his name was Scovell. He said I should not mention meeting him to anyone other than you and then only in private. Rather havey-cavey, don't you think?"

Shermont kept his face impassive with effort. General George Scovell was the chief code breaker and intelligence gatherer for Wellington. He'd played an important role in the victories at Salamanca and Vittoria. Shermont had done a bit of cipher work himself and had consulted with Scovell on occasion. "What was the message?" he asked in a nonchalant tone.

"He made me repeat it, so I would remember his exact words. 'Another in the Ministry. Watch your back. If you need help, I'm your man.' Rather cryptic, eh? I asked him about that last bit. I mean, shouldn't he have said, 'He's your man.' But he insisted I say it exactly that way. What do you suppose it all means?"

"Nothing," Shermont lied with a straight face. Another in the Ministry meant a second French agent had been discovered selling secrets to Napoleon, like the one they'd been watching for the last seven months. Properly identified and carefully handled, such a man could serve as a useful conduit for misleading information.

Since they'd sacrificed the previously known agent by announcing his capture in the *Times*, he guessed the new one would be used to take his place. Since Scovell hadn't indicated how long the new agent had been in place, Shermont concluded the warning meant any number of his prior messages to the Ministry might have been read or intercepted. "Just another loony crying out for attention," he said. "I hope you gave your tailor a stern set-down?"

"How could I do that and not reveal the meeting with Scovell?"

Shermont nodded. Apparently, the general's evaluation of Alanbrooke was correct. Good to know he had a dependable, closemouthed backup if it became necessary. "My advice is to forget meeting him."

"Interesting you should say that. Scovell said after I delivered the message, I should forget the entire incident."

"What incident?" Shermont asked with a blank stare. He slapped a flummoxed Alanbrooke on the back and headed for the picnic area.

Eight

ELEANOR STOOPED, PRETENDING AN INTEREST IN THE wildflowers, and verified that she'd spotted footprints. She was no Indian tracker, but two sets of smaller footprints and the longer stride of a larger set were easy to read in the soft earth.

"Deirdre? Mina?" she said as loud as she dared.

She followed the trail into the shade. Unfortunately, once she was into the woods proper, the footprints disappeared. Hearing voices and laughter, she forged ahead. She concentrated on the ground looking for a clue, any clue, to tell her she was on the right track. Suddenly she noticed the deep silence and realized she'd lost all sense of direction. She looked around. One tree appeared pretty much like another to a city girl. Damn. She should have left a trail of breadcrumbs.

She knew she should stay in one place and let the others find her. Fighting off panic, she located a fallen tree, spread out her handkerchief, and sat down. She folded her hands in her lap and waited. And waited. Without a watch she had no idea how long she'd been in the woods or how long she'd been sitting there, although it seemed like a long while.

"This is silly." She jumped up and paced the length of the log. It might be hours before anyone found her or even missed her and started searching. What sort of animals lived in the woods? Were there bears in England? Wolves?

She shook her head and pushed those thoughts away. She wasn't in Yellowstone National Park. Or lost in the middle of Africa. She was in Hampshire, for crying out loud. If she walked in a straight line, she was bound to come across a cottage, a farmer tending his fields, or a road.

Picking a direction at random, she started off with firm, determined strides. Making her way through the woods wasn't like strolling along a sidewalk, and it was impossible to stay on a straight line. She wound up following barely discernible trails and wandered among the bushes, rocks, and trees. She slapped away branches that caught her hair and stumbled when sharp stones bruised her feet. With each step, she hesitated. She called out, hoping someone, anyone, would hear. Hopefully someone who knew the way back.

"Hello? Deirdre? Mina? Hell-ooo?"

She tripped over a fallen branch and lurched forward, suddenly entering a flower-filled clearing. Tiny yellow blossoms carpeted a meadow not much larger than a ballroom. She took several steps forward, removed her bonnet, and tipped her face to the sun's warmth. A breeze rustled musically through the trees, and thousands of yellow butterflies lifted from their delicate perch to swirl and dance to nature's tune. Not flowers, butterflies! What a magical place! She expected a unicorn or fairies to appear.

She hadn't realized she'd spoken aloud until a deep voice answered. She didn't turn around immediately because the low whisper seemed a part of the magic, rather than an intrusion—words sensed as well as heard. Was Oberon, the fairy king, behind her? Or maybe the speaker was a tree elf, protector of the enchanted forest and meadow?

❧

On their way back to the picnic area, Lord Shermont and Major Alanbrooke had chatted casually as if their previous conversation had not taken place.

"That big-boned filly of Huxley's might not look like much, but she's a real sweet goer," Alanbrooke said.

"If he's serious about taking her on the circuit, bet heavy on that first race. You'll clean up. After that, you won't get any odds because she'll be the favorite."

"Could Dabir have taken her if he hadn't spooked?"

Shermont shrugged. "At two miles, probably. At the shorter distance, it would be a toss-up."

"Have you ever thought of racing him?"

"Not really. The chiseled-in-stone calendar would play hell with my social schedule."

"I can understand that. Rather like military life does," Alanbrooke said with a chuckle as they joined Digby and Rockingham.

"Military life," Rockingham echoed with a snort. "That's an oxymoron. You have no life when you're in the military."

"Come on, mate. It can't be that bad," Digby said.

"Bloody hell if it ain't." Rockingham pulled a flask

from underneath his uniform jacket and offered it around, but got no takers.

"Bit early in the day for me," Alanbrooke said.

"You wouldn't say that if you hadn't slept all night." Rockingham pulled a long swig before tucking it away. "My rotten luck the general's aide got the trots."

"What? You had to nurse him?" Digby asked with a grin.

"Worse. I had to take his place while the general and that damn colonel from the Dragoons discussed that pouch he brought. I was standing at attention all night except when I was acting as his damn personal servant. Fetch drinks, bring food, build the fire, fetch maps, serve coffee, douse the fire."

Alanbrooke laughed. "That's well within the range of duties a general's aide is expected to perform."

"Not the brigadier. Him I wouldn't mind serving. It was that snot-nosed colonel. He kept using phrases like 'based on my experience' and 'from my personal observation.' Bah! His regimentals were so new he probably bought his commission last month. I'd bet my new gaiters Wellington made him a courier to get rid of him."

"Then he came all the way from Spain?" Teddy asked incredulously. "That's a long way to travel to deliver a message. Hasn't the military heard of the mail?"

"Joke all you want," Rockingham said. "Dispatches from the War Office are serious business."

"I hope this doesn't mean you and the others won't be able to stay for the ball. The ladies would be so disappointed."

"I wouldn't want to miss that. We won't be pulling out before maneuvers are over." He lowered his voice. "But the colonel said—"

"Captain Rockingham," Alanbrooke interrupted his subordinate. "I'm sure Lord Digby and Lord Shermont find such tedious military matters quite boring. Shall we talk about—"

"It's quite all right," Digby said to Alanbrooke. "I find the nuances of military service fascinating."

"You would get a firsthand view if you bought a commission," the major suggested.

"If only I could," Digby said with a dramatic sigh. "But I have so many responsibilities. Now, if any of you gentlemen would consider marrying my sisters, I'd be free to don a uniform in time to get in on the action."

Shermont's estimation of Digby's character fell even further with his crass comment. Unfortunately, until he'd completed his mission, he couldn't afford to alienate his host by giving him the set-down he so deserved. He turned his head away and spotted a bit of yellow muslin disappearing into the woods.

"Not I," Rockingham said. "Unlike the rest of you, I haven't any family money expectations. I'm holding out for an heiress with at least five thousand pounds per annum."

"Don't look at me," Alanbrooke said. "I'm holding out for a female without an obnoxious brother."

After a moment of awkward silence, Shermont clapped Alanbrooke on the back and laughed. "Good one."

Then everyone joined in the laughter, and the tension dissipated.

"I believe this is the point where I make a timely exit," Shermont said. He bowed to the other gentlemen. "By your leave."

He headed toward the ruins where Miss Holcum, Miss Maxwell, Miss Hazel, and the two lieutenants had found seats among the large flat rocks and were in animated conversation. The rest of the clearing was deserted except for Mrs. Maxwell dozing in a chair and the servants busy at their tasks.

"Where is everyone?" he asked the group seated on the rocks.

"Oh, here and there," Beatrix said.

He nodded, even though he was sure she'd only kept track of Digby. None of the five had noticed anyone leaving. He announced he was going for a walk and set off at a leisurely pace. After making sure he wasn't observed, he ducked into the woods and made his way to where he'd last seen Eleanor.

Her tracks weren't difficult to follow. What she was doing in the woods he found harder to fathom. At first he was sure she had headed for the ancient oak, taking the trail from the road and approaching the tree from the far side. Was she picking up or leaving a message? Then her trail wandered off in another direction—which was a relief. He found her handkerchief and tucked it in his pocket. She obviously was not an experienced country walker. Evidence pointed to her bumbling her way through difficult terrain when an easier path was nearby, but where she went he followed.

He found her standing transfixed in a flower-filled meadow. The sight of her captivated him. He was content to gaze upon her, but the yellow flowers turned into butterflies that swirled around him and seemed to push him in her direction.

"What a magical place," she whispered in an awed voice. "I expect a unicorn or fairies to appear."

"What would the fairies be doing?" Shermont asked.

"Waltzing with the butterflies," she answered before thinking.

Slowly she turned to face him.

He made an elegant leg, bowing low and sweeping the air with his hat before tossing it aside. "May I have this dance?"

A flight of butterflies swirled around them, casting a magic spell and urging them closer.

To Eleanor it seemed the most natural response in the world to place her right hand in his and step into his arms—as if she belonged there. He held her gently, and their first steps together were tentative, formal. Then she stumbled on the uneven ground, and he caught her up close with an arm around her waist.

As one, they waltzed around the field of clover to nature's music, the breeze in the trees and the warble of a lone songbird. Neither spoke, afraid to break the enchantment of the moment. Slowly, imperceptibly, they came to a stop as the wind gradually subsided. Neither moved.

He held her in his arms and never wanted to let her go. He placed her right hand over his heart. He traced the line of her jaw with his fingers and tipped her chin upward.

The rapid beat of his heart throbbed beneath her

palm, and her pulse echoed its rhythm. Breathless, she slid her hands across his shoulders to the back of his neck.

Shermont wrapped both arms around her waist and tightened his embrace. He waited to read the "yes" in her eyes before he leaned forward. He stopped with his lips a breath away from hers. "I have wanted this every minute since the moment we first kissed," he whispered.

His kiss started gently, exploring the shape of her lips, breathing in her scent, tasting her.

Eleanor gave in to her craving to run her fingers through the hair at the nape of his neck. The warm honey in her veins became lava, pooling in the pit of her stomach. She wrapped her arms around his neck and pulled herself to her tiptoes, pressing her breasts against his rock-hard chest, grinding her hips against the bulge she felt against her belly.

Before her passionate response undid him completely, he thanked his lucky stars she was no inexperienced schoolgirl. Eleanor was all female. Her kiss demanded he give in to his raging desire. He ravaged her mouth, holding her tight against his body, trying to get closer... closer. Her mewls of pleasure egged him on. Groaning her name, he slid his hands down to cup her sweet bottom. He lifted her and could have sworn the minx tried to wrap her legs around his waist, until her clothing prevented further movement. He trailed kisses down her throat to the tops of her breasts, and she tipped her chin up and leaned back.

Eleanor wanted more. She wanted naked skin against naked skin. She wanted to taste and lick and breathe in his essence. She wanted his delicious mouth on places currently inaccessible. She wanted to strip off her clothes along with his—if he couldn't undress fast enough. She released his shoulders and placed her hands on his cheeks, raising his face so she could look him in the eye.

"Put me down," Eleanor said, her voice husky with need, her request a command and a promise.

He gave her a cocky grin and set her back on her feet. He stepped back. "As you wish," he said, but his amused tone implied that he was game. "What do you want me to do next?"

Before she could describe any of the wicked fantasies that flashed through her brain in nanoseconds, she heard someone calling her name from not too far away. "Damn."

He raised both eyebrows.

"Someone's coming."

He cocked his head and recognized Digby's voice. Yet one more reason he disliked the man. Shermont nodded in the direction of the calls. "He'll be here in a minute. Two at the most." Shermont cupped her face in his hands. "Promise you'll meet me later."

"I'll try," she said.

Her response was less than he'd wished to hear, but she left room for hope. He moved to block the coming man's view of Eleanor.

She straightened the neckline of her dress, picked up her dropped bonnet and plopped it on her head. "Am I a terrible mess?" she asked.

When he looked she was nervously smoothing her skirt. Her bonnet was on crooked, her cheeks were flushed, her eyes were bright, and her lips showed signs of being well kissed. And left wanting more. "You are lovely," he said as he straightened the brim of her hat.

She appreciated the sweet gesture. After all, he had to be as frustrated as she was. She ducked her head and had to turn away before she jumped into his arms and to hell with anyone who came upon them.

Trying to regain her composure, she took several deep breaths and blew them out slowly to the count of ten. She quickly had reason to be thankful for Teddy's calls as she noticed Deirdre, Mina, and Huxley crossing the meadow from the opposite direction with waves and wide smiles. How long had they been in the glade?

"Aren't they beautiful," Mina said, twirling around in a circle with her arms held wide in the midst of the swirling butterflies.

"*Colias croceus* of the *Pieridae* family, also known as the clouded yellow," Huxley said. "This is apparently one of the sporadic mass migrations we refer to as Clouded Yellow Years." The butterflies seemed as delighted with him as he was with them. They landed all over his coat, folding up their wings to show the greenish underside with the white dot before taking off again to join the merry dance of their friends.

"We saw a few when we were looking for wild-flowers and followed them here," Deirdre said. "We knew Uncle Huxley would love to see them. He said they were attracted by the clover—"

"Their favorite food," Huxley interjected.

"We know of a huge field of clover beyond that hill

and just had to go see. The butterflies are even thicker over there."

"Millions," Mina said. "So many you can hear them flapping their little wings."

"We should plan a trip to the coast," Huxley said. "There are probably even more there. Maybe week after next."

"I thought butterflies only lived a day or two," Eleanor said.

"Migratory species live for six, eight, ten months, some even longer," he explained. "How else could they fly hundreds, even thousands of miles?"

"Do you want to go see the clover field?" Mina asked.

Before Eleanor had a chance to answer, Teddy stomped up with a scowl. "What in the world possessed you two to wander off alone like that?"

Although he spoke to his sisters, Eleanor had the strange feeling he was really talking about her and Shermont.

Mina and Deirdre apologized immediately, cowering together.

"If I can't trust you at a simple picnic," Teddy continued, building up a head of steam, "how can I take you to London?"

"No, Teddy. Please don't say that," Deirdre begged.

Eleanor could not stand it. She stepped between the girls and put her arms over their slumped shoulders. "It's my fault. It was my idea, and I acted as their unofficial chaperone."

Teddy narrowed his eyes and looked at her as if he could see the imprint of Shermont's lips upon hers.

"Their welfare is my responsibility, and therefore my decision is all that counts. You are not an appropriate choice of chaperone—"

"But I am." Huxley stepped forward with his arms folded, challenging Teddy to deny him.

"This is not the Dark Ages," Eleanor said. "They have every right to make decisions for themselves." She chucked them on the shoulders. "Come on. Stand up for yourselves."

Teddy flashed Eleanor an indulgent smile. "That may work well and good for a widow and an American. After all, what are your prospects? But I entreat you not to spout bluestocking rhetoric within my sisters' earshot. I'll have enough of a problem finding husbands for them as it is."

Shermont stepped forward. "Oh, I doubt that. I think they'll be the toast of the next season." He bowed to the girls.

Eleanor threw him mental kisses. Lordy, lordy, she could just eat that man up. He looked at her as if he heard her thoughts and smiled.

Apparently, Teddy realized he couldn't win the argument against such odds. "I guess we'll see about that." He turned on his heel. "Come along, Deirdre, Mina," he called over his shoulder without looking back.

The girls hesitated only a few moments before scurrying after their brother.

"At least they thought about it for a second or two before giving in to him," Huxley said. "A small step in the right direction."

"There will be more steps," Eleanor said. "They're bright girls."

Huxley nodded. "The daughters I never had." He offered Eleanor his arm.

As Shermont followed behind them, an unexpected thought slammed into his brain. Where did Eleanor learn to waltz? The dance was only done on the continent and had not been deemed acceptable in London. And yet she'd brought it up and had not hesitated for a step. Did they waltz in America? He didn't think so. Did that mean she'd been to Paris?

Of course, it also begged the question: where had he learned to waltz? He rubbed his forehead. As with so many unanswered questions, he was forced to accept that he might never know the truth.

Was Eleanor an agent for the French? That was the question he needed to answer. And soon... before he became even more spellbound by her unique magic.

They returned to the picnic area, and everyone gathered at the tables. Eleanor hoped for a chair next to Shermont's, but Deirdre and Patience had already assigned seats. Throughout the picnic lunch served by footmen on elegant china, Shermont flattered and charmed all the women, all except her.

At the end of the meal, she drew Mrs. Holcum aside and was directed over the hill to where the servants had set up facilities for the gentlewomen. Behind sheets draped in a large square, a chair, washstand, and dressing table had been arranged. A maid provided hot water and clean hand towels.

Eleanor was glad to have a few moments alone. She didn't know what to make of Shermont's hot and cold alternating attitude. One explanation was that he lusted after her, but didn't actually like her. Unable to cope with that dichotomy, he chose to ignore her until his passions could no longer be denied. Or it could be the good girl vs. bad girl mentality. For Regency men the concept was black and white, angel or temptress. A woman could not be both. Neither theory about Shermont's behavior was a flattering explanation. Her only course was to ignore him in return.

She returned to the group and participated in the conversation and games until time to leave. Thankfully, Major Alanbrooke was an attentive friend who raised her spirits, which helped to restore her equilibrium. The trip back was dominated by talk of the play.

Nine

WHEN SHERMONT RETURNED FROM THE PICNIC AT ONE o'clock, his valet waited impatiently with news. In spite of instructions to stay inside and nurse the cold he'd caught after the night in the rain and the mad ride to town, Carl had slipped out and checked the tree. He'd found a note.

"You were right," he said to Shermont in a begrudging tone. "The note referred to the article in the paper about the capturing of Napoleon's agent and said they would have to discontinue operations and leave immediately."

"Let me see the note."

"I left it, so they wouldn't know their secret spot had been discovered."

"Probably a wise move." Shermont leaned back in his chair and closed his eyes. "Tell me everything you can remember."

"No salutation. Female hand. Written on house stationery."

That didn't help. House stationery was left in every room in case the guest had not brought his or her own. That meant every female in the house was suspect. Even the servants had access, though most were likely illiterate. "Perfume?"

"I think so, but to be honest, with this stuffy head I can't say for sure."

Shermont jumped up. "I have to see that note myself." Perhaps he could identify the perfume and that would either clear Eleanor or seal her fate. He found himself hoping for the former. Eleanor was intelligent and beautiful, and the same qualities that made her attractive also suited her to espionage, the work he dreaded she might be doing. He was torn between his attraction to her and his mission. Either way, he had to know.

He couldn't sneak out in broad daylight, so he simply walked out the door and down the drive as if going for a stroll. Once beyond the sight of anyone at the house, he left the road and cut through the woods. At the old oak tree he found a different note. In bold strokes the writer reassured the receiver. *There is no imminent threat. Remain steadfast. We leave as scheduled.* Same paper. Second writer.

He now knew there were at least two persons plus the courier, and they intended to escape, probably soon if plans were already made. He returned to the house determined to catch the agents before that happened. And before he fell in love with one.

He decided to take a role in the play, the better to keep an eye on Eleanor. He found Digby in the ballroom checking on the construction of a rudimentary stage by several footmen and what appeared to be several gardeners.

"I'm willing to take a role in your play," he said,

gritting his teeth and forcing a smile. He'd already heard a good portion, and there was nothing he wanted less than to get up on a stage and emote the inane, self-aggrandizing lines Digby had penned.

"I knew you would come around," Digby said with a satisfied grin. "I'm just on my way to hand out the parts now."

Shermont joined Digby on his way to the parlor, where most of the guests waited to receive their assigned roles. As soon as they entered, Digby called for everyone's attention.

"I have here…" He paused for dramatic effect and raised a sheaf of papers. "Your parts for tonight's play."

Everyone cheered.

"But before I hand them out…"

Everyone groaned.

"I want to explain how this is going to be staged. Due to the short time available, we didn't have time to copy a complete script for each person, so these papers contain an explanation of the story, facts for your character, and only a few key lines to memorize."

Everyone breathed a sigh of relief.

"The rest of the lines you'll make up as we go along." Digby passed out a paper to each young person.

"What if I can't think of anything to say?" Beatrix asked as she took her page with a shaking hand.

"As long as you say those few lines I've given you that are crucial to the progress of the story, everything will be fine." Digby walked by her without apparent concern for her distress and went on to the next person.

Shermont hoped she wouldn't swoon. The poor girl was probably only doing this to please her supposed fiancé, who didn't act as though he was her intended. "It won't be as difficult as you imagine," he reassured her. "We'll all help one another."

Beatrix flashed him a grateful smile.

Shermont looked at his assigned part and stifled a guffaw. A pirate?

"What's all this?" Deirdre asked, thumbing her sheaf of pages. "I can't memorize all—"

"You will be able to read your lines. As the narrator you'll stand to the side of the stage, like the Greek chorus did in ancient times. Your lines will bridge the story action, and you can fill in the gap if someone forgets a line."

Deirdre leaned back in her chair, obviously not excited with her role. Judging by the mostly silent reactions, no one but Digby seemed overly pleased.

"This is not fair," Lieutenant Parker said. "Why do I have to be a soldier? I have to wear a uniform all the time."

"At least you're not the narrator," Deirdre grumbled.

"Why do you get to be the enchanted Frog Prince?" Whitby asked Digby. "You always get to be the hero."

"Because I wrote the play, and I have a green waistcoat."

"So does Uncle Huxley," Mina whispered.

But the play was just for the young people. The older generation and any late arriving guests were the intended audience.

"What we need are costumes," Digby said. He clapped his hands, the signal for four footmen, each carrying a large trunk, to enter. "Each person is responsible for putting together his or her own costume, but these items from the attic may give you some ideas."

There was a mad dash for the trunks. Shermont waited for the rush to die down then picked up an ornate sword and belt. He debated between a black seventeenth-century Musketeer-style wide-brimmed hat with a sad white feather and one with lots of gold braid that looked like it had once been worn by an admiral. Since Digby had named the pirate the Black Blade, Shermont chose the first hat and held out the other to Parker.

"I don't need a costume," he said in a disheartened tone.

"Generals are also soldiers."

It took a moment, but Parker's face lit up. "I could be a general." He stood at attention, stuck out his chin, and gazed into distant battlefields. "Sir Henry Parker, Commanding General, First Brigade."

Shermont plopped the hat on the young man's head.

"Just don't expect me to salute you," Alanbrooke said as he walked by carrying an armor breastplate and helmet.

"Your attention, please," Digby called. "Your chosen items will be taken to your rooms, and you'll have a chance to refine your costumes later. Right now, we're going to walk through the scenes. Please bring your scripts and follow me."

As they walked to the ballroom, Eleanor slowed

Mina with a hand on her arm and whispered, "Where are Fiona and Hazel? Didn't they want to participate in the play?"

"Their mother is scandalized at the very idea of us putting on a play and won't let them take part unless she can read the script first and be present during the rehearsal," Mina whispered back. "Teddy categorically refused."

"I'm surprised Mrs. Holcum didn't insist on chaperoning."

"Did you forget? It's Teddy's project. And anything he does is perfect. At least until her precious daughter gets a wedding ring around her finger. How could she not agree to his terms? But I'd bet she gave Beatrix an earful of instructions. Do this. Don't do that."

"Mostly don't do that," Eleanor whispered, and Mina giggled.

"Whenever you're ready to start," Teddy called to them. He stood on the stage at the far end of the ballroom with his arms crossed, tapping his foot impatiently.

Eleanor hadn't noticed they'd fallen so far behind. All the others stood in front of a wooden platform framed by curtains that looked suspiciously like the drapes from the dining room.

Everyone soon learned Teddy took his theatrics seriously.

Eleanor stood to try on the costume she was making. When her necklace caught on the material, she took it off and laid it on the table. Then, worried it might get misplaced, she set it inside a decorative ceramic box.

"I thought putting on a play was supposed to be fun," Deirdre said. "Like when we were children." She listlessly sorted through the two additional trunks the servants had brought down from the attic. She held up a white silk domino with elaborate gold braid around the edges and peeked through the eyeholes of the mask which covered the upper half of her face.

"You're just crabby because you don't get to dress up in a costume," Mina said without looking up from the black material she was sewing. "I'm not all that thrilled with being the witch, but…"

"Go on. Say it's better than being the narrator."

"That wasn't what I was—"

"What do you think?" Eleanor asked. She walked to the center of the sitting room and pirouetted. She'd found an old ball gown with a nearly sheer overskirt of pink and gold tulle. There must have been eight yards of material in the skirt alone. She'd cut and basted together a tunic with long bell-shaped sleeves that she could wear over her regular dress and still had enough leftover material to use as a veil. "A Camelot-style princess gown. Will it do?"

"It's amazing," Mina said.

A knock on the door forestalled Deirdre's answer.

Beatrix entered, face red and eyes swollen. "I don't know how to act like a gypsy, and I can't make a gypsy costume. Mother is horrified at the very thought of me being displayed on a stage, but she fears if she says anything to Teddy, he will put an end to our engagement. She's so upset that she took to her bed with a headache." She dumped a tangle of brightly colored silk scarves and shawls onto the chair. "What am I to say to your brother? He'll think I ruined his play, and he'll hate me." She blinked away her tears and said to Eleanor, "Your costume is beautiful."

"Thank you. We'll help with your costume." She slipped the dress off over her head carefully, since it was only basted together.

"I wish I could be the princess," Beatrix said with a sigh.

"At least a gypsy is better than—"

"A narrator," Mina and Eleanor finished in unison.

"Of course, Teddy did mention the narrator served the function of a Greek chorus," Eleanor added.

"What's your point?" Deirdre asked. She sat back, crossed her arms, and stuck out her lip in a pout.

"So wouldn't it follow logically that the narrator could be a Greek goddess. The Goddess of Destiny would be an appropriate choice."

Deirdre shook her head. "The Goddesses of Fate and Destiny were old hags. I'd rather be Aphrodite, Goddess of Love and Beauty."

"I always liked Iris, Goddess of the Rainbow," Beatrix said.

"If I have to be a witch, you can be a hag," Mina said.

No one seemed happy with their assigned roles. If this were a Jane Austen novel, one of the women would come up with a clever idea. Suddenly, Eleanor realized how to solve one of her concerns. "I'll be the witch," she volunteered. "You can be the princess." She held out her costume to Mina.

Mina looked horrified rather than pleased. "I'm not going to kiss the Frog Prince. Yuck." She pushed Eleanor's hand back.

"I'll do it," Beatrix said. She grabbed the princess dress and held it to her breast. "Please."

"Fine with me," Mina said. "I'd love to be the gypsy."

"And I'll be the witch," Eleanor said.

Everyone smiled until Beatrix said, "We can't change parts." She gazed fondly at the pink tulle before giving it back to Eleanor. "Teddy would never allow it."

Eleanor refused to take the dress. She didn't want to kiss the frog either. The play called for the princess to kiss the frog mask, a hideous clay and paper head that their father had picked up on his Grand Tour during carnival in Florence. Why anyone would choose such a monstrosity was anyone's guess. Teddy would then lean the princess over his arm, and while his back was to the audience, he would whip off the frog head. They would stand up still in an embrace. A bit of stage hocus-pocus that would change him back to a prince.

Eleanor ducked her head to think of something to say to convince the other women to exchange roles. She spied the white and gold domino Deirdre had dropped next to her on the settee. "We'll all wear masks. What Teddy doesn't know, he can't change. And by the time he does find out, the play will be over and it won't make any difference."

"Great idea," Mina said.

"Let's do it," Deirdre said.

"I don't know," Beatrix said, but she stroked the tulle material of the costume as if she cradled a beloved kitten or puppy in her arms. "Maybe we shouldn't."

"Of course we should. It's perfect," Mina said.

"You have to go in with us or it won't work," Eleanor said. "You are not any man's doormat. Stand up for what you want."

Beatrix bit her bottom lip for a moment. "You're right. I will do it."

Eleanor grinned her approval. Maybe Beatrix had a backbone after all.

"Now... to work on an interesting costume. I'm not sure where to start. You're clever with a needle," Mina said to Eleanor as she sorted through the colorful scarves. "What would you do?"

Eleanor was in her element. She designed each costume to go over the dresses they would wear to dinner, so they could all get dressed backstage. Mina was turned into a gypsy by a wrap-around skirt she could tie around her waist like an apron. To the wide ribbon sash Eleanor tied a multitude of colorful strips of material, ribbons, and silk squares. At assorted spots she sewed on shiny bangles and tiny bells. A large shawl draped over her shoulders and another folded crossways and tied around her hips completed the basic costume.

Mina accented her costume with lots of jewelry, a red domino from the trunk, and another scarf tied around her head turban-style. Eleanor rummaged in the trunk and found a piano shawl with eight-inch black silk fringe that she cut off, twisted together, and tacked under the turban so that it hung over Mina's shoulder like a long braid.

Mina spun around. Her skirt swirled in a colorful circle and the bells tinkled. "I love my costume," she said.

"Me next," Beatrix said.

She already had the basic tunic overdress. To that Eleanor added a chain of coin disks around her hips, a yellow scarf to tie over her hair, and two long hanks of yellow wool yarn that she crisscrossed with ribbons to resemble Rapunzel braids. She placed the veil over the girl's head Maid Marian–style. Mina provided a gold circlet crown from her stash of jewelry to hold it all in place.

"I feel like a princess," Beatrix said. "Oh, thank you. Thank you, Eleanor. Mina, Deirdre. I can't find the words—"

"You're quite welcome," Eleanor said.

"From all of us," Mina added.

"I don't think you have anything in that trunk for me," Deirdre remarked.

"You're right," Eleanor said and then laughed at Deirdre's sad face. "For your costume we need outside help." She summoned the maid and whispered her directions through the door that she opened only a crack. "Once we have the right materials, your costume will be the easiest of all," she said to Deirdre.

Very quickly, a befuddled Twilla returned and handed extra bedsheets through the door. Eleanor draped one length of white material over each of Deirdre's shoulders to hide the small cap sleeves of her dress and fastened them in place with large ornate brooches. A chain of golden leaf shapes was put into use as a belt to keep the sheets from flapping wide. Deirdre insisted on a disguise like everyone else, even though she hadn't traded her part. Eleanor made her a turban of shiny gold fabric, modified slightly to let a long streamer of gold hang over one shoulder. The white domino that had sparked the idea fit the outfit perfectly.

"You look amazing," Mina said to her sister. "Do you want to switch—"

"No," Deirdre said. "The narrator is an important role, and I am honored to be selected for such a responsibility."

For herself, Eleanor basted together another long tunic out of dark purple silk with tiny gold embroidered stars. To that she added a long black cape. She wasn't sure if witches during the Regency wore pointy hats, but she cut a circle of pasteboard from one of the boxes in the larger trunk and glued black material to it. After notching out a pie-shaped piece, she pasted the long sides together. Two holes over each ear allowed her to attach thin black ribbons to tie it on. For a mask, she cut holes for eyes and a slit for a mouth into a piece of green silk and tied it over her face. She needed something to add for hair.

Deirdre found a fly-whisk in the trunk. Three tassels of gray horsehair were attached to a stick, and she explained it was used to swish through the air and chase the flies away. Eleanor attached the tassels to her hat, one over each ear and one so that it made coarse bangs. She wouldn't be able to disguise her height, a good three inches taller than the others, but as the witch she would be sitting by the pretend fire for most of the play. The rest of the time she would have to remember to hunch over.

Loathe to take off their costumes, they fiddled with this, that, and the other detail, adding a last bit of jewelry or another ribbon. A knock sounded on the door. Mina was closest and opened it a crack to peek out. Fiona and Hazel pushed their way into the room. They were already dressed for dinner.

"We finally talked Mother into letting us participate in the play," Hazel blurted out.

"I got so upset I vomited," Fiona said. "It always works."

"Except now we can't find your brother."

Deirdre shook her head. "I'm sorry—"

"Please don't say it's too late," Hazel begged.

"He's already handed out the parts," Mina said.

"And we've already had the rehearsal," Beatrix added.

Fiona and Hazel were close to tears.

"I know what you can do," Eleanor said. "Deirdre can hardly be a Greek chorus all by herself, right?"

"Well, we can't all read it in unison," Deirdre pointed out. "And there isn't time to write out two more copies."

"True, but they can stand at your side."

"And do what?"

Eleanor felt the weight of their collective stares and fumbled for an idea, any idea. "Well, when you get to the end of each section of narrative, you can bow or make a hand signal or something, and they can repeat the last two or three words for dramatic effect. Like a Greek chorus." Her voice trailed off as she ran out of steam.

"We can do it," Fiona said. "Can't we, Hazel? Please let us do it."

"Sounds like a good idea to me," Mina said.

With a little more cajoling, Deirdre agreed. Mina explained the secrecy pact, and the girls were sworn to silence. They too insisted on masks to go with their costumes. Eleanor rang for the maid, made her request, and Twilla fetched more sheets. There wasn't enough gold fabric left to make two more headpieces to match Deirdre's, so Eleanor cut Lone Ranger-style masks from the remnants. She made smaller white turbans for the Maxwell girls while they practiced their routine with Deirdre.

A knock on the door silenced everyone.

"If that's someone else wanting a costume, tell them I'm all sewed out," Eleanor said, flexing her cramped fingers. Everyone had helped with the sewing, but she'd done a lot of work in a short time.

Mina went to the door and opened it a crack. Her aunt's maid stood in the hall. "Yes?"

"Pardon me, Miss Mina, but Mrs. Aubin said to tell you and Miss Cracklebury that the assembly bell has rung and you have guests waiting in the parlor. Miss Austen and Miss Jane have arrived with Mr. Knight and Mr. Austen. Lord and Lady Maybrumble and their daughters are here. And… I forget the other names."

"Don't worry about that. You may tell her we'll be down straightaway." She closed the door a little too firmly. "Good heavens! Where has the afternoon gone?"

"Hurry up, everyone. We have to get downstairs," Deirdre said. She grabbed the bellpull to summon Twilla. "We still have to change into evening dress."

Eleanor had already removed her costume as soon as she'd heard Jane Austen was in the house. "Take your costumes off carefully," she cautioned the others. "They're only basted together. Fiona, if you will empty that smaller trunk, we can put everything in there to have it carried backstage."

Beatrix left, promising to dress for dinner quickly so she could meet them in twenty minutes.

Deirdre and Mina changed clothes faster than ever with Twilla and Eleanor's help.

"But you still have to change too," Mina said to Eleanor.

"I can do that after you two go. It's most important that you get downstairs quickly."

While Twilla put the final touches on Mina's hair, Eleanor went into the sitting room.

Deirdre followed. "Why aren't you changing?"

"I'm looking for a book."

"What book?" Deirdre asked.

"Pride and Prejudice," Eleanor answered. "My favorite." Then she remembered she'd placed it on the table by the window in her bedroom and left to fetch it.

Again, Deirdre followed her. "You're not thinking of taking that book downstairs?"

"Yes."

"Oh, no, no, no. No, you are not."

"But Jane Austen is—"

Deirdre lowered her voice. "I wrote you about that rumor in confidence. Miss Jane has not openly acknowledged that she is… You absolutely cannot mention anything about her… ah… habit. That would be the epitome of rudeness."

Eleanor looked at the book in her hands and sighed. She wasn't sure what she'd planned on saying to Jane Austen if she actually met her, but talking about her books and her characters would have been wonderful. And apparently impossible. She put the novel on the table and gave it a little pat.

"You should take care of that book," Eleanor said. "It's going to be valuable someday. That and anything Jane Austen writes to you, even something as simple as an acceptance to an invitation."

Deirdre gave her a strange look, and then she laughed. "Is that another one of your so-called premonitions? You know they're nonsense. You were so scared about that dream you had of your ship going down, and yet here you are safe and sound." She shook her head. "You always were melodramatic. Forget all that and get dressed. We have to go, but I want you to come down in ten minutes."

Eleanor changed her dress and shoes in two minutes flat. Then she paced the room and watched the clock on the mantle. And worried about what she would say to Jane Austen.

Omigod. Jane Austen!

In the course of her jobs in the costume departments at several major movie studios, she'd met, talked to, and touched a number of big-name stars without a single qualm. But now she had a whole flock of butterflies. *Austenipolo nerviosi.*

The clock ticked ever so slowly, and yet the minutes flew by. Suddenly, it was time to go before she'd thought of something to say.

Ten

Eleanor met Beatrix on the landing. "Where is your mother?"

"Already downstairs," Beatrix answered. "She didn't want me to wait, but I stood my ground for once and insisted I would go in with you. I wanted to thank you for all your help and for switching roles."

"You're welcome, but it's nothing. I'm happy with the changes too."

"Are you all right?" she asked. "You look a little pale."

"Just a bit nervous." Eleanor reached for her necklace as she often did in times of stress and remembered she had taken it off earlier and left it inside the decorative ceramic box. She made a mental note to retrieve it as soon as she returned to her rooms.

"I know the feeling. I get butterflies every time I see Teddy—I mean Lord Digby. And Lord Shermont is so much more… intense."

"Oh, no, it's not him. It's… it's…" Eleanor couldn't explain she was anxious because she was about to face the woman she had come so far to meet.

"Keep your secrets. I don't mind." Beatrix took

Eleanor's arm and linked elbows. "Everything will be fine. We'll go in together."

The parlor had been expanded. What Eleanor had thought were wooden walls turned out to be floor-to-ceiling sliding panels. The parlor, adjacent music room, and library at the rear of the house were now one large space filled with people.

Deirdre must have been watching for them because she immediately sought them out. Beatrix excused herself to join her mother.

"Let me introduce you to your favorite author," she whispered in Eleanor's ear. Deirdre took Eleanor by the arm and led her to a group of three women near the pianoforte. She slowed her steps so as not to interrupt the conversation in the middle of a sentence.

Eleanor tried to determine which woman was Jane Austen since no real portrait had ever been made. Her sister Cassandra had done a sketch, and during the Victorian period an artist had added details to that, but no one could say for sure if the second artist had ever seen the famous writer. There was a serious question as to the accuracy of any depiction.

One woman was tall, taller than Eleanor, big-boned, and ostentatiously dressed. Eleanor counted her out. The other two must be Jane Austen and her older sister Cassandra. The one with the darker hair must be Jane.

She was tiny in stature, not even five feet tall. Slim. High arched brows, straight classic Grecian nose, small mouth with thin lips. Ordinary. Someone you might pass by without a second thought. Except for the lively sparkle in her eyes.

She wore a lilac dress of smooth cotton fabric historically referred to as sarsenet. It had black satin ribbon trim. A lacy cap covered most of her hair, but a few unruly curls peeked out around her face.

Eleanor knew Jane Austen was thirty-nine years old in 1814. She was saddened to see the patch of pigmentation below Jane's lower lip and an irregular area of darker skin with white spots under her chin. The blotchiness was a symptom of Addison's disease, the likely cause of her death in July 1817.

"I can't really say much on recent fashions," Jane Austen said to the robust older woman seated across from her. "We rarely socialize anymore except for family functions, but I was in Bath... April last. Satin ribbon trim on dresses was all the rage there, and I cannot see the styles in London being much different."

"Very nice. But so plain. I like the what-do-you-call-it... the froufrous." She patted her large bosom adorned with ruffles, lace, ribbons, beading, and lots of jewelry. "I have the physicka for it, no?"

While the tall woman brayed with laughter at the joke only she appreciated, Deirdre pushed Eleanor forward. She introduced her cousin from America to the Countess Lazislov from Russia, Miss Austen, and Miss Jane.

Eleanor was tongue-tied, but Deirdre picked up the slack as would any competent hostess.

"We're having a light informal supper tonight because we have a special entertainment planned. Eleanor is in our play and made many of the costumes," Deirdre said to start a conversation before she excused herself and left Eleanor on her own.

"I love homespun theatricals," Jane Austen said. "We used to put on plays at home when we were growing up."

"We've seen some that rivaled professional productions," Cassandra added.

Eleanor shook her head. "I'm afraid this one involves more enthusiasm than actual talent."

"Good," Jane said with an impish grin. "That sort is always more entertaining."

"Oh, my," Countess Lazislov said. "Who iss dat?"

Without being as obvious, Jane and Cassandra looked toward the door. Eleanor peeked over her shoulder. Shermont had entered, and the man looked good. The high collar of his charcoal gray cutaway coat framed the fall of snowy linen under his strong chin. The silver embroidery on his sky-blue brocade vest was several shades lighter than his form-fitting silver gray slacks. The subdued hues stood out among the red uniforms and peacock colors of the other male ensembles.

"I vant him for a dinner partner," the countess said. She immediately stood and went in search of Deirdre to make it happen.

"Definitely eye candy," Eleanor said without thinking.

"That's an interesting turn of phrase," Cassandra said.

"Ah… that's what we call stunningly handsome men where I come from. In America."

"Well, Lord Shermont is that," Jane said. "I always thought he had something more important than looks. Character. Moral fiber to back up his charm."

"Then you know him?" Eleanor asked.

"Pardon me. I should not have spoken. We've

met a few times, but my opinion is merely an intuitive evaluation."

Eleanor was trying to think of a way to bring the conversation around to books. Two elderly women joined the group, inquiring about Jane and Cassandra's family. Then Teddy arrived.

"I'm sure you'll excuse Eleanor," he said. "I must have her resolve an issue between myself and Alanbrooke, a bet, if you will, concerning America." He held out his arm.

"Oh… I'd rather not," Eleanor said, even though the others demurred to Teddy's request. She was perfectly happy where she was. "I… I…"

"Come, Cousin. Dinner will be served shortly, and I would like to take care of this before then."

"Lord Digby is the author of our play tonight," she said, hoping to open a conversation on writing.

Teddy chuckled. He picked up her hand, put it on his arm, and held it there. "A fact you should reveal only after the play is a rousing success. By your leave," he added with a bow and literally pulled Eleanor away.

She tried to ease her hand out from under his.

"You can thank me later," he whispered.

"For what?"

"For rescuing you from the old maid's corner." He jerked his head to indicate the area behind them.

"I was perfectly happy with the company and would prefer to go back," she said. "Now release my hand before I cause a scene."

He dropped her hand as if it had turned red hot. "Bit ungrateful, I'd say."

"Then let me thank you for your previous concern, albeit misplaced. I'm quite capable of walking away from a conversation if it is not to my liking." She turned on her heel and took several steps before she realized the dinner gong had rung. Everyone else was moving toward the door.

As on the evening before, Eleanor was seated near the middle of the table that had been expanded with additional leaves to seat twenty-eight guests. On her right, her dinner partner was a very young lieutenant so awed by his surroundings he could barely manage to stutter one-word questions and answers. On her left, Mr. Foucalt, the dancing master, had been drafted to fill out the table despite his sniffling and sneezing. She did learn he planned to hold a dancing lesson early the following morning.

From her position she could clearly see Shermont, now at the opposite end of the table. The countess had gotten her wish and spent much of her time fawning over him, apparently to his amusement and enjoyment. Eleanor ate little and emptied her wineglass a number of times. Nerves over the coming play, she told herself. Thankfully, Deirdre's definition of casual dining meant there was only one remove before she led the women into the parlor.

Eleanor expected another chance to talk to Jane Austen, but her efforts were foiled again. Deirdre turned her hostess duties over to Aunt Patience and herded the female cast members into the ballroom, so they would have plenty of time to don their costumes and disguises. The women were already lined up stage left when the gentleman arrived in costume and awaited their cues stage right.

Shermont's pirate outfit consisted of a loose white lawn shirt open at the neck, a red satin sash under his sword belt, well-fitted black leather breeches, and knee-high boots. A wide-brimmed hat with a large blue ostrich feather worn cocked at a jaunty angle completed his costume. Eye candy. With difficulty, Eleanor pulled her gaze away.

She heard the audience come in and get settled. Eleanor peeked through the curtains. Deirdre, as the goddess Aphrodite, followed by Fiona and Hazel, walked solemnly up the center aisle and mounted three steps to line up on the audience's right.

"Our story," Deirdre said in a serious tone, "as are many stories, is of the quest for love. Our hero is an enchanted prince cursed to bear the likeness of a frog by a wicked witch. He has traveled the world seeking a cure and has almost given up hope, until he meets a gypsy fortune-teller."

"A gypsy fortune-teller," Fiona and Hazel said in unison.

Two footmen stagehands pulled open the curtains. Center stage, Mina danced and twirled in a circle.

The Frog Prince paced wearily across the stage carrying a well-used portmanteau. The hideous green mask covered his entire head, but the protruding jaw gave room for his words to escape. "My heart is filled with despair," he said, bringing his fist to his chest. "I have searched far and wide for the cure to this terrible curse. Please help me. I must know if I will ever succeed."

Mina sat at the small table and gestured for the Frog Prince to do the same. "Cross my palm with gold, and I will tell your future."

He handed over a small pouch that clinked. The gypsy tucked it in her belt. Then she waved her hands over her crystal ball, actually an overturned opaque glass bowl, but a reasonable facsimile.

"I see the witch who cursed you living in a cottage in the woods near here."

The frog jumped up. "I will—"

"That is not all," the gypsy said. "Sit down. The witch holds a beautiful princess prisoner. The princess is the key to your salvation. Only a kiss of true love from her will cure the wicked enchantment."

"But how can she love me when I am so ugly?"

"You will be tested five times, and if you prove worthy, she will love you. But beware. You must outwit, outfight, out-reason, out-trick, and out-charm your opponents to win the princess's love."

The frog jumped up. "I will do it."

He exited.

As the curtains closed, the gypsy fortune-teller called after him, "Good luck." Then she added in a stage whisper, "You're going to need it."

Eleanor scrambled to her place on a three-legged stool by the pretend fire, and Beatrix sat on a throne-like chair.

Deirdre said, "And so the Frog Prince searches high and low until he finds the witch's cottage in the woods. He enters, ready to claim his true love."

"His true love," the chorus echoed.

The curtains opened and the Frog Prince entered

and knelt in front of the princess. "Your kiss alone can break this terrible curse."

She turned to the witch. "Must I kiss him? He is so ugly."

"A kiss that is not freely given is worthless," Eleanor said in a high trembling voice.

"Then I choose not to kiss you," the princess said to the frog.

"Begone," the witch said. "You have your answer."

"I will fight for your love," the frog said to the princess.

"You will take the Five Tests of Worthiness?" the witch asked slyly.

The princess gasped. "Don't do it. If you fail, you will forfeit your life."

"If it is the only way to end this curse, then I will do it," he said.

"Very well. The first test is one of wits," the witch said. "Bring on the wise man."

Parker, wearing a monk's cowled sackcloth robe and carrying a book at least six inches thick, entered stage right.

"Ready?" the witch asked. "What has four legs in the morning, two legs at noon, three legs in the evening, and is weakest when it has the most legs?"

Both men acted as if they pondered a weighty matter. Eleanor rolled her eyes, but fortunately, no one could see beneath her mask. It had to be the oldest riddle on earth, literally, since Sophocles had posed it in *Oedipus Rex*. She was surprised everyone in the audience didn't shout the answer before Teddy had a chance to respond.

"A man," the Frog Prince answered triumphantly.

"I am rightly and justly defeated," the wise man said with slumped shoulders. He left, dragging his feet.

The frog knelt before the princess.

She leaned away from him. "That was only the first test. I still choose not to kiss you."

"The second test is harder," the witch said. "A test of your fighting ability."

The pirate entered with long strides. "I have come to claim the princess as my prize."

The frog stood protectively in front of the princess with his arms spread. "The princess is no man's booty."

The pirate drew his sword. The frog drew his. They sparred back and forth across the stage. Shermont had the bigger sword and longer reach, and for a moment Eleanor thought the fight was in earnest. She scooted her stool back to the edge of the stage, and Beatrix jumped out of her seat and cowered against the curtain.

The script predetermined the winner, and so the pirate finally had to drop his guard. The frog smashed the sword out of his opponent's hand and stabbed him in the heart. Even though the tip of his sword was blunted, the effect was quite realistic due to a chicken's bladder filled with blood fastened under Shermont's shirt. The pirate fell to the floor, dying with dramatic flair as he crawled toward his sword and ended by rolling off the rear of the stage.

The audience spontaneously applauded, and as Teddy took a bow, Eleanor could not help being concerned for Shermont. Was he really hurt? She leaned back to look over the rear of the stage. Suddenly the stool slipped from beneath her. With a yelp of surprise, she tumbled backwards, feet over head.

Shermont had been squatting behind the stage, wondering how to make a dignified exit without being seen, when the witch did a backward somersault off the stage. He lunged forward, got his right arm and shoulder under her, wrapped his left arm around her legs, and stood.

The audience broke out in applause and cheers.

"Put me down."

"Not just yet." He shifted her so he could hold her with one hand, turned to face the audience, and said in a loud voice, "I do believe I have the real princess." With his free hand he picked up his sword and jammed it into the wooden stage. "Let that be a warning to any who would follow." He exited around the back carrying her over his shoulder.

Eleanor braced her hands on his waist and pushed herself up with her arms. The other players stood stock still with their mouths hanging open. Deirdre at least had the presence of mind to smooth over the incident.

"And the witch enchanted the pirate into believing she was the princess, and he carried her away."

"Carried her away," the chorus echoed.

Shermont did not stop at the edge of the stage, but strode the length of the ballroom.

"Off to his ship," Deirdre said.

"To his ship."

Shermont turned at the door. "The play must go on," he said.

"Must go on," the chorus said.

Eleanor didn't know what happened to the play after that because Shermont carried her out of the ballroom and into the hallway.

"Put me down," she said again, her voice strained due to the fact that his rock hard shoulder pressed into her stomach.

He hitched her up a bit higher.

"Ho, there. What's this?" someone asked. Eleanor recognized Patience's voice, though her words were quite slurred.

"I'm taking her to the library," he said. "To recover from her faint."

"Faint, my—" Eleanor stopped speaking when he placed a hand on her derriere. "Hey!"

"She might have hit her head and could be delirious," he said.

"Then by all means, carry on." Patience giggled. "See, I can be witty, too. Carry on."

Shermont started walking, and Eleanor looked up to see the older woman taking a long swig from a flask. Obviously not her first. Some chaperone.

Suddenly it occurred to her that Shermont believed her to be Mina, who had originally been cast as the witch. Was this the seduction that had resulted in the duel? Despite her tingle of excitement, or maybe because of it, she didn't reveal her identity as he carried her into the library. He closed the door and set her on her feet.

"I have thought of this all day," he said, cupping her face and lowering his lips to hers.

The feel of his kiss through the silk of her mask was an interesting sensation and just as magical as it was in the meadow. She leaned into the kiss, but as much as she enjoyed it, something was wrong. And it wasn't the silk that separated their lips. She couldn't get past the fact that he thought she was someone else. As much as her body screamed for more... more, she forced herself to push away from him.

She spied the blood on his shirt and looked down to see a blotch had transferred to her costume. Suddenly she realized it might have seeped through to her beautiful dress. The seams of her tunic, merely basted together, had already been torn apart in spots by the rough handling, so she ripped it the rest of the way off. And breathed a sigh of relief.

Shermont watched her with a raised eyebrow. "Don't stop on my account," he said in an amused tone.

"We should get back to the others now."

"I don't understand. First you kiss me—"

"You kissed me."

"Merely semantics, but I'll rephrase that. You kissed me back with true fervor, and then seconds later you want to walk away. You run blazing hot and then freezing cold like—"

"Me? You're the one who ignores me one minute and then tries to seduce me the next."

"Oh, come on, Eleanor. You can't—"

"What did you just call me?"

"Eleanor. Your name. What is your—"

"How do you know it's me? I mean, Mina was supposed to play the witch, so why don't you think I'm her?"

"Did you not think I would recognize you? The tilt of this stubborn chin…" He touched her bottom lip and drew his finger down to her neck. "The curve of your cheek that my palms itch to caress." He took her face in his hands. "And even if I had not recognized your scent and the feel of you when I carried you in my arms—"

"Over your shoulder like a sack of potatoes," she corrected, her dignity still bruised.

He ignored her sarcasm. "One kiss and I would know your lips, the taste of you." He kissed her long and gently before breaking away. He pulled on the ribbon ties of her hat, and the bow under her chin disappeared as fast as her resistance to his charms. "Please take off that mask."

She stepped back, removed her hat, and worked on the knots of the mask.

"I can't believe you'd think I didn't know who I kissed." He shook his head, then stopped and looked at her with a quizzical expression. "As a matter of fact, I cannot fathom why you'd even consider my seducing Mina as a possibility. She's little more than a child." By the end of the last sentence, his eyes narrowed and a muscle in his jaw clenched. "What sort of man do you think I am?"

Eleanor could hardly explain that she knew it had happened. Now she thought it wasn't Mina after all and had been Deirdre, the older of the two sisters, he had seduced. "Based on the evidence—"

"Your so-called evidence was circumstantial at best. I should think you would have believed better of me despite the situation." Even as he said the words, he realized he'd made judgments concerning Eleanor, believed she might be one of Napoleon's agents based on evidence that was shaky at best. He ran his hand through his hair. "My apologies. I've never felt... whatever this is between us." He turned away, unable to think clearly while looking into her eyes.

Eleanor couldn't define what was happening between them, but she knew it had no future. Long distance love affairs were an uphill struggle at best with a gaping chasm at the summit. When the gap to cross was two centuries wide, any relationship was impossible. She'd never thought of herself as a one-night stand, but if she didn't grab this chance to be with him, she might never have another. At least she would take the memory of him back with her.

She stepped around his body to face him. "I've never felt this way before either. I burn for your touch." She put her hands on his chest. "Does my boldness shock you?"

He sucked in a breath, and the muscles beneath her palms tensed. "Your audacity enthralls me. But I cannot promise you—"

"I'm not asking for promises. No strings, no regrets." At least none he would ever know about.

He whispered her name and wrapped his arms around her with a groan. Then he set her away from him and rested his hands on her shoulders. "If we aren't back for the curtain call in fifteen minutes, your reputation will be ruined."

"Not yours?"

He shrugged. "It is the way of the world."

"I don't care about my reputation."

"Ah, so you say now, but if you're judged guilty of immoral behavior, the other guests would shun you. You might even be forced to leave the house. Is that what you want?"

"Oh." That would mean she wouldn't have another chance to speak to Jane Austen. Hmm... hot sex or the real, live Jane Austen? Hell of a choice. Eleanor backed away to put space between herself and Shermont so she could think clearly. If she had to leave the house, how would the ghosts find her to take her back to her own time? Damn.

"I want more than a few stolen moments with you."

What did he mean by that? His words sounded suspiciously like a brush-off. She sat properly on the edge of the seat, her back yardstick-straight, ankles and knees together, hands folded in her lap. "Why did you bring me here?"

"I don't know."

He ran his hand through his hair as he sat next to her, close enough for her to feel his body heat but not touching. He knitted his fingers together as if to keep from reaching for her and rested his forearms on his knees.

"I am not habitually inclined to spontaneous, ill-considered conduct, however..."

She recognized his attempt to distance himself from her. "Oh, for Pete's sake, speak plain English."

"It was a spur of the moment decision."

At least he was honest. They sat in silence. She couldn't fault him. He'd only caught her when she fell. She placed her hand over his.

"I forgot to properly thank you for saving me yet

again." She used her free hand to turn his head, so she could place a kiss on his lips.

He looked surprised.

"Did I shock you?" she asked.

"Your boldness enchants me beyond measure." He embraced her and kissed her long and hard, tasting her, teasing her tongue with his.

She wrapped her arms around his neck. He lifted her onto his lap and ran his hand up her leg.

Eleanor smiled against his lips. Regency women didn't have an article of clothing similar to modern panties, and he would find no impediment. She concentrated so hard on willing his hand higher... higher, she nearly missed the sound of a scratch at the door and the latch opening. Shermont didn't.

Suddenly, he stood with a twisting motion that dropped her flat on her back on the sofa.

"Yes, Tuttle," he said, his voice a lot calmer than she felt.

"Pardon, milord. Mrs. Aubin said Mrs. Pottinger fainted. I've brought cold compresses, a vinaigrette, and the housekeeper. Mrs. Otto has some skill dealing—"

"That will not be necessary," Shermont said. "You may leave the cart by the door."

Eleanor realized he was trying to keep the servants from coming far enough into the room that they could see over the high back of the settee. And discover his obvious arousal.

She quickly made sure all her clothing was in place and then stood, forcing Shermont to take a step back. She assumed a position between him and the door, flashing a smile at the butler and housekeeper.

"Thank you for your concern," Eleanor said, making sure her tone was gracious. "I was a bit light-headed for a minute, but I'm fine. We will be rejoining the others now."

"That will be all," Shermont added, and the servants bowed their way out of the room without any change of expression.

The brief respite had brought Eleanor back to her senses. What was she thinking? Anyone could have interrupted them.

"Eleanor?

She turned to face him. "I'm afraid our time is up."

"Can we meet later tonight?" he asked. "After everyone has gone to sleep? I will come to your room."

"Yes. No. I mean, yes, we can meet, but you can't come to my room. I'm sharing a suite with Deirdre and Mina." If one night with him was all she was going to get, she would grab the chance. "We must be discreet. I'll come to you."

He raised an eyebrow. "You never cease to surprise me… delightfully so."

She ducked her head. "You make me want to be daring, wild, and wanton."

"The next few hours without you in my arms are going to be hell, and I am not usually a patient man."

She looked at him from underneath her lashes. "Maybe I'll make it worth your wait," she teased, stretching onto her toes to kiss him on the chin before dancing out of his reach. She picked up her hideous hat, discarded the ruined mask, and paused at the door. "Ready to return to reality?"

If he had asked her that question, her answer would have been "no." She wasn't ready to go back to her world. Not yet. Please, not yet.

Eleven

ELEANOR JERKED AWAKE WHEN HER HEAD FELL forward. Either that or the raging thunderstorm outside had woken her. The single candle had guttered out, and she couldn't see the clock on the mantle. How long had she slept? Would Shermont still be waiting? She stood, dumping the book in her lap onto the floor with a thump.

Damn. She hoped the girls were sound sleepers, or that the noise would blend with the thunder. She picked up the book. Moving slowly, using the fairly frequent strikes of lightning to orient herself, she made her way to the door and across the sitting room. She put her ear to their bedroom door. Silence.

She peeked in. Two lumps under the covers reassured her that the girls had not woken due to the noise. She eased the door closed.

With a sigh of relief, she carefully made her way to the exit. She opened the door and saw a movement in the hallway, then pulled the door shut except for a tiny crack. Omigod. Was that Count Lazislov leaving Patience's room? Eleanor put a hand over her mouth to stifle a giggle. She'd heard the Count and Countess had insisted on separate rooms, and now she knew why.

Eleanor waited as she counted slowly to one hundred and then opened the door enough to make sure the hallway was empty. She slipped out and pulled it shut with a soft click. When she reached the stairway, she saw lights below and heard talk and laughter, though the sleeping footman at the front door seemed oblivious. The clock in the entrance said two-twenty-five. Could people still be awake? And partying?

She started to head back to her room, and then, at the sound of uneven footsteps, turned and stopped.

Shermont reeled out of the parlor door and stumbled on the first step. "Whoa." He shook a finger at the step. "If you must move, make it upward."

"Wake Stevens and let him help you to your room," Digby called from the parlor.

"Noooo. I'm never too drunk to put myself to bed." To the sound of laughter, on the third try he got his foot solidly on the step, grabbed the banister, and pulled himself up. After awkwardly negotiating half the steps, he ran nimbly up the rest.

"I was beginning to think you'd changed your mind," he whispered to Eleanor.

She shrank back a step. "Are you drunk?" she whispered.

"That? Only an act to get out of playing cards. Everyone knows I never drink while I gamble." He took her arm and gently guided her down the hall in the opposite direction from her room.

Eleanor dragged her feet. She was having second thoughts. This seemed so... so premeditated. And she was getting nervous. The first time with a man could go either way. What would he think of her naked? Should she get naked? What sort of lover would he be? What would he like? So many questions ran lickety-split through her brain. Then something totally off the track occurred to her. "How did you know I was at the top of the stairs?"

"Ahh. I could say I sensed your presence."

She rolled her eyes.

"Or that I recognized your perfume?"

"From that distance, I should hope not."

"Or I could admit I coerced Alanbrooke into a chess game. I set up the board and positioned my chair so that I could see the stairway in the convex mirror located in the entrance hall."

"A rather small, distorted image," she said. "What if it had been… the Countess Lazislov?"

"Then I would have been surprised. She is downstairs playing cards."

Normal conversation, even if it was in whispers, calmed her nerves a bit. "Why weren't you in the game? I'd heard…"

"Ah. Don't believe everything you hear. Not only would I rather be with you, if I'd stayed, it would have broken several of my cardinal rules for gambling. Never gamble with anyone who wants to learn how to play. If you think there's a patsy at the table, it's probably you. And never gamble with a female—"

"Don't tell me you're—"

"I was about to say… never gamble with a female willing to bet her jewelry. Either she's cheating, or her jewels are paste."

"So, which is it? Is the Countess cheating, or are her jewels fake?"

He laughed. "Both. As Digby, Rockingham, and Parker will find out soon."

"You didn't warn them?"

"Not my place to save a grown man from his own foolishness, which rarely works even if you try. Some lessons must be learned the hard way." They reached the end of the hallway, his door the last one on the right. He reached for the knob and paused. "Someone has entered my room since last I left."

"How can you tell?" she asked, her voice matching his barely-above-a-breath volume.

"I always leave a thread or hair on the doorknob for just such an incident."

Eleanor wasn't sure what to make of that. He hadn't seemed paranoid. "Your valet? One of the servants?"

He shook his head. "Not only would they have no reason, they would have used the servant's entrance." Shermont crossed the hall, opened the mica filter on the wall sconce, and took out the lit candle. "Wait here."

He opened the door and stepped inside.

The door swung nearly closed, and she couldn't see anything. Eleanor got goose bumps. Were the ghosts in his room?

She heard a scuffling sound. She was listening so hard she almost missed the sound of footsteps on the marble floor downstairs.

"Good night, gentlemen," the countess trilled from the stairway. "Perhaps you can vin your money back tomorrow."

Oh dear. Eleanor didn't want to get caught loitering outside Shermont's room. She slipped inside, closing the door behind her.

The single candle was stuck in a holder on a small table and gave only a weak light. Flashes of lightning lit the windows and the anger on Shermont's face, giving him a sinister air as he strode toward her, hauling Mina forward by a grip on her upper arm.

"Mina?"

"I found her in my bed," Shermont said.

"Mina! What are you doing here?" a voice from the other side of the room said. Deirdre stepped from behind the drapes.

"Deirdre?" Eleanor cried.

"What the bloody hell!" Shermont said. "Is someone going to drop from the ceiling next?"

"What on earth are you two doing in Lord Shermont's room?"

Deirdre's chin shot into the air and her mouth set in a stubborn line. Mina tried to mimic her sister, but Eleanor stood her ground, crossing her arms and tapping her foot.

Mina was the first to cave in and confess. "Teddy was so mad this afternoon. I figured he'd never take us to London and I'd never get married," she babbled. "I don't want to die an old maid. Shermont was so nice and said we'd be the hit of the Season, so I thought he wouldn't mind if I was discovered in his room and he had to marry me. Then he could take us to London."

Eleanor turned to Deirdre.

"My reasoning was much the same," the other girl mumbled.

"That... that illogical, convoluted thinking cannot be called reasoning," he said.

"If it had worked, it would have been brilliant," Mina said.

"I would have refused to be coerced into marriage," he said.

Deirdre seemed less concerned with Shermont than arguing with her sister. "As the oldest it's my place to take care of you. Why would—"

"I can take care of myself. You—"

"Girls!" Eleanor said, stepping between them. "You can settle this later. Right now, we need to get back to our rooms. Quietly." Thankfully, neither girl had thought to ask why Eleanor was there.

She turned to Shermont. "I regret this disruption of your plans for the evening," she said, hoping the look in her eyes conveyed how disappointed she was.

He nodded as if he understood and opened the door.

She pushed both girls into the hall and followed them out. Footsteps alerted her to trouble coming. She turned to face Shermont, and the girls did the same. "Thank you, Lord Shermont, for that ah... scientific explanation of thunder and lightning," she said in a formal tone loud enough to carry down the hallway. "I'm sure we'll be able to sleep now. Come along, girls." She hooked one arm with each and marched them away.

As they approached Teddy, backed by Rockingham, Parker, Whitby, and Alanbrooke, Eleanor acted surprised. "Seems everyone is having trouble sleeping with the terrible storm," she said without slowing her pace and towing the girls with her.

She came face to face with Teddy. Dropping her voice, she said, "Friends should not let friends wander around drunk. Fortunately, we were awake when we heard someone fumbling with our door latch. Shermont is so drunk he had no idea where his room was. I find such drunkenness repulsive, don't you? Well, all's well that ends well. We must be going. Good night, gentlemen." Without giving him a chance to reply, she pulled the girls along, powering through the group of surprised men who stepped out of their way.

Deirdre opened her mouth to say something, but Eleanor whispered, "Not until we're inside our room." She slammed the door open, pushed the girls into their suite, and then paused to smile and wave to the gentlemen who had turned to watch them, still stunned by the turn of events.

She followed the girls into the bedroom they shared. Deirdre lit a candle, revealing two misshapen lumps on the bed. As each girl removed the pillows they had arranged to take their place, Eleanor put her hands on her hips.

"I'm not going to say how stupid your actions were because I'm sure you know it. I hope both of you have learned a valuable lesson."

"We have," Deirdre said.

"We have," Mina echoed. "Do you think Teddy believed your playacting?"

"I hope so," Eleanor said. "If not, then…" Omigod! Was this the basis for the duel? Had she stopped it? Only one way to know for sure. She spun toward the door.

"Where are you going?" Deirdre asked.

Eleanor paused with her hand on the doorknob. "To make sure Teddy isn't going to do something stupid in response to hearing that Shermont tried to enter your rooms."

"But he didn't. You made it up," Mina pointed out.

"What do you mean something stupid? Oh dear! He wouldn't challenge Shermont, would he?" Deirdre asked.

"Challenge? Do you mean, a duel? Like to the death?" Mina covered her mouth with her hands.

Deirdre shook her head. "Teddy was miffed about the sword fight in the play—I mean Shermont showing him up and all, but still he wouldn't..."

"I hope not, but I want to make sure."

"We'll go with you," Deirdre said.

"No, you won't," Eleanor said. "You two stay here, and until morning do not set foot outside this room for any reason. I think you've stirred up enough trouble for one night."

After securing their promise to stay put, Eleanor went to Shermont's door. She tapped lightly.

While she waited for a response, she turned to look up and down the hall. Suddenly the door opened behind her, and Shermont pulled her backwards into his room. He shut the door and turned the key in the lock before spinning around and gathering her into his embrace.

"I was afraid you wouldn't return," he said. He found her lips with a hungry kiss that ravaged her mouth.

Despite her physical reaction, she had to make sure Teddy wouldn't die in a duel. She pushed on

Shermont's chest. "Wait. First we have to talk. I'm here on a particular mission."

Her use of that last word acted like a bucket of cold water. He dropped his arms and stepped away to pour a drink and gather his thoughts. Was she here to pass on information about the foreign agent ring? Why would she come to him? He didn't think anyone here, other than maybe Alanbrooke, knew he was working for the Crown, but Scovell had sent a warning that his security may have been breached. "Won't you sit down? Can I get you a drink?"

She shook her head and bit her bottom lip.

He returned to stand in front of her. "I can see the wheels turning." He tapped her on the forehead. "What's on your mind?"

She took a deep breath. "I wanted to make sure that if Teddy did something incredibly stupid like challenge you to a duel, you wouldn't—"

"A duel?" He breathed a sigh of relief. "I remind you of your earlier words. This is not the Dark Ages."

"But dueling is not uncommon?"

"I wouldn't say it's frequent, but on occasion, when the matter is serious enough and cannot be resolved any other way…"

"Then Teddy didn't challenge you?"

"Of course not. And if he had, I would have simply apologized for the imagined slight, and that would be the end of it."

"Hmmm, so you say now," she said. "But if he does—"

"Why are we talking about him? There are so

many other things I'd rather talk about." He set his untouched drink on the table near the door and cupped her face in his hands. "Such as your lovely forehead." He kissed her there. "If I were a poet, I would recite a sonnet about your eyes." And he kissed each eyelid. "Your attractive ears. Your charmingly stubborn chin." He touched and kissed each spot he named.

Now that she'd been reassured, she was free to enjoy his attentions. She wiggled in anticipation. "Hurry up and get to the good stuff."

"I want to take my time and adore every inch of you."

"I think I like that plan." She wrapped her arms around his neck and returned his kiss with fervor.

A loud pounding on the door caused them to jump apart.

"Open up, Shermont," Teddy called from the hall.

Shermont laid a finger over his lips to signal for silence. He pointed to the large bed and helped Eleanor scamper up the steps. He pulled the heavy tapestry bed curtain halfway closed, motioning for her to draw the rest of the curtains to enclose the bed, while he messed up the coverlet and punched the pillows. Eleanor sat cross-legged on the foot of the bed where she would be out of sight from the door. He gave her a smile and a wink.

"Shermont," Digby called. "I would have a word with you."

"What, ho?" Shermont responded. He undid the tie of his robe and mussed his hair. "Bloody hell. Keep your pants on." He paused to glance behind him to make sure the room looked as if he'd been asleep. He assumed a squinty-eyed, slack-jawed expression and opened the door just as Digby raised his fist to knock again. "Is the house on fire?" Shermont closed his robe over his nakedness and retied the sash with deliberate fumbling.

"No," Alanbrooke answered from his stance behind Teddy. "We saw the light under your door and thought you were still awake. We wanted to talk—"

"You have dishonored my sisters," Digby said.

Eleanor couldn't see what was happening, but she heard. She covered her mouth to keep from speaking out. The truth would only make matters worse.

Shermont felt the muscles in his shoulders tighten. Digby's accusation besmirched the Shermont name. His gut reaction was to tell Digby to sod off, but thanks to Eleanor he'd been forewarned the fool might take matters to an unreasonable conclusion. Adding another insult would only serve to escalate the problem.

Instead, he blinked a few times and said, "Don't be ridicluu… ridcluu…" He brought up a respectable belch. "I would never do such thing."

"Alanbrooke has agreed to act as my second," Digby continued undeterred.

"Only to dissuade you from this course of action." Alanbrooke turned to Shermont. "Your apology—"

"I demand satisfaction." Digby removed a glove from the pocket of his waistcoat and raised it to slap Shermont's cheek.

According to the Code Duello of 1777, Rule Number Five, no verbal apology could be received after such an insult. Shermont ducked the blow by stumbling sideways. He bumped into the table and acted surprised to see his glass there. "So that's where I left it," he muttered under his breath. He picked it up and drained the amber liquid with one gulp before flashing the others a supercilious grin. "Ah! I think we all need a drink. Won't you come in?" He bowed low and stumbled forward a step, forcing Digby and Alanbrooke to back up.

"Perhaps you've had enough," Alanbrooke said.

"I'm not so drunk as to forget the Code forbids a challenge to be delivered at night," Shermont said, speaking slowly and slurring his words. "Rule Number Fifteen."

"He's right, Digby. Let's leave him to sleep it off." Alanbrooke put a hand on the hothead's shoulder.

Digby shook it off. "There is still the matter—"

"Not tonight," Alanbrooke said. "The Code provides a time of reflection for good reason. Obviously no disrespect was intended. In fact, we should have ensured our foxed friend made it to his room without incident. If you must blame someone, perhaps we should look in the mirror."

Shermont set his empty glass back on the table and leaned against the doorjamb.

"I suppose you have a point." Digby's shoulders sagged. "As the host I should not have been so reluctant to fold my hand and leave the gaming table."

"And it would have saved you twenty quid," Alanbrooke said, clapping Digby on the back good-naturedly, turning him away from the door. "Let's just forget the matter, as I'm sure Shermont will. At least I had enough sense to not play cards with the countess."

Digby laughed and shook his head. "I swear she was cheating. No one is that lucky. Impossible odds for her to have four queens against my four tens."

Alanbrooke glanced over his shoulder as he propelled the younger man down the hall toward the master's suite in the north tower. "Improbable, maybe, but I've come to believe nothing is impossible."

Shermont had the distinct feeling Alanbrooke had seen through his playacting. He nodded his thanks for his friend's role in averting a disaster that would have done only harm. He stepped back into his room, closed the door, and turned the key in the lock. He made a point of blowing out the lone candle that had betrayed his lack of slumber. The nearly full moon provided more than enough light for what he had planned.

Several long running strides took him across the room, and he launched himself onto the bed, landing on his left side and propping himself on his elbow. "Now, where were we?"

Eleanor had been standing to open the bed curtains. The sudden weight in the middle of the bed knocked her backwards, and she sat down facing him.

"Hello," he said with a grin.

"You were wonderful." She giggled as the tension of the previous situation dissipated. "The belch was an especially effective touch."

"A talent that has come in handy a time or two."

"I'll bet. Do you suppose Teddy will forget the matter?"

"By morning Alanbrooke will have convinced him he owes me an apology, which I will graciously accept, even though I will profess to remember nothing."

She smiled. "Thank you."

"For what? Your name was never mentioned. Do you care for Digby that much?"

"Not at all. I was speaking for the girls," she said.

"I am not interested in them. I am, however, very interested in you." He rose to a kneeling position and leaned over her. He brushed her hair from her forehead and placed a kiss there. Then eyelids, nose, cheeks, and chin. He lingered a breath away before gently touching his lips to hers.

Her blood, kept on simmer for hours, erupted to the boiling point, lava heat pooling low in her stomach. She pulled him closer, kissing him deep and long.

He thrust his tongue into her mouth, and she did the same to him, a private duel with no rules.

He pulled away and took a deep breath. "My sweet, I wanted to take it slow to—"

"To hell with slow," she said, burrowing her hands underneath his open robe and running her hands up and down his chest. "Take that off." She wanted to feel skin and lots of it.

He answered her with an animal noise torn from deep within his throat. He ripped loose the knot on the sash and shucked his robe. She sat up and scooted onto her knees to face him. He unbuttoned her long brocade robe and shoved the material off her shoulders, but the close fitted sleeves stuck on the ruffles of her nightgown.

Eleanor stood in the middle of the great bed.

She tugged each arm free and tossed the robe aside. Then she pulled the frilly white cotton nightgown over her head, pitching it into the darkness. A bright arch of lightning highlighted their nakedness and mimicked the electricity between them.

His lips were at the perfect height to reach her breasts. He leaned forward, steadying her with his hands on her hips, branding her flesh with his fevered touch. He swirled his tongue around the peak of one breast and then the other. "You are so beautiful," he whispered, his breath causing her nipple to pucker into a tight bud.

He raised his head, and the look in his eyes made her feel beautiful. Her knees turned to warm butter. She placed a hand on either side of his face and sank down to lie back on the feather mattress, pulling him with her, spreading her legs to welcome his weight between her thighs.

A streak of lightning sizzled nearby, and the immediate boom of thunder muffled their groans as their bodies moved together. She wrapped her legs around him. Grabbing fistfuls of coverlet, she raised and rolled her hips, matching his rhythm. She pulled him deeper with each stroke, encouraging, demanding the increasing tempo. She felt as if she were running headlong toward the rim of a cliff. At the edge she flew into space, soaring through the storm raging inside and out.

Shermont wanted to last longer, but her silken sheath vibrated with contractions, a rhythm he could not resist, a pull so strong he couldn't hold back any longer. He reared back, every muscle in his body braced. An animal growl escaped his lips as his release exploded and exploded.

He collapsed on top of her, rolling to the side and flopping onto his back, drained and sated. No need to ask if it had been as spectacular for her as it had been for him. She, too, was breathless and limp. He reached out to take her hand, not wanting to lose the connection between them, even as he refused to analyze its meaning.

Eleanor fought the urge to roll toward him and snuggle. No promises, no strings, she reminded herself. Just sex. Okay, great sex. But that was all. She kept repeating the "just sex" mantra silently, even though she knew she lied to herself. After a few moments of shared stillness, she was the first to move, using a corner of the pillowcase to wipe a bead of sweat from her temple.

"I wish I'd brought my fan," she said, proud that her voice reflected the no-commitment tone of her comment.

Only then did Shermont notice the stuffiness. The storm had done little to lower the temperature. Knowing he would fall asleep if he didn't move, he gave her hand a squeeze and then rose from the bed and padded naked across the room. He threw open the French doors that led to a balcony facing the north lawn. A breeze wafted inside, bringing with it a refreshing mist of raindrops.

Eleanor watched him silhouetted in the moonlight. She got out of bed and wrapped the sheet around herself sarong-style, tucking in the end and letting the length drag behind her as she followed him, drawn to his side by the cool air and the sound of running water. Peeking out the double doors, she discovered the gargoyle decorations on the side of the house were actually downspouts. One was located just to the left of the terrace. She stepped outside and reached up to put her hand in the running water spurting from the grotesque horned monster's mouth.

"It's practically warm," she exclaimed.

"It's coming from the roof, so I imagine the slate tiles held the warmth of the sun. It won't last long."

Like so many things. She cupped her hand in the stream of water, directing the spray to her face, and laughed in delight.

He disappeared for a moment and returned with a scoop that looked like it belonged to the fireplace. He held it into the spurting water, and a deluge hit him in the face. She laughed at his surprised expression. After moving his arm, he shook his head, splashing water like a dog.

She jumped back, still amused, and then he turned the scoop to direct the spurting water toward her. She shrieked, grabbed his arm, and tried to pull it away from the spout. Rainwater sluiced down their bodies.

He wrapped his free arm around her waist to pull her away and only succeeded in loosening the sheet she wore. It dropped to her waist, and then the soaked material slid to the floor of the balcony. He pitched the coal scuttle over the railing and wrapped her in his arms. Their playful wrestling quickly turned into a fevered discovery of rain-slick bodies as they explored each other with their hands, lips, and tongues.

He was of a mind to go back to the bed, but she didn't want to leave the fresh breeze. They made it as far as the thickly carpeted floor just inside the French doors.

His plan to take it slow this time was easier made than played. First, he planned to kiss every inch of her body, bared to his hungry eyes in the moonlight. He started at her toes, then ankles and knees. When he reached junction of her thighs, she pulsed almost immediately. He backed off a little.

Eleanor burned for him. So close, so close. Like climbing a mountain, yet she couldn't reach the top. She dug her heels into the carpet and raised her hips. With his tongue and hand he brought her to the brink and back, to the brink again and again, until she was a mindless mass of quivering need. "Now, Shermont, damn it, now," she demanded, even though it sounded more like breathless begging.

"James. My real name is James." For some reason, he needed to hear her say his name.

She did... as he entered her... and as she soared to the heights. And again, softly, as she slid down the other side of the mountain.

He held her close. Eleanor felt so right in his arms, fit exactly as if she belonged there. He wanted to sleep with her in his arms and wake with her. He must have dozed off to that pleasant dream, because he woke to find her, stubborn chin resting on the back of her hands folded on his chest. He'd never understood the feminine need to talk at such a time. Now he realized it was a piece of biological good fortune that gave the man a chance to regenerate for the next session.

She smiled. "What did you mean when you said your real name is James?"

He hesitated.

"Does this have to do with the elder Shermont finding you on the road?"

"I see the gossips' tongues have been wagging."

"Within the hour of my meeting you," she said with a grin. "An unbelievable story."

"That part is true. When I came to my senses and Shermont asked my name, I remembered nothing. He insisted I must have a name, so I chose James. Somehow it felt right." He picked up her hand and placed it over his heart. "In here. Not that it's been any help determining my identity, but at least I know part of the name I chose is truly mine."

"Part?"

"I chose Bond as a last name."

She couldn't stop a guffaw.

"What's so amusing? James Bond is a perfectly good name."

"Yes, yes. It is."

"Then why are you—"

"There is a rather famous... character by that name in my... country. Wait until my father..." She rolled to her back. Her father would find it amusing, too. If she ever got a chance to tell him. What would he think if he didn't receive her usual Sunday night phone call? Would he worry?

Shermont rolled to his side. "I heard you lost your father in the war. I'm sorry."

She blinked away tears. "It just sort of hit me. How much I miss him."

She sat up, but he wrapped his arms around her waist.

"Stay with me," he said.

She turned and looked at him. So tempting. For a few moments she was lulled by the thought. But… what did Shermont really mean? Her common sense returned with a jolt. She gently broke his hold, scooted off the bed, and gathered her clothes. "I have to get back before I'm missed." Both to her room tonight and to her own time.

"I understand, even if I'm not pleased. We'll find time to be together during the fortnight I planned to stay. After that, we'll think of something. Until then, name a time and place and I'll be there."

"I… I'm afraid that won't be possible. I'll be leaving to my own… for home, I mean, London, and then back to America, probably right after the ball."

Her statement was a kick in his gut. In order to give himself a few moments to process what she'd said, he rose from the bed, donned a robe, and poured himself a drink. Did he need more proof she was one of the foreign agents? Who was she working with? His heart argued with his brain and lost.

He turned to face her and toasted her with his glass. "Well, then, my sweet, perhaps we'll run across each other in London before you sail."

Her stricken expression punched him in the chest. Then he remembered she was his lead to the other agent or agents, and he certainly shouldn't alienate her. He forced a smile to his lips. "My apologies. I allowed my disappointment to speak uncensored." He took her in his arms and held her gently, despite her poker-stiff spine. "Please say you forgive me and will let me make it up to you."

He gave her a charming smile and caressed her cheek, but to her his words rang insincere. Eleanor tried to hide her confusion by dressing as quickly as possible. Did she do something wrong? She'd thought the lovemaking had been pretty damn good, the best. He couldn't have expected her to be inexperienced. Maybe men of the time didn't have a high opinion of women who responded enthusiastically. Unable to voice a lie at that point, she nodded quickly, before ducking out of his embrace and scooting out the door.

Eleanor dashed away her tears before they could fall. Making love with him had been a huge mistake on many levels. At least getting pregnant was out of the question because she had kept taking birth control pills after her breakup, and even though she'd missed a few days, that possibility was remote. There was the issue of unprotected sex. Stupid, stupid. STDs were quite present during the Regency.

But her biggest mistake was not guarding her heart against falling in love. She would have to remember that, for whatever time she had left. She refused to consider it was already too late.

Shermont watched her safely back to her room. She didn't turn around or glance back. He wasn't sure what he would have done if she had. Wave? Blow a kiss? Ha! He would have to do more than that to get back into her good graces. Even if he must woo her relentlessly, he needed to stay by her side as much as possible to learn the identities of her possible cohorts. At least, he chose to believe this was the reason motivating his decision.

Twelve

Eleanor had fallen into an uneasy sleep by repeating a litany of all the things she missed: sneakers, toilets, M&Ms. When she woke with a toothache, she added twenty-first-century dentistry to the list. Apparently, using her finger to apply the tooth powder had not been effective, even though she'd mixed it half and half with salt as instructed on the can. Twilla had proudly pointed out the wooden toothbrush with boar's hair bristles, but Eleanor, who hadn't known boars even had hair, couldn't stand the idea of putting such an offensive substance in her mouth.

She sat by the window, her hand cupping her sore jaw. She also missed extra-strength Tylenol. To take her mind off the pain, she added items to her catalog. Her car. Shopping online. Dove dark chocolate. Lights and music available at the flick of a switch. And her cell phone. How could she have forgotten to add that to the list? It was one of the top ten—right up there with hot and cold running water and flush toilets.

A knock on the door interrupted her mental exercise.

"You're not dressed," Deirdre said, entering Eleanor's bedroom.

"Thank you for that statement of the obvious."

"Oooo. And grumpy," Mina said as she followed her sister. "I hoped after the hours you spent with Teddy last night that you and he—"

"I did not spend time with Teddy. I didn't even see him."

Deirdre flashed Mina a smug look. "See. I told you so."

"Then who—"

"Why don't you two go downstairs and deal with your guests. I didn't sleep well due to this toothache and won't—"

"I know what to do for that," Deirdre said. She used the bellpull to summon the maid and requested oil of cloves, red flannel, and willow bark tea. She ordered Eleanor back to bed, and Mina set up a small table within reach for some books and fetched a warm shawl.

"I'm not an invalid," Eleanor complained.

"We're just trying to make you comfortable."

Twilla brought the supplies. Even though Eleanor doubted the archaic remedies would work, she submitted to their ministrations for no other reason than it distracted the girls. After dousing the tooth with oil of cloves, Deirdre wrapped the flannel under Eleanor's chin and tied it on top of her head, which looked positively ridiculous. The willow bark tea was bitter and tasted, no surprise, of cloves.

"Now, you try to get some rest," Deirdre said.

"You look terrible," Mina added.

"We'll check on you in a few hours, and if you're not any better, we'll send someone to fetch the barber from the village."

"The barber?" Eleanor asked.

"Very experienced in tooth extractions," Deirdre said. "Takes care of all the locals, but, of course, if you'd rather wait, we can fetch one of those modern trained dentists from London. I'm sure Old John will do as good a job."

"No, no. I'm sure everything will be fine." No way was Eleanor going to let the local barber near her mouth. He probably didn't wash his hands and most likely had never heard of sterilizing his equipment. "I'll try to sleep now," she added, hoping the girls would take the hint.

They left, and Eleanor immediately got up and paced the room.

Despite the attractions of the time period, including one too sexy Lord Shermont, she wanted to go home. She could never be happy without the conveniences she'd taken for granted all her life.

"All right, you ghosts," she said. "Manifest yourselves or whatever it is you do. We need to talk."

No response.

"I did what you asked, and now I want you to send me back."

No response.

Then she heard movement in the sitting room and rushed to slam open the door, startling Twilla as she set a large arrangement of pink and white roses on the table. She almost caused the girl to drop the porcelain vase.

"Oh, miss, I didn't mean to wake you," Twilla said, using her long apron to wipe up the water she'd spilled from the vase. "Lord Digby sent you these." She pulled a note from her pocket and handed it to Eleanor.

"They are beautiful," she said. The note from Teddy was a formal wish for her speedy recovery—reserved, proper, and impersonal. She tossed the note on the table.

After Eleanor reassured her she didn't need anything, Twilla left.

In truth, the treatment had made her feel a bit better. She wandered to the window and watched the other guests playing at archery. Shermont scored a bulls-eye, and all the women cheered. Eleanor was almost thankful for an excuse not to be down there. She wasn't sure she was strong enough to resist his charms.

Even from a distance, she could see Mina and Deirdre seemed determined to catch his attention. And their so-called chaperone was nowhere in sight. The naïve girls could still get into trouble.

Was that why the ghosts had not yet sent her home? Would they send her back if she failed?

Eleanor paced again. She couldn't do anything cooped up in her rooms, and she had to do something other than mope around in self-pity. She spotted the girls' sewing boxes and got a brainstorm. Digging in one, she found white embroidery thread. She cut a length of fourteen inches and separated one of the six twisted strands to use as dental floss. She dislodged a piece of food. After several saltwater rinses, she felt well enough to get dressed.

She heard Mina and Deirdre moving around in the sitting room and opened the door from the bedroom to find the girls had brought a guest.

Shermont stood in the open doorway to the hall and refused Mina's invitation to enter. He extended both hands, one with a simple bouquet of cheerful daisies and the other with a recently published book, *Mansfield Park*. "I thought you might enjoy this."

"Thank you," Eleanor said, touched by his thoughtfulness. Just seeing him brought back vivid memories of the previous night, causing the back of her neck and other body parts to heat. She didn't want to get any closer, so she asked him to lay the gifts on the table by the door.

"I'm glad you're feeling better," he said.

"Of course, we are, too," Deirdre said. "What a rapid recovery. One might even say miraculous."

"Yes," Mina said. "When Lord Shermont insisted on bringing his trinkets in person, we told him you were probably asleep. Where is your red flannel?"

"I believe you are mistaken," Shermont said. He leaned against the doorjamb. "I asked you to deliver my best wishes personally, and you insisted it would mean so much more if I accompanied you. Though I admit, due to my concern, I wasn't difficult to convince."

Deirdre glared at Mina as if the younger girl had let the cat out of the bag. Indeed, she had.

"How sweet of both of you." Eleanor smiled with insincere sweetness at the sisters. They had meant for Shermont to see her swollen and wrapped in red flannel.

"Come in," Mina said to him. "Make yourself comfortable. Eleanor can act as our chaperone."

"Yes," Deirdre said. "We'll order some tea and have a nice cozy chat."

"No, thank you," Shermont refused again, maintaining his position in the doorway. He covered a fake yawn with his hand. "I hate to admit it, but I think I'll take a little rest. I didn't get much sleep last night."

He said it with a straight face, but a hint of a cat-that-got-the-cream smile curled the corners of his mouth.

"Apparently the storm made for a restless night for everyone," Deirdre said.

"Yes," he agreed. "A tempest of a night."

"Hopefully we'll have good weather for the ball tonight," Deirdre said.

"Oh, I don't know," he said. "I now have a certain fondness for storms. I was rather hoping for a repeat of last night."

"Don't even say that," Mina said, horrified. "We must have good weather, or we can't set off the fireworks we ordered. Oops! I wasn't supposed to let out the surprise. Please don't tell anyone, especially Teddy."

"Why? Doesn't he know?"

"Of course he does. He made the arrangements, but I don't want him to know I told you."

"My lips are sealed," Shermont promised. "However, I will take my leave before any more secrets are revealed."

He bowed, but Eleanor caught his glance.

"I have no secrets worth revealing," she said with what she hoped was a nonchalant shrug.

He raised an eyebrow and would have said something, but Mina grabbed his arm, demanding his attention.

"I can't let you leave without promising me a dance tonight," she said.

"Mina!" Deidre said with a horrified expression. "A girl should never, ever ask a gentleman for a dance."

"Then how will he know I want one?" Mina replied and stuck out her bottom lip.

"Very sensible," Shermont said. "I shall be honored to ask you to dance this evening."

"And me," Deirdre said.

"A promise gladly given to both of you," he said. His gaze touched each face, but his look to Eleanor promised much more than a dance. "By your leave." He stepped back and bowed before walking away.

Mina closed the door and sagged against it. "He is sooo handsome. He makes my knees weak."

"Well, don't faint now," Deirdre said. She stood. "We have lots to do today. Change your shoes quickly. Mr. Foucalt is scheduled to start the dancing lesson in ten minutes."

Eleanor fought the urge to roll her eyes. She'd just put on her walking boots to go outside. At least her day dress was appropriate. She changed into soft leather dancing shoes, and the three of them hurried downstairs to the ballroom, where the other women of the party waited. She was disappointed to note the Austen sisters were not in attendance.

"Excellent," Mr. Foucalt said. "Now we begin." The dancing master waved the late arrivals forward.

The tall, gaunt dancing master reminded Eleanor of an exotic bird with his large hooked nose, heavy-lidded dark eyes, bright yellow coat, and royal blue satin knee breeches. Sparse wisps of hair escaped his combed-forward hairdo and stuck straight up like the feathers on a parrot's head. Red stockings covered his thin legs. Eleanor suspected his talented tailor had added strategic padding to his ensemble, even to supplement the calves of his hose. Although obvious to a seamstress who had been called upon more than once to perform costume magic to make an actor look better, a casual observer would assume the man was in fantastic physical shape.

Mr. Foucalt had them stand at arm's-length in two lines six feet apart. Eleanor, Mina, Beatrix, and Fiona made one set of four, and Deirdre, Hazel, Countess Lazislov, and a mousy girl named Cecily made up the second group. Patience sat at the harpsichord in the corner, and the other chaperones sat in the chairs along the wall.

"Now take the hand of your imaginary partner," Mr. Foucalt said, demonstrating by raising his left hand to almost shoulder height, elbow slightly bent.

"My partner is Raoul Santiago De Varga, aide to the Spanish Ambassador," Mina said.

"Lieutenant Whitby," Fiona said, batting her eyelashes to her left.

Beatrix didn't have to announce, though she did, that her imaginary partner was Teddy.

"You are with Lord Shermont," Mina said to Eleanor with a knowing smile.

"No, this dance belongs to Mr. Darcy," Eleanor said.

"Your attention, please," Mr. Foucalt said, pounding his tall walking stick on the floor. "Thank you. This dance is one I composed for the Prince Regent and is now all the rage in London. I call it "On a Midsummer Night," and it is included in my new book of dances available next month from Corinthian Publishers on Fleet Street. *Maintenant*, salute your partner." He demonstrated a half turn to his left and a curtsey.

All the dancers copied him.

"Now, all take two steps forward and clasp your hands behind your back. You will promenade to your right around the men in a lively step–close–step. Right foot first. Music please. *Allez-vous.*"

Eleanor followed Mina, imitating her footwork, while Patience pounded out a fairly fast pace.

Mr. Foucalt called, "Right, close, right, left, close, left. Non, non, non. Mademoiselle Maxwell. Do not lift your knees so high like the prancing horse."

"How dare you," Mrs. Maxwell said, jumping up with fisted hands. "My daughter—"

"It's all right," Fiona said to her mother. "He's only trying to help me."

Mrs. Maxwell sat down, but she glared at the dancing master.

"You are gliding… gliding," he said. "Better."

As the dancers returned to their original positions, Eleanor could see why the Regent would like the dance. She could just imagine him ogling the pretty girls parading in front of him.

"And salute your partner," Mr. Foucalt said. *"Très bien."* He rapped his stick on the floor twice and the music stopped. "Then the gentlemen will have their turn, which we will, of course, skip over."

"Perhaps you should have a gentleman demonstrate," said a deep voice. Shermont entered the ballroom from the open French doors that led to the terrace. He took the spot next to Eleanor, usurping poor imaginary Mr. Darcy.

Mr. Foucalt bowed low. "Milord. Thank you for the offer—"

"But we do not condone mixed lessons," Mrs. Maxwell said, stepping forward.

Eleanor could see her point. Who would want her daughter called a prancing horse in front of a potential husband?

"Are you French?" Shermont confronted Mr. Foucalt directly.

"I am from Belgium," the dancing master said, raising his chin. He clicked his heels together and bowed.

"Same difference, isn't it?"

"Just because that odious little Corsican annexed my country does not make me French. I have been in this country for twenty years, a political *émigré*."

"Now, if you will excuse us," Mrs. Maxwell said, a not-so-subtle hint for Shermont to skedaddle.

"There you are," Teddy called to Shermont from the door. He was backed by the entire military contingent. "We wondered where you'd got to. Are we interrupting?" He looked around as if the gathering was a total surprise. His voice seemed hopeful rather than expressing regret.

Mrs. Holcum practically ran across the room as he spoke. She took his arm. "You are just in time," she said, towing him toward her daughter. "I think having the gentlemen participate in the dancing lesson is a marvelous idea."

The other men scrambled to take a place in the lines of dancers. Alanbrooke bowed and asked Deirdre for the honor of the dance. Parker and Whitby jockeyed for position next to Fiona, Whitby winning when she took his arm. Parker rushed down the line to partner Hazel. The countess snagged Rockingham's arm as he made his way to the heiress Cecily's side.

There was a moment of awkwardness when everyone realized Mina and Cecily stood alone.

"I think my imaginary partner Raoul is the best dancer here," Mina said. She motioned Mr. Foucalt toward Cecily. He bowed and took her hand, and she sent Mina a grateful look. Seeing she was defeated, Mrs. Maxwell retreated to the sideline.

Mr. Foucalt explained the dance, starting from the beginning, not forgetting to mention it was the Regent's current favorite, and again plugging his upcoming book. He rapped his stick on the floor, and Patience played with more enthusiasm than talent. After the gentlemen did their promenade, each couple, alternating sides, made the circuit in the same step–close–step manner. "While you are waiting your turn," he said loudly as he danced down the line with Cecily, "it is appropriate to chat with your partner."

"I missed you this morning," Shermont said to Eleanor.

"Perhaps it was for the best," she replied. "I can't shoot a bow and arrow, and I might have injured an innocent bystander."

"I missed you at archery, too," he whispered.

Eleanor hoped her blush wasn't obvious to all as she and Shermont took their turn and promenaded between the other couples. They resumed their places.

"May I have the first dance at the ball tonight?" he asked.

She shook her head. "If I count this, I know the steps to a grand total of one dance. There's no guarantee "On a Midsummer Night" will be the first dance of the evening."

"I remember another dance among the butterflies," he reminded her. The spark in his eyes said he remembered other activities as well.

"The waltz is considered too risqué and not—"

"Ah, you are wrong," he said with a smile. "I did some checking, and it seems the rules at country parties are much more lax than at Almack's."

"Even so, I truly doubt the first dance will be a waltz."

"That depends on who calls the first set. Who do you suppose will be the ranking female at the ball?"

"I have no idea," she replied. She had assumed Deirdre would be the one to open the ball and call the dances.

Shermont looked thoughtful as the steps of the dance caused them to separate and link up with the person across the line.

She raised her left hand as Teddy lifted his right, and they walked in a circle, fingertips touching.

"Unfortunately, I must open the ball, but I would dance the second set with you," Teddy said when his back was to Beatrix, a statement rather than a request.

"I must decline the honor due to lack of dancing knowledge," Eleanor replied with an insincere frown. "So sorry."

"What did he say?" Shermont asked when she returned to her starting point.

She was taken aback by the fierceness of his expression. Regency men were so possessive and presumptuous. "None of your business."

"My apologies. I phrased that wrongly. You seemed upset."

"I am quite capable of taking care of myself," she assured him as they clasped *hands across*, left hand to left and right hand to right.

"I'm sure you are." He twirled her under his arm, so their opposite hands were now on top. "That doesn't mean I can't be concerned."

They sashayed ... slide, slide, slide... up the line, twirled, and then came back. While the others took turns with the same moves, they stood quietly in place.

As a grand finale, the dancers made a large circle. Each gentleman swung his partner around before twirling her under his arm and passing her to the man on his left. Another reason for Prinny to love the dance.

Eleanor went from Shermont to Teddy to Whitby, who held her too tight and stared down at her décolletage while asking her for a dance later that evening. She declined without remorse. Rockingham acted as if she were a mere imposition, his attention glued on the heiress Cecily. Foucalt swung her expertly and handed her off to Alanbrooke.

"You could smile when you step toward me," he said with a teasing sparkle in his eye.

She did just that. "Sorry. My mind was a million miles away."

"How flattering," he said in a dry tone. But he returned her smile before passing her to Parker, who stammered out his invitation to a dance that evening. She regretted she could not accept and explained her ignorance of the popular dances.

Then she had a moment to breathe with Mina's imaginary partner Raoul. Eleanor reminded herself that if she wanted to keep an eye on Shermont, she would have to mend a few fences. She approached him with a smile.

"Am I forgiven?" he asked.

"My apologies. I've gotten so used to being on my own. I forget life is different here."

"No need to apologize. I should remember you aren't like other females. I'm just glad we're back on good terms." The music ended and he bowed. "I look forward to the evening ahead." His wicked smile promised more than his polite words.

The music stopped, and everyone applauded. "That is all we have time for today," Patience said with a bow.

Deirdre closed her mouth.

Eleanor wanted to help Deirdre regain the status that Patience seemed determined to usurp. "What does our hostess have to say?" Eleanor asked in a loud voice, pointedly looking in Deirdre's direction. "Do we learn another dance?"

Deirdre sent her a grateful look. "Regretfully, Aunt Patience is right."

Eleanor hid a smile at the double meaning. Did Deirdre regret that time was up or that Patience was right?

The gentlemen gave their polite *adieus* and left. Then the women meandered back to the entrance hall and up the stairs in twos and threes, chatting about everything that must be done to get ready for the ball.

"Shall we bathe before our naps or afterward?" Mina asked as they entered their sitting room.

"Bathe?" After washing in a basin, Eleanor was all for a bath. "Let's do that first."

"Good idea. There might be a rush on hot water later," Deirdre said as she rang for Twilla to ready the bathing chamber.

"Rochambeau for who goes first?" Mina asked.

Deirdre agreed, so Eleanor nodded without knowing what she was agreeing to do. Deirdre gathered them into a circle of sorts and held out her fist toward the center. Mina followed suit, so Eleanor did too.

"On three," Deirdre said.

She raised and lowered her hand on each slow count, so Eleanor copied her. On the count of three her hand was still fisted like Deirdre's, but Mina had made the two-fingered sign for scissors. Eleanor immediately understood the game played by a different name.

"I hate bathing in used water. Why do I always have to lose?" Mina stuck out her lip and marched off to the bedroom.

"Because she always does scissors," Deirdre whispered.

"Now what?" Eleanor asked.

"Loser goes second in the tub?" Deirdre asked as she sized up her new opponent.

Eleanor reasoned out her next move. Since Mina always took scissors that meant Deirdre always took rock. But since Deirdre had just told her that, then she wouldn't take rock next. But if she took scissors, then she would be mimicking her sister, something Eleanor didn't think she would do. But Deirdre wouldn't expect her to use rock twice, so…

Omigod. She was turning into Vizzini from *The Princess Bride* with his convoluted logic. Eleanor decided to wing it.

"Ready?" Deirdre asked, staring at Eleanor as if her choice would be flashed on her forehead a second before her hand dropped.

"Go for it."

After the count, Eleanor ended with a fist. And her rock beat scissors.

"Congratulations," Deirdre said in a tight little voice, unaccustomed to losing, but keeping the traditional stiff upper lip. She spun on her heel and went into the bedroom, head held high, passing her sister without a word.

In the process of donning her robe, Mina came into the room wearing her chemise and slippers. She stared after her sister as she tied her belt. Turning to Eleanor, she asked, "What's wrong with Deirdre?" A slow smile of comprehension lit her face. "You won!" She clapped her hands. "I love it. Well, what are you waiting for? Go on. Get ready. I'm going to enjoy this."

"I don't know what—"

"Go on." Mina shooed her into her bedroom.

Eleanor still didn't know what to expect, but she did what she'd been doing since she arrived and mimicked one of the girls. She disrobed down to her chemise, took off her shoes and stockings, and donned her robe and slippers. She was ready to go to the bathing *chamber*, an unfortunate name. The only other ones she could think of were a judge's chamber, a decompression chamber, and a torture chamber, none of which sounded like a pleasant experience.

Shermont propped his feet up and accepted the drink his valet handed him. "I can't be one hundred percent certain without a letter by letter comparison, but I'd bet my new Hessians the handwriting on Digby's note was the same as the one from the tree."

Carl shook his head. "It doesn't make sense. Why would a peer risk everything? Could someone else have written the note for him? His steward? His valet? I've written notes for you."

"To complete a mundane task such as ordering stationery or to decline an invitation from a stranger, but not a personal note. And never a missive to a lady."

"I agree. He probably wrote the note himself, but that still leaves the question of why," Carl said.

Shermont shrugged. "I don't really care why. If he's guilty, we arrest him."

"If we know why, it may help us identify the other foreign agent or agents."

Shermont was fairly certain he knew who the other was, but he held his tongue. Since omission was a form of lying, his silence counted as the first time he'd lied to his partner. He took a swig of his tea. "Probably one of the big three motivators—money, love, or revenge."

"My research on Digby didn't turn up any incidents that could even remotely incite a need for revenge. Just a normal, aristocratic childhood."

"His mother was French," Shermont reminded his friend.

"And she brought him to England in order to escape Dr. Guillotine's diabolical invention. Well, not exactly his mother. She died on the journey, but his aunt brought him."

"So that leaves money. We know Napoleon pays well for information."

"You must be joking. The estate, the house, the servants—"

"All of which cost *beaucoup sous* to keep functioning. Digby is a strange mixture of extravagance and economies."

Carl gestured around the luxurious room. "Economies?"

"I've told you. It's all in the details. For instance, the bed linens the girls used for costumes had been mended multiple times by different seamstresses, some more skilled than others."

"Extras. With so many guests…"

"Possible. But lots of little details add up. The house and grounds, though grand and well-maintained, have not been updated for many years—nothing in the newer styles of furniture and no modern conveniences. I noticed the drapes used on the stage were sun-faded on the back and had not been replaced or even relined. Several pieces of furniture need to be reupholstered. At dinner last night my chair wobbled so badly I feared I might land on my backside if I crossed my legs."

"Perhaps Digby has no interest in furnishings. Many men leave that to a wife, which he doesn't have."

"Does he also take no interest in the gardens? New plants are the rage every year. He has none. The paths remain quite wide, a style popular twenty years ago, so that a man could escort a lady wearing the voluminous skirts of the time without stepping into the grass or flowerbeds."

"Gardening may not—"

"I'll give you only one more example, even though I could go on for hours."

"Please, no."

Shermont smiled. "The wine cellar."

"Surely you have no complaints regarding the wine and potables served. Digby has an excellent nose. The stock is first-rate, maybe even exceptional."

"You are a better judge than I am in such matters, but I agree. However, on the tour Digby gave me when I first arrived, I noticed something peculiar. No new vintages have been laid away for future use."

"Hmmm."

"I see you're still not convinced. Start looking, and I'm sure you'll find examples of your own. Especially in behind-the-scenes areas."

"What about the third motivator? Who does Digby love?"

"Other than himself?"

"But it is a possibility?"

"Love?" Shermont leaned back and closed his eyes so Carl wouldn't see the truth reflected there. "You never know what a man will do for love."

Thirteen

ELEANOR HAD NO IDEA WHAT TO EXPECT. EVEN THOUGH the thought OF a bath was appealing after washing from a basin, she walked to the bathing chamber with all the enthusiasm of a prisoner shuffling to the firing squad.

What was so difficult about a shower that it took so many years to invent? Shermont had done it with a gargoyle and a coal scuttle. More important, why had she complained about her tiny little bathroom with the ugly Pepto-Bismol pink tiles and the showerhead that whined and sputtered? She sighed at the heavenly memory.

Mina walked beside Eleanor and asked, "Is something the matter?"

"My mind is hundreds of miles away, that's all."

"Thinking about your home in America?"

"Yes." At least that part was true.

Approximately halfway toward the end of the hall a screen had been set up to block the view. On the other side, they ducked past a curtained entrance into a wide alcove. A brass tub at least eight feet long and three feet high dominated the area. Warmth radiated from the fireplace that covered the entire wall to the left. Several big iron pots hung over the flames, and steam filled the air. Five maids bustled around the room, busy with various tasks. Deirdre and Mina sat on the bench that ran around the other two walls.

Eleanor hesitated. She'd never been a fan of group cleansing rituals. As a chubby teen, gym class had been torture.

"Step to it," the old crone seated by the fireplace barked. "Water's not getting any warmer."

One maid took Eleanor's robe and hung it on a hook. Another bent down to remove her slippers. Then two others each took one of her elbows and guided her up the steps leading to the foot of the tub. Three more steps led down into the deep water, and she wasn't given time to take off her chemise. Apparently, Regency women didn't bathe naked.

While Deirdre and Mina chatted, Eleanor chose honeysuckle-scented soap and a cloth from the tray offered. After she'd quickly washed herself, one maid scrubbed her back with a soft brush, and then another washed her hair. She was instructed to stand, and a bucket of fresh warm water was poured over her head to rinse her off. She climbed out of the tub. They wrapped her in a large sheet and guided her to a place on the bench beside Mina.

Two maids each dipped a bucket of water out of the tub, and two others adding steaming hot water.

"Step up. Step up," the crone said.

Deirdre jumped up to take her turn.

"I'm glad you're quick," Mina said. "Mrs. Tuttle doesn't like us to dawdle." She indicated the crone by the fireplace.

"Then she's the butler's wife?"

"Good heavens, no. She's his mother and very strict about the rules. We humor her because she's been with the family forever. She was father's nursemaid, maybe even grandfather's." Mina partially covered her mouth so no one else could hear her whisper. "We heard that at a certain house party, an unmarried couple was found bathing together, in the middle of the night no less."

Eleanor eyed the large tub, and her imagination provided an inviting image of Shermont soaking there. Several enjoyable aquatic activities came to mind. "Oh, that's… astonishing."

"Something like that would never happen in Mrs. Tuttle's bathing chamber."

Too bad. "Of course not."

A maid brought another tray with an assortment of creams and oils, but since Eleanor didn't know what they were for, she shook her head. She also refused a cup of lemon verbena tea.

When Deirdre was done, she took a seat on a small stool by the fire, and Mrs. Tuttle brushed her long blonde locks.

"Whenever I think about cutting my hair, I reconsider," Deirdre said to Eleanor. "However did you get the nerve?"

Eleanor shrugged. She'd worn her hair long most of her life, but after her breakup, she'd decided she needed a drastic change. She'd donated fourteen inches of hair to Locks of Love and decided she preferred it short. "It's so much easier to take care of this way." She fluffed her curls with her fingers and wished she'd brought a comb.

"A gentlewoman's hair is her crowning glory," Mrs. Tuttle said, her voice little more than a rasp. "If you cut it, you cut your chances of an advantageous marriage."

"Well, I'm going to cut mine," Mina said as she took her turn in the tub. "Not really short as in the Titus style, but I want those adorable little curls that frame your face. I'm going to wait to see the fashions when we get to London."

In the warm bathing chamber, Eleanor's thin chemise dried quickly and she feared she would sweat, thus negating any good done by the bath. "I'm going back to our room," she announced as she stood.

"Have a good rest," Deirdre said. "I'll tell Twilla to wake you in plenty of time to get dressed for the ball."

A maid rushed to hold Eleanor's robe and another brought her slippers. As she ducked through the curtain, she encountered Fiona, Hazel, Beatrix, and their mothers.

After the normal pleasantries, Beatrix started toward the curtain. Mrs. Holcum blocked the way and folded her arms over her ample bosom. "We'll wait until they are done. I don't hold with public bathing. We're not ancient Romans, you know."

Eleanor fought the urge to roll her eyes. Obviously, Mrs. Holcum didn't consider the servants members of the public.

"I don't know why young people today are so obsessed with bathing," Mrs. Maxwell said. "It's unhealthy to immerse yourself in water so often. In my day, twice a year was considered more than adequate."

"Moth-ther," Fiona and Hazel said together.

"I agree," Mrs. Holcum said. "It's the schools that put these preposterous ideas into their heads. Before she went to Miss Simpkin's Academy, my daughter hated bathing and had to be bribed every spring and fall."

"I was a child then," Beatrix said. The whine in her voice disproved her claim to maturity.

"My daughters were the same," Mrs. Maxwell said. "But once in the tub, I had the devil of a time getting them out."

Knowing from experience with friends and coworkers that motherly bonding could extend to hours of comparisons, Eleanor used the lame excuse of damp hair and the possibility of taking a chill to escape. As she walked down the hall, she heard Mrs. Holcum say, "See, Beatrix. You could learn from such a sensible, old-fashioned girl."

Eleanor was still smiling when she entered her bedroom. The drapes had been drawn and the bed turned down in preparation for her nap. Even in the dim light she recognized her visitors.

"No need to ask if you're having a good time," the ghost of Mina said with an answering grin.

"Where have you been?" Eleanor asked. "I've called and—"

"You made us promise not to interfere," Deirdre's ghost said. "We're only keeping our word."

"Oh, yeah… well… then why are you here?" Were they going to take her back? Now that the time was near, she realized she wasn't quite ready.

"We wanted to let you know how pleased we

are with your progress so far," Mina said. "You've adapted amazingly well."

"We will return at midnight tonight," Deirdre said. "So you have to chaperone us for only ten more hours. But the most difficult hours are ahead. With so many people at the ball, you must pay close attention and not allow yourself to be distracted."

"But we have every confidence in you," Mina added.

"Do you mean it hasn't happened yet? I haven't stopped it? What about last night in Shermont's room? You do know what happened there?"

The ghosts looked at each other. Deirdre nodded to Mina.

"Yes, we saw. As to whether only one incident can predicate a duel, we can't be sure," Mina explained. "Since we're here with you, we won't have any memories of what you do until we return to the future."

"But we have every confidence you will be successful," Deirdre said.

"You could make this easier if you'd tell me exactly where and when this seduction happened."

Again, the ghosts looked at each other before answering.

"That's impossible to determine," Deirdre said. "You see, there are certain pivotal points in each person's life. In between those points, events can shift around without making a huge difference. You prevented one incident, but another may yet occur. However, if Shermont does not seduce one of us by midnight tonight, then it won't happen."

"That's when we met Ackerly and Clifford and decided we should marry brothers," Mina added.

"Not them," Deirdre said.

"Good heavens, no. But they did give me the idea that—"

"It was my idea."

"No, it wasn't."

"Girls!" Eleanor said in exasperation. "It doesn't matter whose idea it was."

"Quite right. Anyway, it was a pivotal point and one that will prevent the duel. After that, neither of us wanted to pursue Shermont any longer."

"Fine. But it would be easier if I knew which girl to follow. If they… you… separate before midnight—"

"We cannot break our sacred vow," the ghosts said together.

"Arrrgh! How do you expect me to follow both of you?"

"There's only one of him," Deirdre pointed out.

With that cryptic comment, they winked out of sight.

Eleanor hadn't expected to sleep, but when Twilla entered with a tray of food, she woke from a dream. She had been Cinderella, Shermont her Prince Charming. The refrain from the musical stuck in her brain: *Impossible things are happening every day.* She tried reciting a poem and the multiplication tables to dislodge it, but until she hummed the Oscar Mayer jingle, that song wouldn't budge. Then, of course, she was stuck with the commercial tune, but at least it didn't make her think of her midnight deadline.

After eating the light dinner Twilla had brought, Eleanor dressed in a deep yellow silk dress she'd made to go with her amber cross necklace, which was back in place around her neck. Twilla insisted on helping with her hair. The maid attached a gold ribbon three times across the crown of her head for a diadem effect. Mina had lent a white feather rosette with a pearl center that Twilla pinned over Eleanor's ear.

Since elbow-length gloves were not *de rigueur* as they would be in the Victorian Age, Eleanor chose the more comfortable short ones made from netted lace. With her turquoise tulle evening shawl, beaded reticule, and ivory fan, she was ready.

"Thank you for your help," she said to Twilla.

"My pleasure. You look lovely."

Eleanor knew guests usually left money for those who had provided for them, one reason why servants didn't mind the extra work events such as house parties and balls caused. She would be leaving, but she had no money to give the maid. Instead, she pulled the string of blue glass beads from her case. "I want you to have these," she said to Twilla.

"Oh, no. I couldn't—"

"I insist."

The maid reached out and took them as if they were precious jewels. "I ain't never had anything so fine," she whispered.

"Put them on." Eleanor wanted the others to see Twilla wearing them before she left. Not so they would know she'd tipped the maid, but so no one would think the servant had stolen them.

They joined the others in their bedroom as the girls put the finishing touches to their own outfits.

Both wore the white appropriate for their ages. Deirdre's dress was trimmed with embroidered edging and a sash of braided ribbons in several shades of green from mint to forest. Mina's dress had pink satin trim and tiny ribbon roses scattered around the square neckline and along the three-inch hem.

Deirdre sat at the dressing table and rubbed a red-tinted paper on her cheeks.

"Lightly," Mina cried. "We don't want Teddy to know we bought rouge papers."

"I look like a Punch and Judy puppet," Deirdre said, leaning forward to peer closely in the mirror. She picked up a damp cloth and scrubbed her cheeks clean.

"Are you going to try again? Let me. It's my turn."

"If I can't do it, you can't do it either," Deirdre said without relinquishing her seat.

Before they escalated into a full-blown argument, Eleanor noticed Mina's paint case and had a brainstorm. "Wait a minute."

She rummaged around until she found the largest brush in the case. Thankfully, Mina kept her watercolor brushes scrupulously clean.

Eleanor laid the rouge paper on the table, rubbed the brush over it in a circle, and then swirled it lightly over the girls' cheeks. She wasn't a makeup expert, but everyone agreed the effect was quite attractive and natural looking.

As Twilla helped the girls gather their accessories,

Mina suddenly stopped. She turned from Twilla to Eleanor with a sharp look. "Are those your—"

"I think they look very nice on her," Eleanor said.

Mina shrugged as if the gift was of no consequence, exactly as Eleanor had hoped.

She followed the girls down the hall, butterflies of anticipation tickling her stomach. Shermont waited below, and the look on his face told her all her trouble had been worthwhile. He made her feel beautiful and desirable with nothing more than his smile. She nearly had to pinch herself to make sure she wasn't dreaming. Ordinary Eleanor Pottinger was going to the ball. She hoped she would have another chance to talk with Jane Austen and might even risk a dance with a handsome lord. She touched her necklace for luck and descended the stairs.

Even though the ball was scheduled to begin at eight o'clock, a number of guests had already arrived and more poured in as fast as the full carriages could unload them. Since country affairs were less formal and almost everyone already knew everyone else, the butler did not announce each arrival. Deirdre and Mina joined Teddy and Aunt Patience in the entrance hall to greet the guests. Shermont offered his arm and escorted Eleanor into the ballroom.

Armless gilt chairs had been placed around the perimeter of the room, and several chaperones had staked out their positions. Mrs. Holcum and Beatrix sat near the door, all the better to snag Teddy on his entrance. Mrs. Maxwell had chosen a spot halfway down the length of the room and sat with Fiona and Hazel on each elbow. Gentle music wafted through the air and Eleanor located the musicians in a loft at the far end.

"Shall we walk the circuit?" Shermont asked.

Those not seated promenaded around the room in couples or small groups of three or four. The glittering society was everything she could have imagined. The clothes. The jewels. Hard to credit the idea that this wasn't everyone's best and that a ball in London would have more of... everything. "Why aren't they dancing?" she asked.

"The host will open the dancing shortly. Until then, we walk, perhaps stop to chat. See and be seen. Take those young bucks, for instance," he said, indicating with a nod the group of four gentlemen sauntering along a dozen feet ahead. "They're sizing up the new crop that will go on the marriage mart next season."

"That's a bit predatory."

"Not the half of it. There's not a full pocket among the lot. If they want to continue the life they've been accustomed to, they must marry well, an heiress preferably."

"What about love?"

"Ah, a love match does seem to be the current ideal according to the doctrine of sensibility, but when a man must choose between a ladylove and his tailor..." He shrugged.

"Sounds as though you think of marriage as a business deal."

"I don't think of marriage at all," Shermont lied. How could he ask someone to share his future when he didn't remember his past? He rubbed the scar on his forehead with his free hand. "I take it your marriage was a love match."

Eleanor hesitated. "I believed I was in love with the man I got engaged to. Unfortunately, I later found out he wasn't the man I thought he was."

"A testimonial for long engagements?"

"Not necessarily. It wasn't his fault I bestowed qualities on him he didn't possess." And as she said it, she realized it was true. He couldn't live up to her expectations because she had tried to make a Darcy out of a Wickham, which made her think of Jane Austen. She looked around the now crowded ballroom, but didn't see her favorite author.

There were so many people in the room the temperature had risen several degrees, undoubtedly helped by hundreds of candles on two chandeliers. Eleanor opened her fan and plied it for a bit of breeze. One detail the glittering illustrations of the time period had not been able to show was the air tainted by so many perfumes. Even though liberally used, the fragrances did not conceal the underlying odor of unwashed bodies.

Teddy led a bejeweled Countess Lazislov to the front of the dance floor. As the highest-ranking female present, she had the honor of calling the first set. The Countess indicated her choice to Mr. Foucalt.

"May I have this dance?" Shermont asked.

Eleanor shook her head. "I don't know the steps to most—"

The dancing master rapped his walking stick on the floor three times. "Gentlemen, choose your partners for the first dance, 'On a Midsummer Night,'" he said in a booming voice, quite unexpected from such a skinny frame.

The announcement caused whispering among the crowd, but the men who had been in attendance at the earlier class and those who had been to recent town parties took positions on the floor.

Shermont held out his arm with a smug smile.

"How did you know?"

"Know what?" he asked with an innocent air as they took their places in the line of dancers.

"That the first dance would be the only one I know the steps to," she said as the music started.

"Ah, yes. I don't suppose you'd believe it was a grand coincidence," he said as he bowed in the salute.

"No." She curtseyed. He didn't have time to explain. The dance required her to follow the other women and promenade the length of the ballroom in the step-close-step movement she'd learned earlier. The countess gave her a broad wink as they passed each other going in opposite directions. What was that about?

Eleanor returned to her starting place. "You were saying?" she said as she curtsied again, returning to their earlier conversation as if it hadn't been interrupted.

He bowed. "The countess owed me a favor," he said with a mischievous grin. Then he stepped out for the gentlemen's promenade.

Leaving Eleanor to wonder exactly what he'd done for the countess. She watched Shermont as he danced the steps with masculine grace, and she noticed a number of other women ogled him as he passed by. A surge of jealousy took her by surprise.

She had no claim to him. The respite from his presence gave her the opportunity to pull herself together and rein in her wayward feelings.

When he returned, they had a few minutes to chat as they waited for their turn for the couples' promenade.

"The music is lovely," she said.

She felt the muscles of his forearm tighten under her hand as he shot her a quizzical glance. The amusement in his eyes said he recognized her attempt to depersonalize the conversation.

"I hardly noticed," he said. "The dance is only an excuse to be by your side."

He wasn't making it easy. "From what I hear, the weather is particularly balmy for this time of year," she said, trying again to move to a safe subject.

"Is it? I feel only the heat of your touch. Do you deny you feel the same?" he asked as he led her out for their turn at the couples' promenade.

She did not respond to his taunt.

"I do not need to hear you say in words what I can read in your eyes," he said. "After what we have shared—"

"No strings," she reminded him as well as herself. "We have only the moment—no past, no future."

After thoughtful hesitation, he replied, "As you say. Then we should enjoy these moments to the fullest."

The finale of the dance called for him to twirl her around, which he did doubly fast, making two full turns before spinning her toward the gentleman on her left.

By the time she returned from making the round

and being twirled by all the gentlemen, she was dizzy and more than grateful for his steady presence as the music ended.

"Just stand there for a minute," she said, politely applauding the musicians. "I need to catch my breath before walking off the dance floor."

"We can't leave yet," he said. "There is another dance in the set."

She shook her head and started to remind him she didn't know any other dances when Mr. Foucalt rapped his stick on the floor.

"The second dance of the opening set will be the waltz," he called in his loud voice.

The first dance had caused whispers, but the announcement of the waltz caused a minor tumult. A number of couples committed a breach of decorum and left the dance floor. Some were forced to do so at the insistence of overzealous chaperones, including Fiona and Hazel and their partners. A few couples eagerly took their places.

Mr. Foucalt rapped his stick. "We will have order."

As the orchestra played the opening bars, Eleanor stepped into Shermont's arms. "I fear the countess has created quite a commotion by her choice of dances," she said.

He laughed. "From what I know of her, Countess Lazislov enjoys making a spectacle and being the center of attention." They moved to the music, making small circles as he led her around the dance floor.

"I don't," Eleanor said, ducking her head, her body stiffened by awareness of the censorious stares she received. The magic of the butterfly field was missing.

"Look at me." After she complied, he smiled down at her. "We are the only two people here. You are in my arms, and that is all that matters."

She decided to stop worrying about everyone else and concentrate on her partner. She returned his smile. "Then let's enjoy the moment."

With that he tightened his embrace and lengthened his stride, swinging her around in wider and wider circles, even lifting her feet off the floor. No inane chatting, no verbal sparring—just a man and a woman moving in harmony with the music and with each other. Although there were no overtly sexual moves, as in the dances she'd known in her time, she now understood why the waltz was considered scandalous.

They created a world of their own within the circle of each other's arms, moving as one, responding to the slightest touch. Swinging apart and then swaying back together. A sensual, unspoken interchange. Then she stopped thinking and gave herself up to dancing in his arms. She laughed with pure joy.

By the time the music ended, she was breathless. She heard applause and turned to add her clapping to the accolades for the orchestra, which she had barely noticed. To her surprise, the dance floor was empty except for the two of them.

"Smile and take a bow," Shermont prompted.

"How can you be so calm?" she asked, dropping into a deep curtsey and hoping her cheeks were not as fiery as they felt. She remembered her fan still attached to her right wrist and opened it to create a cooling breeze. "This is so embarrassing."

"Why?" he asked as he offered his arm.

"Because it feels as though we just made love in a public place in front of a roomful of people," she said behind her fan as they walked off the dance floor.

He grinned and leaned over to whisper in her ear. "We did."

She spotted the countess barreling her way toward them with purpose in her stride. "I think Countess Lazislov wants her turn on the dance floor." Even though Eleanor didn't want him to, she felt obligated to excuse him to dance with someone else. "Please don't feel as if you have to stay here with me."

"I don't want to dance with anyone else. Shall we walk out on the terrace?"

"Fresh air sounds appealing," she said. She turned and practically ran toward the open French doors. Shermont beat her to the exit.

Stepping outside was like entering an air-conditioned movie theater for a summer matinee. Cool and dark with music seemingly all around. Several couples ambled leisurely across the length of the terrace from one curved stairway leading down to the garden to the other. Shermont guided her to a corner of the stone balustrade overlooking the grounds.

"The garden was designed especially for a moonlit night such as this," he said, offering his arm. "Shall we take a stroll?"

She glanced over her shoulder. The countess had appeared determined, and if she had seen them exit, she was sure to follow as far as the terrace. Eleanor wasn't sure why she didn't want that woman to dance with Shermont. Obviously he hadn't learned to dance in a vacuum and he'd had other partners. She just didn't think she could stand by and watch him hold another woman in his arms. Not right after their intimate dance. "That sounds perfect."

She placed her right hand on his forearm and they descended the terrace steps to the path leading into the gardens. The white shells beneath her feet were crushed almost as fine as sand. Her fabric dancing shoes made no noise, his steps only a slight crunching sound.

"It's dark."

"That's by design. To enhance the experience, no lanterns are lit along the path. Another reason why it's so popular among young couples." He gave her an exaggerated leer before relaxing into a grin. "The designer of a moonlight garden chooses plants with white flowers that bloom at night and foliage that provides delight for the sense of smell," Shermont explained as they strolled along the path, bowing and nodding politely as they passed couples returning to the ballroom. "Such as this night-blooming cereus from the West Indies with vanilla-scented blooms."

"Lovely." She paused to touch one of the large flowers that lent an aura of magical fantasy to the garden.

As they strolled from one garden "room" to the next, he pointed out the intensely fragrant night jasmine, evening primrose, angel's trumpet, and Nottingham catchfly.

"I didn't know you were so into flowers," she said.

"Into? Oh. I understand. I'm not really *into* gardens. Although I admit to spending an hour with the gardener this afternoon in the hope I would entice you into taking a stroll with me. In fact, I hate gardening. It took forever to get the dirt from under my finger-nails." He gave her that oh-so-charming smile that made her toes curl. "Are you into gardening?"

"I enjoy flowers but I know practically nothing about them. I've had little opportunity to garden," she said. The sum of her gardening knowledge was a few unfortunate potted plants that she'd received as gifts and had quickly killed by overwatering or forgetting. No green thumb.

He glanced around and saw they were alone. He cupped her face and kissed her lips. "I've been waiting all day for that." He slid one hand to the back of her neck and moved the other to her waist. "And this." Tightening his embrace, he kissed her jaw just under her ear.

Shrill laughter signaled the end of their privacy. Shermont jerked away.

Unfortunately, a button on his sleeve snagged on her necklace. She caught the amber cross before it fell. The clasp of the chain was broken.

He apologized. "Let me have that repaired. I know a trustworthy jeweler in town and I'll get it back to you in a few days."

"No." She shook her head. She would be leaving tonight after midnight and would never see him again. She blinked the tears from her eyes as she put the amber cross and the chain into her reticule.

"The necklace obviously means a lot to you. I'm so very sorry."

"Easily fixed," she said. "Don't give it another thought. Shall we continue our stroll?" The Cinderella time limit made each minute with him more precious.

The group of laughing people passed, soon out of sight beyond a curve in the garden path.

"Let's wait a few minutes," he said, leaning against a marble pillar carved to resemble a Greek ruin. "What shall we do to pass the time? No chess set handy. Can't dance. Let's see. Read any good books lately?" he asked with a lopsided grin.

Guessing he didn't really expect an answer, she shook her head. Her eyes had adjusted from the brightness of the ballroom to the gentler illumination of the full moon. In the moonlight, colors paled to shades of gray, yet she could see clearly, like being inside the classic black and white movie version of *Pride and Prejudice* from 1940. She almost expected Greer Garson and Laurence Olivier to approach along the garden path.

Shermont looked so yummy standing there in the moonlight. Eleanor clasped her hands behind her back to keep from reaching for him. She had to look away. Another couple approached and passed with polite nods.

"No ideas for an activity to pass the time? Well, then I have one," he said, taking her hand and leading her at a quick pace to the far corner of the garden, where a humongous plant took up the entire area.

"What's this?" she asked, touching one of the large three-foot leaves.

"To be truthful, I've forgotten."

She chuckled. "You know, you could have told me anything, and I wouldn't have known the difference."

He brushed an armful of leaves aside and with a bow waved for her to go in front of him.

With a quizzical look, she ducked under his arm and walked through a green tunnel. Across from the entrance, two walls made of rough stone met behind a small bench. The plant itself formed a semicircle, making a third wall and a partial ceiling, enclosing the area into a cozy fairy room about ten feet across.

"How did you find this place?"

Shermont walked past her. "I gave a gardener twenty shillings and asked where he went to take a nap after lunch." From under the bench in the corner he pulled out a folded quilt and spread it on the ground. "I thought it would be a nice place for a moonlight picnic."

"I suppose I should count myself lucky he doesn't nap in the toolshed."

From a basket beside the bench, Shermont took out a bottle of champagne, opened it, and filled two crystal glasses. He held one out.

"You've thought of everything," she said before taking a sip of the cold bubbly. His machinations looked suspiciously like a seduction. Not that he needed to go to so much trouble. She hadn't been shy about her desire for him. But it was flattering. Anticipation shivered deliciously up her spine.

"Won't you have a seat," he said with a courtly bow worthy of the grandest courtier.

She hesitated. Rolling around on the ground would

wrinkle her precious dress beyond repair. The material alone had cost her two months of brown-bagging her lunch, and she had invested uncounted hours into sewing the intricate pattern of beads on the bodice. To risk ruining it was unthinkable. And no matter what happened, they would return to the ball.

Eleanor practically heard the minutes tick away toward midnight. Just like Cinderella, she would have to go home, so she made the decision to enjoy what little time she had left. She set her glass on the bench. After taking the beaded reticule from her left wrist and the ivory fan from her right, she set them beside her drink. Then she added her folded turquoise shawl and gloves to the neat stack.

Then quickly, before she could change her mind, she undid the hooks and snaps and slipped off her amber silk gown, laying it gently next to her accessories. Her chemise, corset, underdress, and stockings covered her more than if she had worn a pair of shorts and tank top to the grocery store. Not to mention what she would wear to the beach or at the pool. When she turned to face Shermont, he raised an eyebrow.

"One should never wear a ball gown to a picnic," she said in imitation of Mrs. Holcum's most proper upper crust tone. Eleanor retrieved her glass and sat on the blanket, her legs decorously curled to one side.

"Correct attire is always essential," Shermont agreed, removing his coat and laying it on the bench beside her dress. He sat down on the blanket across from her.

Eleanor clasped her hands in her lap. "What does one do on a moonlight picnic?"

"Drink champagne," he said, holding out her glass after topping it off. He raised his glass in a toast. "To your beautiful eyes."

"Thank you." Although she had a good idea where he was leading, she wasn't going to let him off easy. "What else?"

"Your delectable lips."

"No," she said with a little shake of her head. "I wasn't fishing for another compliment, but I do thank you. I meant, what else do we do?"

"I thought we might get to know each other. You are quite a mystery."

"Me?"

"What do you enjoy doing? I only know you don't play the pianoforte or croquet, and you don't shoot a bow."

"Was I that bad at croquet?"

"Actually, you did quite well for someone who watched others for direction on what to do."

"You noticed that." She ducked her head.

"I am aware of everything you do."

Unsure how to respond, she directed the focus of the conversation to him. "What do you like to do?"

"You first."

"I like to read and sew." She could hardly tell him she liked to rollerblade or go bicycling with friends. "I like to watch the sunset on the beach." And drink margaritas on the patio of a little Mexican restaurant. She smiled at the memory of the *bon voyage* party her friends had thrown there.

Shermont furrowed his brow. "If you live... how could..."

Oops. She realized she couldn't have lived on the West Coast of America during the Regency period, and the sun would rise over the water on the eastern shore. "It's something I remember from my childhood and hope to do again soon. When I get back to a place where that's possible," she said to cover her *faux pas*.

"Oh. Do you have a trip to the coast planned? I remember Huxley said something about going to see the butterflies in a fortnight."

Eleanor shook her head. "I hope to be hard at work in a few weeks."

"Work?" He was taken aback.

Another slip of the tongue, but one she couldn't cover easily. "I'm starting my own dressmaking business. I suppose you think that scandalous."

He shook his head. "No. And that's one reason I'm fairly certain I wasn't born to the aristocracy. I don't have their inbred aversion to commerce."

"Enough about me. What do you do for recreation?"

"The usual. I typically ride in Hyde Park early in the morning before the see-and-be-seen set hits the Serpentine Path. Spend time at my club. I spar several times a week at Gentleman Jim's. Keep up with social obligations." He shrugged. "I enjoy the racing season."

"You play cards?" she prompted.

"On occasion."

"That all sounds rather frivolous. And you don't impress me as a trivial person."

He gave her a sharp look that said he wasn't used to his façade being questioned. His astonishment was quickly replaced by a bland expression. "I am cognizant of the responsibilities of my title. A great number of livelihoods depend on the success of the Shermont estates. If Parliament is in session, I attend to my duties in the House."

She sensed he was hiding something. "And do you find that fulfilling?"

Shermont glanced down at his now empty glass. Her question went directly to the heart of his issue with the title. He understood hobnobbing with the nobility was the only way to ferret out those who had no problem betraying their country for Napoleon's gold, the privileged few averse to doing an honest day's labor. Scovell was certain the foreign agents reached into the highest level of the aristocracy.

If she had been any other female of his acquaintance, he would have brushed aside her question with a witty reply, dismissing good deeds. But, for whatever reason, he wanted her to think better of him.

"To my surprise, I found myself involved in the cause of compulsory education for all children," he said. "Although we are years away from passing an act, the groundwork is laid. I think nationwide literacy will influence the future for the better, and I find that rewarding."

"I think that's admirable."

Although he basked in her approving smile, he knew he should change the subject before he revealed too much. His goal was to get her to divulge her secrets, not vice versa.

"We are too serious for a discussion held in the moonlight." He pulled the basket toward him and unpacked it. "One must have food on a picnic. Sandwich?" He held out a plate.

Eleanor was baffled by the sudden change. Yet her time with him was limited, and she wanted to get to the seduction part of the picnic that she'd expected and hoped was coming. She played along. "What kind of sandwich?"

Shermont opened one. "Some sort of paté."

Although the little triangle and circle shapes were attractive, she declined.

"Here we go. Biscuit?"

Eleanor took a cookie from the second plate and nibbled on the edge.

"And the *pièce de résistance*." He removed two more objects from the basket with a flourish. From one bowl he chose a perfect strawberry, dipped it in the smaller dish of clotted cream, and held it out.

Her hands were full, so she opened her mouth to take a bite. Thankfully, she didn't close her eyes. A big dollop of cream slipped off the strawberry. With a small cry of dismay, she dropped the cookie and caught the gooey blob in her palm before it landed on her clothes.

Shermont tried to prevent the messy accident by lunging forward. Halfway prone, his outstretched hand came up underneath hers.

That spark, no less intense because of its familiarity, leaped at first contact.

He gazed at her and after a heartbeat flashed a mischievous grin. He tipped her hand toward him and licked the cream from her palm, lapping with quick thrusts and then using the length of his tongue.

The touch of his mouth sent goose bumps up her arm. He followed with warm kisses from her wrist to her shoulder, stopping at that sensitive spot below her ear. Strange how shivers could heat her blood so quickly.

She tipped her head to allow him easier access. She melted and raised her arms to wrap them around his neck.

Suddenly he rolled away, thereby avoiding the stream of champagne she would have dumped inadvertently down his back.

"Oh, I'm so sorry," she said, watching the wet stain spread on the blanket and scrambling backward to get out of its path. "I totally forgot I had the glass in my hand."

"No harm done," he said. In truth, he'd been saved only by a stroke of luck. His attention had been diverted by the sound of heavy footsteps nearby, as if the owner of the large feet had wanted to be heard approaching. Then he'd recognized that the nightingale he heard was actually warbling "La Marseillaise." Napoleon might have banned the tune for its revolutionary associations, but it was still the French people's unofficial anthem. Was it a signal for the foreign agents to meet nearby? Or was it a warning for Eleanor? "I think the possibility of interruption has passed."

But the magical mood had been spoiled.

"We should get back to the others before we are missed," he added.

"Just what I was going to say," Eleanor lied.

She turned her back to him to slip into her dress,

gather her accessories, and regain her composure. A few more hours and she would never see him again. Perhaps it was for the best that he'd turned cool toward her again. She could think the words, yet her heart still ached.

She turned and headed toward the entrance, but the broad leaves had closed ranks. She couldn't see a way out. He grabbed her hand and spun her into his arms.

"I'm sorry we must leave," he said.

"Me too." Her words held a different meaning than his, but her regret was genuine. She forced herself to breathe through her mouth, hoping to forestall her tears.

"We will have another chance to be alone later," he said, promise in his voice.

"Possibly."

"We must make it happen."

Eleanor nodded, unwilling to trust her voice.

He gave her a long, gentle kiss and then stepped away to push the leaves aside and clear the path back.

As they walked up the steps to the terrace, she spotted Jane Austen and her sister Cassandra wandering around the terrace, looking for something on the stone floor.

"Can we help you?" Eleanor asked.

Miss Jane looked up. "Oh. Are we intruding? I'm sorry. We'll come back later."

"No. What's wrong? Did you lose something?"

She put her hand to her throat. "My necklace. An amber cross, similar to the one Cassandra is wearing. Our brother Frank is in the Navy, and he brought them from Spain. The chain on mine must have broken." She looked around her feet. "I was wearing it when we came downstairs, but we've looked everywhere."

It seemed a bit presumptuous for Eleanor to ask what Jane Austen would do when the very woman was standing in front of her. She knew Jane would take the honorable path even if it hurt, and in her heart Eleanor knew what was right. She took her necklace out of her reticule and held it out. "Is this yours?"

"You found it!" Jane picked up the amber cross reverently and held it to her breast with both hands. "How can I ever thank you?"

Eleanor felt a sharp spasm of loss, but that was quickly replaced by a glow of satisfaction. The necklace had been returned to where it belonged. "No thanks are necessary." Giving joy to the woman who had provided her with so many hours of reading pleasure was enough.

But when the Austen sisters turned to reenter the ballroom, Eleanor could not let the opportunity slip past. "Please…"

Jane turned. "Yes?"

"May we speak privately?"

She nodded, and they walked ten paces away from the others.

"I just wanted to…" Eleanor paused. How could she tell Jane Austen how very much her novels meant to her without revealing she knew Jane was the author? "I wanted to recommend a book. My favorite. It's titled *Pride and Prejudice*."

The flash of wariness in Jane's eyes was instantly masked behind feigned indifference. "Well, thank you. I will remember your suggestion. If you will—"

"I am compelled to tell you how much I enjoy reading the story. I find the characters so filled with life. Every time I read it, I fall in love with the hero Mr. Darcy all over again." Eleanor knew she was speaking too fast and verging on babbling, but this was a golden opportunity that would never be repeated. "I want to have Elizabeth Bennet for a sister or at least for my best friend."

"Ah, but if you were her friend, then you might wind up marrying Mr. Collins." Jane smiled. "You see, I am... familiar with the work of which you speak."

Eleanor let out a sigh. Jane hadn't given her the cut direct, or worse, run in the opposite direction. "Aside from pure enjoyment, I really think the story helped me learn valuable lessons, or at least helped me cope when life gave me an education in relationships the hard way."

"A book did that?"

"Elizabeth's journey taught me I should listen to my brain and my heart and to neither exclusively. Love does not demand perfection because imperfections make each of us unique. Appearances can be false, and what is important comes from the inside."

Jane chuckled. "That's quite a lot for an unpretentious little volume about unimportant people."

"A person does not have to be of great consequence to be influential."

"I suppose you're right." Jane took a half step back as if she was about to close the conversation.

Eleanor wasn't ready to let her go. "Where did you… where do you suppose the author got her ideas?"

Jane narrowed her eyes and gave her a long look that said she realized Eleanor knew who the author was, but didn't understand how. Then her expression cleared as if she'd decided not to admit anything. Then the other woman could not be sure.

"I suppose this author is much like any other," Jane said. "I once… heard an author describe writing as taking bits and pieces of her experiences and observations, then she questions, dissects, and analyzes them. She extrapolates from them, stretching the thought out. Then she adds from her imagination a big dose of what might have been, a good measure of what would never be, and spices it all with wishful thinking."

"So… you don't think an author must experience everything she writes about?"

"Absolutely not. Daniel Defoe was not shipwrecked on an island for years as was his character in *Robinson Crusoe*, although it is known he interviewed sailors who had been shipwrecked. Jonathan Swift, as he portrayed through Gulliver, did not actually find on his travels tiny Lilliputians, giants, immortals, or a utopian society built by horses endowed with reason. Now that's imagination."

"Of course, you must be right," Eleanor said. After all, logic dictated Tolkien couldn't have visited Middle Earth, Mary Shelley hadn't built a Frankenstein from body parts, and the Baroness Orczy hadn't been an English spy during the French Revolution like her Scarlet Pimpernel. "Although I'm disappointed because that means there probably wasn't a real Mr. Darcy or Mr. Knightley."

"Live heroes have the distinct advantage of being able to… dance with you." Jane glanced obliquely at Shermont, conversing with Cassandra at the other side of the terrace. "Perhaps you have found your own version of a male protagonist better than any novel could portray."

Eleanor smiled sadly and shook her head. "He's some lucky girl's Mr. Darcy, but unfortunately not mine. I must return to my… home soon."

"Then I wish you a good journey," Jane Austen said. "And, if you will excuse a bit of advice from a stranger, life is short, and the opportunity of love rarely comes around a second time."

Was she referring to the plot of a book? In *Persuasion* Anne Elliot was given a second chance at love with Frederick Wentworth eight years after turning him away. Or was she just referring to the fact that she thought Eleanor was a widow? Did it make a difference?

Was *Persuasion* a bit of wishful thinking on the author's part or simply a big dose of what would never be? To ask her was not only impossible because the novel would not be published for another three years, but it would be an impertinent invasion of privacy she most likely would find abhorrent.

"Thank you for the advice," Eleanor said. "I'll remember our conversation."

Forever.

Jane must have somehow signaled her sister because Cassandra excused herself and approached. "I you will excuse us, we should let Edward know we've found Jane's necklace."

"Of course," Eleanor said politely, even though she would have liked to prolong the conversation.

After again thanking her, Jane and Cassandra left. Eleanor walked back to join Shermont.

"Do you want to explain what just happened?" he asked.

"Nope. You have to trust me. Everything is as it should be."

"But you gave her your—"

"Trust me."

The music ended and flushed dancers flooded the terrace, including Deirdre and Mina. They spotted Shermont and headed directly toward him, their partners in tow.

Shermont leaned over and whispered in Eleanor's ear. "Meet me in the library in fifteen minutes." Then he swung his long legs over the balustrade, pushed off with his hands, and landed on the shell path below with a crunch. He turned and gave her a deep courtly bow before disappearing into the darkness.

"Where's Shermont?" Deirdre asked as they approached.

"He was right there a minute ago," Mina said.

Eleanor simply smiled. Who could blame the guy for escaping after the mess the girls had nearly incited the night before? "I suppose he had an errand."

"Let's go for a walk in the garden," one of the dancing partners eagerly suggested and offered his arm to Mina, who giggled her response as she placed her hand on his arm.

"It will be much cooler there," the other youth said, and Deirdre laid her hand on his forearm.

"Ahem." Eleanor cleared her throat, but neither girl took the hint. "Not without your chaperone."

"We thought you were on our side," Deirdre said.

"You're supposed to be our friend,' Mina added.

"I am. That's why I don't want you to ruin your reputations before you get to London. I mean, I don't want you to ruin your reputations at all. Propriety is important if you want to have a wonderful, successful Season. Do you want to ruin any possibility of that?"

"Then you come with us," Mina said.

"No, thanks," Eleanor answered. "Not only have I been told I do not qualify as a chaperone, I can't think of anything I'd like less than the responsibility of keeping you two in check." And keeping track of them was a near impossible task—something she knew from experience.

She took Deirdre by the shoulders and turned her toward the ballroom. "You know I'm right, so let's go find your Aunt Patience." Eleanor gave the girl a gentle push. She snagged Mina's elbow and pulled her after her sister. "Come along." Then she added, "How will new dancing partners find you if you're outside? Did you think of that?"

Mina stopped struggling. The boys followed with sour faces, their amorous plans foiled.

They found Patience holding court with three older women. "And believe you me, I told him exactly what he could… oh, here are my darling nieces. Come sit by me. You know everyone, don't you?"

But she made a point of introducing poor, unfortunate Eleanor to everyone. The boys excused themselves, leaving her standing alone in front of the others.

Two young men arrived to ask the girls to dance, and they jumped up eagerly. A third man showed up and offered his arm to Eleanor. She declined, explaining with real regret she didn't know the steps. She didn't want to make a fool of herself stumbling and bumbling through the complicated dance maneuvers.

"You'll never find a new husband like that," Patience said much too loudly.

Eleanor forced herself to nod politely. "If you will excuse me, my toothache has returned with a vengeance," she lied. "I'm going upstairs to have a cup of willow bark tea and a bit of rest."

"Put a dollop of rum in it, my dear," one of the gray-haired women advised. "Quicker with liquor," she added with a giggle.

"Brandy is better," another said.

"Where are you getting brandy with a war on? Bourbon is best."

Eleanor left, unnoticed by the women as their argument continued. She went to the library.

Shermont circled around the moon garden and joined Carl on the other side. They spoke in hushed tones as they walked around to the back of the mansion.

"What was so important that you had to throw a rock at me?" Shermont asked. A ping on the back of his neck had caused him to turn and catch sight of his valet, who motioned for him to follow.

"You didn't respond when I whistled."

"That was you?"

"Apparently you were so preoccupied, a rock to your head was the only way to get your attention."

"Fine. What do you have?"

"You were wrong about Digby. While everyone else's servants were running around readying fancy clothes for the ball, his valet was cleaning and pressing traveling clothes."

"So I'm right, and he's planning on leaving tonight," Shermont said.

Carl shook his head. "His valet hinted at a trip to Gretna Green. That validates my theory that the oak tree was a trysting spot."

Shermont avoided contradicting Carl for now. "The best time for him to leave would be just before supper is served—no, during the fireworks."

"There's going to be fireworks?"

"It's supposed to be a surprise. I was out in the gardens this afternoon and saw them setting up the displays. I talked to one of the workers, and he said they were to start firing the rockets at eleven o'clock."

"I love fireworks."

"And they provide an excellent distraction." Shermont shook his head. "I know I'm right about Digby."

"Then let's take him into custody."

"Not yet. We can't arrest a peer of the realm without solid evidence."

"What about the female?"

"Not her either. I never tip my hand until all the cards are dealt and the bets are on the table."

"So now what do we do?"

"We check his rooms for evidence."

They entered by a back way and took a deserted servants' stairway up. The lock on Digby's door proved only a moment's delay against Carl's lock-picking acumen. Moonlight flooded through the windows, and Shermont used the night lantern on the hearth to light a candle.

"Nothing seems out of place," Carl said. "Maybe he really is just going on a trip."

"In secret."

"Eloping to Gretna Green is not usually announced ahead of time."

"Details," Shermont reminded him. He pictured the way the room had looked several days earlier when he'd joined Digby for a drink before the card game started. The first objects that struck him as out of place were the works of art on the walls. "Those two paintings used to be in the hall." He pulled out a chair that had been shoved back, and two empty frames fell forward. "The Gainsborough landscape and the Rubens unicorn have been cut out of their frames. Probably rolled up and packed into a small trunk."

Carl threw up his hands. "How can you know the trunk size?"

"Because the large Reynolds over the fireplace would be of equal or even greater value, so there must be a reason it was left behind—hence, a small trunk."

Carl could only shake his head.

Shermont went to the desk and flipped open a case that had been left out. "If a man leaves his jewel

case accessible it means there is nothing of value left
to steal."

"Or he trusts his servants."

He flicked though the items lying on the velvet
lining before closing the lid. "Not in this instance."
He stared at the top of the desk. He remembered
Digby fondling a letter opener with a diamond- and
emerald-encrusted handle before placing it in a leather
sleeve in the first drawer, using a tiny key on his watch
fob to secure it. The drawer was no longer locked, and
the leather sleeve was empty.

Shermont checked every drawer in the desk, exam-
ining for false bottoms or secret hidey-holes. Then
he picked up the candle and carried it into Digby's
dressing room. Two large armoires flanked a cheval
mirror. Both were still crammed full of clothes.

"Interesting."

"What? It's clothes. Oh, I know. He hasn't taken
his clothes, so that must mean—"

"But he did."

"There's so much. How could you—"

"If you were in charge of this wardrobe, wouldn't
you keep the number of clothes in each armoire
relatively equal?"

"You don't think the valet is in on—"

"Actually, no. Look here. Every hook has three or
four items, except this one on the far left. And every
shelf is crammed full, except for one. This tells me Digby
planned carefully what he wanted to take and placed
those items together. He could grab them and pack
quickly without help. My guess, based on what appears
missing, is two changes of clothes and four shirts."

Shermont looked around the room. Luggage would have been stored in the attic until needed. If the valet wasn't part of the plot… "Aha! The play! Digby had a servant fetch a portmanteau from the attic to use as a prop in the play, and then, none the wiser, it would be available for his trip. Clever."

"Then let's arrest him."

"Unfortunately, this is all circumstantial. A man can't be arrested for keeping plans for a trip secret or for stealing his own paintings."

"So… now what?"

"We wait. Our one advantage is that he doesn't know we're onto him. We watch and wait for him to make a move that will convict him."

"And hope we don't lose him."

"That will be your job. Find him and stick with him."

"What are you going to do?"

"Look for evidence."

"Oh, I almost forgot," Carl said, turning back. "I heard from our contact in the Admiralty. They have no record of a Captain Pottinger in the United States Navy. He suggested Pottinger may have sailed under letters of marque."

"A pirate?"

"A privateer. A private ship, outfitted at the owner's cost, whose captain is authorized by President Madison to take our ships as spoils of war. Lucrative if they are successful. However, a number have disappeared without a trace under fire from British warships."

That made sense. If Eleanor's husband had invested everything in such a risky venture, she would have been left penniless when he failed.

"Thank you," he said to Carl. "Since that line of inquiry has hit a dead end, let's concentrate on Digby."

Shermont scanned the room one last time before blowing out the candle and leaving Digby's suite. There was still a missing piece to the puzzle. Minimal clothing, jewelry, and two rolled up paintings. Not enough to fill the luggage piece he remembered. What was Digby leaving space in the portmanteau for?

❧

Eleanor paced the library, trying not to watch the clock. Not wanting to appear anxious, she sat on the settee, carefully arranging the skirt of her dress. She checked her breath and armpits. Should she be waiting in a seductive pose? She put up her feet and laid back, one arm over her head. But unless she scrunched up her legs, her head had to rest on the arm of the settee. After a few minutes, the position gave her a cramp in her neck. She tried a stance near the fireplace, but that felt pretentious. She wandered around the room.

What would Jane Austen do if she were waiting for a suitor to call? She would want to appear nonchalant, not indifferent, but not overly eager. Eleanor decided to sit on one of the wingback chairs, an open book on her lap. That way she could close it when he entered, a signal that he was more interesting than the book, but when he wasn't there she was pleasantly occupied. Perfect.

After twenty minutes, her anticipation faded. She made excuses for his delay. He met an old friend and couldn't break away. Maybe the countess cornered him and demanded a dance. After thirty minutes, she concluded he wasn't coming.

Probably for the best. In a few hours she would be going home, and then her memories of him were all she would have. She blinked away tears. She set the book on the table and stood, then paced the room again to get hold of her emotions. Was he even worth her tears?

Although her heart said yes, she forced her brain to deny it. The man had stood her up—couldn't even find a servant to bring her a message. He didn't have to dance with the countess or spend time with an old friend. Shermont wouldn't have if he'd really cared about her. She fanned her anger because it helped her cope.

Well, she certainly wasn't going to wait any longer. Did he expect to find her an hour from now, welcoming him with open arms and grateful for his belated attention? Like hell he would. If she happened to see him in the ballroom, she would give him the cut direct. She stood and stomped to the door, but paused with her hand on the knob. There was still the matter of keeping track of him until midnight. Damn.

The girls or him.

She'd come to care about the girls and wanted them to have their wonderful Season untainted by their brother's death in a duel. It wasn't as if she thought all her recent actions had been in noble self-sacrifice. There had been plenty of selfish, lusty satisfaction. Well, she would find Shermont and stick by his side a little longer, but she would be strong and resist her physical attraction to him.

She left the library intending to find him, wait with

him until midnight, and then meet the ghosts in her room for the trip home. Six steps outside the door, she stopped at the sound of Deirdre and Mina's voices drifting from above.

"Aunt Patience said she went to lie down in her room," Mina said. "Where can she be?"

"You're the gypsy seer," Deirdre said.

"I knew you were upset about that."

"I am not."

Eleanor certainly didn't want to explain why she wasn't in her room. She did an about-face to return to the library and nearly ran over a couple headed toward the same place. But she didn't want to go back to the ballroom because that's probably where the girls were headed, and she wanted a chance to find Shermont without them. She spun around and took off in the opposite direction, even though that took her to a hallway she'd never been down before. Her evening shoes with the soft leather soles made no noise on the thick carpet.

Yet the voices followed her. The hall dead-ended without an exit. She had to turn around and start back. She tested the first door on her right. When it opened, she ducked inside. And encountered a surprise.

Fourteen

ELEANOR TRIED TO MAKE SENSE OF THE SCENE BEFORE her. Teddy, who had changed into plain traveling clothes, knelt in front of an open iron cabinet built into the wall behind a movable section of wainscoting. He unloaded items and threw them into the portmanteau he'd used in the play and didn't notice she'd entered.

"What are you doing?" she blurted out without thinking.

She startled him, and he dropped an oblong green velvet box. A necklace, bracelet, and earrings fell out. She recognized the emerald necklace as the one Mina had a paste replica of in her drawer upstairs. Those must be the real emeralds.

Teddy jumped up, grabbed a pistol off the desk, and pointed it at her. "What in bloody hell are you doing in my estate office?"

"Rather a long story. I—"

"Never mind. It doesn't matter. Sit down and keep silent," he demanded, his expression hard and ugly.

Shocked, Eleanor slipped into a nearby chair.

He returned to his task, laying the pistol on the

floor next to his knee, and occasionally glanced up to make sure she hadn't moved.

She realized he was stealing the girls' jewels, and she was a witness. Not a good omen for a long life. She couldn't expect anyone to rescue her. Deirdre and Mina would never think to look for her here and would likely be distracted from their search in next to no time. Weren't the fireworks supposed to start soon? Once they did, he could shoot her with impunity, and no one would even notice. She had to escape before then. She looked around the estate office and noticed the door leading outside, which was used by tradesmen so they didn't come through the front entrance. If she could distract him from the weapon, she might have a chance to run for it.

"Why are you taking Deirdre and Mina's jewelry?" she asked.

"I told you to keep silent."

"I will, if you tell me why you're stealing from your sisters."

"Adoptive sisters," he said in a derisive and contemptuous tone. "If Father had married my mother as he should have and brought her back to England, she wouldn't have died."

"You can't know—"

"By the time I arrived here, he'd already married that insipid, mewling female and produced those two whining brats. I hated her for taking my mother's place, and I hated him for stealing my true inheritance."

"Those jewels are from their mother's family and not part of your—"

"They stole from me first. Every bit of food in

their mouths and every piece of clothing on their backs came out of what was due me. These jewels are scant repayment."

"If you do this, where can you go? You'll be hunted as a thief."

"Hah! Let them search. I'm returning to the land of my birth and the land of my ancestors. I will stand with Napoleon and find my real family."

Eleanor was confused. "But your father was English."

"The man who raised me was not my real father. My father died on the guillotine before my parents could marry. Mother feared her aristocratic blood would lead to the same end for herself and me, so she wrote to the Englishman she'd met while he was on his Grand Tour and claimed the child was his. Lord Digby was so desperate for a male heir, he sent for the mother and child immediately, even though he knew he could not marry her."

Teddy's emotional outburst wasn't making logical sense. "How do you know all this is true?"

"Aunt Patience confessed the truth when I came into the title. How Mother died to see me safe and how she honored Mother's wishes and brought me here and stayed to help raise me after my stepmother died."

"If Digby wasn't your father, shouldn't you have refused the title? The girls should rightfully—"

"No! The title and all it entails is mine! Digby legally adopted me, though he named a bastard in the process, shaming my mother's memory. As an American you should understand my hatred for the English. Your people are at war against them, as are mine. We are on the same side. Come with me. I have a carriage waiting down the road and two berths on a fast ship to Holland. From there…"

Eleanor shook her head. Her memory of her history classes was a bit weak on Napoleon, but she was sure any man who crowned himself emperor and tried to take over the world was no George Washington. "Stealing isn't honorable, no matter what the cause or justification."

Teddy gave her a hard look. "If you are not with me, then you are my enemy. Unfortunately, I cannot leave you behind to raise the alarm." He closed the portmanteau and directed her at gunpoint to pick it up.

The fireworks hadn't started yet. A gunshot might be noticed, but that would do her no good if she were dead. So she did as she was told. As long as she stayed alive, she might have a chance to escape.

He motioned her toward the tradesmen's door.

❧

Shermont entered the estate office to search for evidence and found not only Digby, but Eleanor. They appeared to be on their way out. Both spun around at the sound of the door closing.

"Oh, Shermont," Digby said. "Your bloody timing is fortuitous. I just caught this female stealing my sister's jewels. I'll hold her while you fetch the constable, but quietly, so as not to disturb the festivities."

Eleanor dropped the portmanteau and stood up straight. "He's lying," she said in a quiet, dignified voice.

"Silence, thief," Digby demanded. "She is obviously an imposter who has wheedled her way into our affections for her own nefarious purposes."

Shermont had only a moment to make a decision. He wanted to believe her, but could he trust his heart? She could still be a foreign agent, and Digby could be sacrificing her to make his own escape.

When Shermont hesitated, Digby said, "Better yet, you keep her here, and I'll go find the constable." He slid the pistol across the desk, and Shermont caught it before it fell off the edge.

A bold move, especially since Shermont had decided to believe Eleanor.

"I should not be gone longer than an hour." Digby headed toward the exit, pausing to pick up the portmanteau. "I'll take this for safekeeping."

"Halt," Shermont said, raising the pistol. Once he'd made the leap of faith, the details he always drilled Carl to notice vindicated his belief in Eleanor. Digby was dressed for traveling, but she was still dressed for the ball. She looked pale and scared, while he appeared flushed and frustrated. She'd dropped the portmanteau like a hot potato, and Digby had refused to leave it behind. "Put the portmanteau on the floor," Shermont said, the steel in his voice brooking no defiance.

Digby complied, but before Shermont could demand an explanation, the tradesmen's door opened. Patience entered, armed and in a towering rage. Digby flashed Shermont a smug look and opened his arms to his Aunt Patience.

"*Ma chère tante.* Your timing is impeccable. Keep these two under guard for half an hour, and then join me at the meeting place," Digby said as he again picked up the portmanteau. His cocky grin faded as he realized she had her weapon aimed at him.

"Leaving without me, I see," Aunt Patience said.

"Not at all. I just said I'd meet you at—"

"And you think I believe you, you ungrateful little guttersnipe. If not for me, you'd still be wandering the streets of Paris stealing crusts of bread or prostituting yourself like your mother."

"My mother was an aristocrat!"

"Ha! Victorine was a *soubrette*."

"You said Digby met her at court."

"He did. Aristocrats often invited actresses to their wild parties. Rent the right clothes, put on a few false airs, and they fit right in. It usually resulted in a romantic assignation and gifts of money and jewelry. Most women of the stage did it. Your oh-so-sanctified mother was one of the best."

"You malign your beloved sister?"

"Not my sister." Patience laughed. "I was the one with breeding who had fallen on hard times. I was the one who belonged at court. But Victorine got everything she wanted simply because she was beautiful. The vicious little bitch treated me like dirt beneath her shoe. Your father could have been one of dozens or even hundreds. She forgot one as soon as another better looking, richer, and more generous one appeared."

"Stop it. I don't want to hear more of your lies," Digby said, putting his hands over his ears.

"I find it fascinating," Shermont said. Patience had a lot to get off her mind, and he knew the longer they stayed in one place, the more likely his valet would find them. He laid his pistol on the desk, propped one hip on the top, and crossed his arms. "I've always said the lady with the weapon has the floor for as long as she wants it."

Patience nodded with a smug smile. "After Victorine and her sickly baby died, I went through her possessions, hoping I could sell something to pay my long overdue wages. When I found a great number of love letters, I hit on the scheme of writing to each as if I were her, claiming the child as his and asking for money to aid in his care."

"You mean you blackmailed them in her name," Digby sneered.

Patience shrugged. "While I waited for the money to arrive, I had to sell her fine clothes and jewelry. Months passed until finally one wrote back and sent money. My neighbors were jealous of my bounty and were going to turn me in as an aristocrat in hiding. So I decided to emigrate to England, but I could hardly appear on Lord Digby's doorstep without an appropriate child. So I went out and found you—filthy, dirty, snot-nosed, dressed in rags, crying on a street corner. You had the white-blond hair Digby had mentioned in one of his letters as a family trait. I promised you a good meal, and you said you would do anything I wanted. I'd say you're lucky it was me and not some white slaver who—"

"You lie." Digby shook all over.

"Yes, I admit I lied to you when you were a boy, but it was for your own good. Fat lot of profit in it for me. You can take the boy off the street, but you can't take the street out of the boy. You will always be an ungrateful guttersnipe. Now hand over that portmanteau, and we'll all go outside quietly in single file."

Eleanor glanced at Shermont and could tell he was thinking what she was. If they left the house, they would never return.

"What happens then?" he asked.

When Patience glanced toward Shermont, Digby lunged forward, grabbed the bag, and headed toward the door. Shermont tackled him by the ankles and the two fought, rolling around on the floor. When they stood, trading blows, Patience took aim with her pistol at Shermont's back.

Eleanor jumped forward and seized Patience's arm. They struggled for control of the weapon, but the older woman outweighed her by a good fifty pounds and shoved her aside. She fell to the floor as Patience again took aim.

"Look out," Eleanor cried as she got up and went after Patience again.

The pistol retort bounced off the walls of the small room, deafening the inhabitants. The echoes seemed to go on and on, but Eleanor realized the fireworks display had started outside. When the roomful of acrid smoke cleared, Teddy was on the floor, his chest a bloody mess. Shermont knelt beside him and pressed his handkerchief over the gaping wound.

Patience dropped the pistol and put her hands to her mouth, not quite stifling her cry of dismay. She turned from the sight and ran outside.

"Give me your handkerchief," Shermont said, shrugging off his coat.

Eleanor still had her reticule looped over her wrist. When she found her handkerchief and held it out, he had covered the other man's face with his coat. She swallowed. She didn't have to ask if Teddy was dead.

Shermont took her handkerchief and said, "I'm afraid I'll ruin it."

"Go ahead." She pressed it on him. As he dabbed at his bleeding lip and wiped his hands, she said, "Hurry. Patience is getting away."

"We'll deal with her later."

As soon as his hands were clean, he tossed the handkerchief to the floor and wrapped Eleanor in a tight embrace. "Are you all right? For a moment there…" He choked up and couldn't put into words the terror that had swamped him while Digby aimed his pistol at her.

"I'm fine."

He knew she lied because she was trembling.

"Patience is a murderer," she said, her quivering voice rising in pitch. "And she's getting—"

"Eleanor!" He took her by both shoulders and looked deep into her eyes. "Right now we have other problems. I need you to remain calm. Take a deep breath. That's better. Undoubtedly, any number of people heard the gunshot—"

"The fireworks…"

"Military men and hunters will know the difference and will likely investigate the source. We can't keep this disaster quiet for long, but I don't think the girls deserve to hear about this from a curious crowd."

"Of course not."

"I'm glad you agree. I want you to find them and use whatever excuse you can to get them someplace private."

"Our rooms?"

"Excellent. You can tell them—"

"I don't think I should be the one to tell them. It should be someone who knows them well and loves them, like their Uncle Huxley."

"Good thinking." He kissed the tip of her nose and gave her a quick, tight hug. "I knew I could count on you to keep a cool head. I'll send Huxley to your rooms as soon as I can."

Carl was the first to arrive in the estate office. Eleanor left on her errand. Outside the door, she leaned against the wall, her knees like Jello and her hands shaking. All her bravado of earlier had drained away.

Omigod. Shermont could have died. She could have died. She wanted to run back into the room and hold him. Just being with him gave her strength. But he was depending on her, and she had a job to do. She took a deep breath and straightened. She had to be strong. Her friends Deirdre and Mina needed her.

Eleanor found them in the ballroom about to line up with their partners for the next set.

"I need to speak to you," she said. "Privately."

"But it's the supper dance," Mina said.

That meant it was close to midnight, her deadline. But she hadn't prevented Teddy's death. Did that mean the ghosts would not take her back? She couldn't worry about herself now.

"You look terrible," Deirdre said. "Is your tooth-ache worse?"

"We looked for you," Mina said. "But you weren't—"

"I know. This is important." Eleanor looked at the young men. "If you gentlemen will excuse us." She stepped between them and took each girl by the elbow, guiding them out the door and toward the stairs.

"What—"

"I can't tell you here. We're going to our room where we can't be overheard."

As they walked up the stairs, Deirdre said, "I know the secret. Shermont has asked you to marry him, right?"

Eleanor shook her head but didn't slow the pace.

"I don't think it's a happy secret," Mina said.

"Oh dear," Deirdre said. "You're carrying his child, and he refused to marry you."

Eleanor started. "Whatever gave you an idea like that?"

"I'm not as naïve as you think," Deirdre said smugly. "If you hadn't found us in his room, you would have been there alone with him. And then you left again, but the next day you said you hadn't seen Teddy."

"That's right," Mina said. "I didn't even think of that."

"I'm not pregnant," Eleanor assured them as they entered the sitting room. Both girls sat on the settee and looked at her with expectant expressions. Where was Huxley? She needed to stall for time. "We need tea." She used the bellpull to call the maid.

While Shermont explained to Carl what had happened, Huxley entered and listened. Shermont then sent his valet to apprehend Patience, both assuming she would head to the oak tree to meet her contact.

Huxley looked down at the body of the man who had pretended to be his nephew. "My brother thought the world of him, but I always knew he was a bad apple. I've always said, never trust a man who mistreats animals."

"What story do you want to tell the girls?"

"The truth. There have been enough lies already. The girls are stronger than you think, stronger than they themselves know. No, I won't have them grieving for a beloved brother when he never deserved their regard."

"I'll support whatever you decide."

"I would appreciate it if the facts did not become common knowledge. No sense dragging the girls' names into his disgrace."

"A few need to know the truth, but I guarantee their discretion."

Huxley gave him an assessing look before nodding. "I'll make a succinct announcement, canceling the balance of this evening's festivities. The story will be that Digby was fatally wounded during a robbery attempt."

"As you say."

"I'll make funeral arrangements befitting his former position. But I refuse to have him buried in the family plot. His true grave will not carry my brother's name."

"My lips are sealed."

"Will you make it look—"

"I'll straighten up in here. The scene will reflect the story."

The two men shook hands.

"One moment," Shermont said. "I'd like you to witness that I'm returning all this jewelry to the safe. If anything is missing, I want you to know I'm not responsible."

"I trust you with my family's name. Compared to that, those baubles are inconsequential." Huxley left without another word.

Shermont unpacked the portmanteau and was surprised to find two red leather portfolios. He recognized the folders used for diplomatic dispatches. The seals had been broken. He opened one and found it addressed to Wellington and signed by the Prince Regent.

Major Alanbrooke and Captain Rockingham burst into the room. Alanbrooke quietly assessed the situation, but Rockingham blurted out, "What happened? Hey! What are you doing with those?" He started forward with his hands outstretched.

Alanbrooke stopped him. "Give the man a chance to explain."

Shermont faced Rockingham with a stern expression. "You're supposed to be on your way to Spain, aren't you?"

The captain's ears turned as red as the folders. "I leave at dawn. Digby promised me his fastest horse. Said I could make up two days during the trip, and no one would ever know."

"So you gave him these?"

"To keep safe. Away from prying eyes. Like yours. How dare you open—"

"Just a moment." Alanbrooke laid his hand on Rockingham's shoulder. "Now would be a good time to start talking," he said to Shermont.

"I'm an agent of His Majesty. And I expect you, Major Alanbrooke, to arrest Captain Rockingham for dereliction of duty."

"Hell you say," Rockingham said. A rivulet of sweat ran down his temple. "We don't believe your cock and bull—"

"The less you say, the better off you'll be," Alanbrooke said to the belligerent captain. "What happened here?" he asked Shermont.

"Lord Digby was fatally shot during a robbery attempt."

Shermont could see Alanbrooke didn't believe him either, but not for the same reasons as Rockingham.

The door opened, and the two lieutenants who had also heard the shot entered. Alanbrooke ordered them to take the captain into custody and to keep him under guard in his room until further notice. Rockingham protested until Alanbrooke silenced him by whispering something in his ear. The three men left.

The two remaining men looked up when the music came to a sudden halt. Shermont stood. "Huxley has made the announcement. I would appreciate it if you and any men you can round up could facilitate the rapid exit of the guests. Less time for gossiping. And send a footman for the constable."

"What are you going to do with those dispatches?"

"Return them to the sender."

"Are you going to tell me what really happened?"

"No."

"I can guess. Digby is wearing traveling clothes. The hidden wall cabinet is standing open. The portmanteau he used during the play is packed with his clothes, jewelry cases, and I assume those dispatches were in there. Only one shot was fired. And a government agent is found standing over his body."

While Alanbrooke talked, Shermont put the jewelry cases back in the secret cabinet, locked it, pocketed the key to give to Huxley later, and replaced the wainscoting. Although he was impressed by the other man's observations, he kept his face impassive.

"I'd say you were tracking Digby for some reason," Alanbrooke concluded. "He was probably selling information to Napoleon. You caught him trying to escape and shot him."

"I didn't shoot him."

Alanbrooke nodded and headed toward the door. He stopped and turned at the sound of Shermont's voice.

"If you ever decide to try a different career, contact Scovell. I'll write you a recommendation."

Alanbrooke raised an eyebrow. "I think not. I wear my country's colors proudly. I've no respect for agents who skulk in dark corners buying and selling military information like loaves of bread."

"Actually, I agree. What would you say about those tasked with catching those same agents?"

"I'll have to think on that."

"That's all I ask. By the way, what did you say to Rockingham?"

Alanbrooke smiled. "He's always had a fondness for rum, and I reminded him that I had half a bottle stashed in my room." He turned on his heel and left.

❧

"Just tell us," Deirdre said, a bit of exasperation sneaking into her tone. "Whatever it is, we'll…" Her voice faded as the music stopped mid-song on a discordant note. She cocked her head. "What is that?" She started to stand.

But Eleanor couldn't let her leave to investigate. She quickly pulled a footstool to a position in front of the girls and took their hands between hers. "There's been a terrible accident," she said, her voice hoarse with emotion.

A scratching on the door preceded Twilla's entrance with a large tray. Nothing else could be said while the servant was in the room. Eleanor hoped it would take the maid a long time to serve the tea, but Deirdre curtailed any fussing.

"Just leave the tray on the table," she said. "That will be all." As soon as Twilla left, Deirdre turned to Eleanor. "Just tell us." This time her tone was gentler, but wary.

Mina added her other hand to the rest. "I'm scared."

"I hate to be the one to tell you," Eleanor started, but a knock on the door interrupted her. "Enter." She hoped it was Huxley. She glanced over her shoulder. The poor man looked as if he'd aged a decade in the last hour.

Shermont wrapped the dispatches in one of Digby's shirts, so he could carry them to his room with no one recognizing them for what they were. He hid the portmanteau under the desk where Huxley would find it when he sat there to go through Digby's papers.

Carl entered from outside. "Patience wasn't at the oak tree. They must have had a different prearranged meeting place for the escape, but no horses are missing from the stable."

"She may have decided to make her own way, so she wouldn't have to explain his absence. Check any stage stops within a two-mile radius. I don't expect she got any farther than that without a horse."

"There's only one stop in a five-mile radius. The mail coach stops daily at nine o'clock in the morning. That's it. I checked the inns, and they promised to let me know if anyone answering her description appears looking for a room."

Shermont wrapped the pistol that had been fired in another shirt and moved Digby's weapon to a spot a few inches from his hand. He used a penknife to scratch the outside of the lock on the tradesmen's door.

"What are you doing?"

"The official story is that Digby was fatally shot during a robbery attempt. I'm helping the constable come to the desired conclusion." He gave his valet the shirt-wrapped packages. "Please drop these off in my room."

"What's in the other one?"

"Diplomatic dispatches."

Carl raised a questioning eyebrow.

"I'll explain later. One of us will have to take them back to the Prince Regent tomorrow. Where are you going to search next?"

"I'm thinking she might be hiding on the estate, waiting for daylight to travel cross-country to the coast. I'm going to check the outbuildings and then the neighbors."

"As long as you're going upstairs, look in her room for clues first. Letters from friends might point to a possible escape route or hiding place."

Carl nodded and started to exit by the door to the hall.

"You'll have to use the tradesmen's door again," Shermont said. "Tuttle and Digby's valet are guarding that door until the constable arrives. I recommended they allow an officer of the law to view the scene of the crime. They didn't appear to agree, but couldn't argue with me."

"Who is guarding the other door?"

Shermont grinned. "I am."

The session with the constable went as Shermont expected. The country lawman was more used to dealing with stolen pigs and taproom brawls than murder. Shermont's title gave him an advantage. The obsequious constable accepted everything he said unchallenged. The investigation took only minutes, and the body was released to the servants for preparation to be laid out in the front parlor.

Shermont left, intending to go directly to his room. He passed servants stopping clocks and draping mirrors as he approached Eleanor's door instead.

Fifteen

ELEANOR BACKED OUT THE DOOR TO THE GIRLS' bedroom and pulled it gently shut. When she turned around, Shermont waited inside the door to the sitting room. She walked directly into his arms.

"I had to see you," he whispered.

"I wanted to see you, too." Eleanor needed to touch him and know he was alive. So very alive.

"Huxley was here?"

"Yes. He… he really loves those girls and was so gentle and considerate."

"But he told them the truth?"

She sighed. "Yes. Everything. He left about ten minutes ago to see to the arrangements."

"How did the girls take it?"

"Pretty much as one would expect. No matter which way you look at it, they lost a beloved brother tonight." They'd all shed more than a few tears, not for the thief and traitor, but for the boy he'd once been and for their expected future that now would never be. "They finally fell asleep, emotionally exhausted. Huxley insisted they drink a special herbal tea for strength, but I think it had a mild sedative effect."

Shermont tightened his embrace. "And you? How are you holding up?"

"Better now," she said, snuggling against his chest. How could something so hard be so comfortable and so comforting?

"I should go," he said. "I need to help Carl search for Patience. She seems to have disappeared into thin air."

"Not yet," she said, holding onto him as if she would never let him go.

He tipped her face up for a kiss. Pleasure ignited an explosion of passion.

Eleanor grabbed his hand and dragged him into her bedroom. They started stripping off their clothes before the door latch clicked shut. The dim moonlight coming from the window gave just enough illumination to see. She untied the ribbon belt below her breasts, unhooked the wrap front, and shrugged off her dress as easily as he shed his coat.

Next came the demi-corset she'd designed with the lacing in the front. She could manage it herself, but when she pulled on the bow it tangled. The more she tried to loosen it, the more it knotted. "Damn it."

"Wait." He reached behind the nape of his neck and pulled out a long thin knife from the sheath strapped to his back.

She took a step back. "No wonder you weren't afraid of Teddy."

He shook his head. "Only an idiot isn't afraid of a pistol pointed at his head. A knife isn't faster than a bullet, but it does come in handy sometimes, especially up close."

"I assume you know how to use that thing."

"Yes," he answered simply. "Do you trust me?"

"With my life," she answered without hesitation.

When he stepped forward, she stood still, arms locked to her sides. He inserted the tip of the knife under the bottom edge of the corset and slit the laces straight up the middle. She felt only a slight pressure almost like a shiver, and her corset fell away. Her chemise dropped off her shoulders and gaped over her breasts because he had cut the ribbon that gathered the neckline. She grabbed at the thin material and held it in place.

He flipped the stiletto over his shoulder, and it stuck in the door with a soft thud. Without breaking eye contact, he kicked off his shoes, removed his vest and tie, and unbuttoned his high stiff collar.

Even though she enjoyed the show, the banked fire deep in her belly blazed to life, hotter than the July sun on Santa Monica Beach. "Too slow." She reached for him. Her chemise fell to her elbows. He ripped off his shirt. "Better," she said with a smile.

She dropped her arms and her chemise slid to the floor, leaving her clad only in her white silk stockings with red ribbon garters and her delicate dancing shoes.

He undid the buttons of his trousers, and the flap fell open. His penis sprang forward, but try as he might the tight trousers resisted his efforts to pull them past his thighs. "Bloody newfangled styles."

"Forget them."

He swept her off her feet and carried her to the bed, kissing her as he laid her down, rolling her to lie on top of him as he joined her. She bent her knees so she could straddle his hips, found the exact position, and took him within her. The pleasure of his fullness caused her to push herself upward with her arms and downward with her hips, taking more of him inside, stretching and sliding, quivering and pulsating.

He jerked his hips upwards, filling her, seating himself deep within her. Again and again.

She arched her spine and threw her head back. He tweaked the tip of her breast, rolling it between his thumb and forefinger. He slid his other hand between their bodies so the tip of his finger rubbed against her clitoris with each movement. Her orgasm came quickly, stunningly. She felt as if she would explode into a million pieces. She flopped forward, needing to hold him, to have a tether to earth, while she flew into space, detonating into blazing fireworks.

When he felt her internal pulsing, he wrapped his arms around her and rolled her under him, driving hard and fast toward his satisfaction, staying with her, becoming one. He bit his lip to keep from crying her name to the world.

Spent and breathless, he rolled to his back, cradling her to his side. She felt so right within the circle of his arm. He wanted to sleep thus, wake up thus.

As soon as his pounding heartbeat slowed to near normal, he said, "Several years ago, I read an ancient Oriental love poem, but I didn't understand its meaning. In it, two clay figurines represent lovers. One magical night the moonlight shines upon them, and they come to life. During the act of making love, they fall from the shelf into the darkness and out of the magical moonlight. They shatter into tiny shards. The next morning the sculptor scoops up the pieces, adds water, kneads the mixture, and forms it into two figures identical to the originals. But in the one are bits of the other and vice versa. Forever altered, each will always have some essence of the other molded into their existence. Now I understand. And believe it to be true."

He tipped her face up to kiss her. "Are those tears?"

"No. Yes." She blinked and sniffled. "That was beautiful."

"The poet said it better. I'll find a copy for you."

She laid her hands on his chest and propped her chin on them. "I'd rather remember it in your words."

He caressed the side of her face, tracing the line of her jaw. "I should go."

She pressed his hand to her cheek. "Not yet." She wiggled closer and propped her knee on his hip.

He chuckled. "Keep that up and I won't be able to leave."

"If I could, I'd stay like this forever."

"Like this?" He pulled her upward until they were a breath apart. "Or like this?" He kissed her, long and gentle, tasting her lips and the inside of her mouth.

She pulled on his shoulder until he rolled on top of her, fitting his hips between her thighs. Starting at her forehead he kissed every inch of skin, moving lower and lower, spending extra time on each breast until she squirmed with need.

He relished her little kitten mewls of pleasure and moved lower, across her belly to the sensitive spot in the vee of her legs. He bent her knees and spread them wide, licking the nub with his tongue, tasting her essence, delighting in the uncontrolled bucking of her hips. He pulled her knees over his shoulders and then slid two fingers inside her, in and out, faster and faster. When he felt her orgasm begin, he quickly levered himself upwards, lifting her hips and plunging into her. He knelt upright on the bed, her heels on his shoulders. Felt deeper than ever, the rhythmic vibration of her pleasure milked him of every drop of semen.

Her body went limp. He rolled her onto her side and spooned protectively around her. Although he wanted nothing more than to go to sleep holding her, he knew if he didn't move soon that's exactly what he would do. And he had other obligations to fulfill before the night was through. He kissed the back of her neck and the delicate spot below her ear. "Eleanor?" he whispered.

"Don't go, James," she mumbled sleepily. "Not yet."

"I hate the thought of leaving you, but I promise I'll come back. Will you wait for me?"

She turned over to face him. She'd told him the other evening she was leaving after the ball, but now she wasn't so sure. Teddy had still died. The girls didn't meet the pivotal brothers. She didn't even know if the ghosts would take her back since she'd messed everything up. Surely they wouldn't fault her for events beyond her control. Would it be so terrible to stay with him? Could she deal with the often grim realities of Regency life if he was by her side? She didn't know what to say.

He placed a finger across her lips. "Don't answer. I know I have no right to ask. I have so little to offer you." He rubbed his forehead. "I don't even remember who I really am."

She took his hand and held it between hers. "It's who you are now that matters, not who you were or who your family was. You are a good and honorable man, and you deserve happiness."

"Then if the universe is just, you will be here when I get back, for that is what will make me happy." He kissed her. "I will return as soon as I can."

She wrapped her arms around him and held him tight. When she kissed him good-bye, somehow she knew it would be forever. He rose from the bed and dressed. She sat up, drawing the coverlet over her shoulders, suddenly cold. Blinking away her tears, she smiled. She wanted him to remember her smiling.

"Sleep well, my love," he whispered and blew her a kiss.

As soon as the door clicked shut, she rolled over and buried her face in the pillow. Too heartsick to sleep, her tears flowed freely, and sobs wracked her body.

Sixteen

ELEANOR WOKE LATE IN THE MORNING, HEAVY AND groggy from her restless night. Then she remembered the ghosts had not come for her. She was still in the past and would see Shermont again. Her heart soared. Energized, she sat up, ready to face the day.

"Good morning, sleepyhead," Deirdre said.

Eleanor's hopes evaporated as she realized she was in a different room, and the two ghosts were seated primly at a small table near a window that faced the rear, rather than the south lawn where they'd played croquet and where the archery targets had been set up.

Disoriented, she asked, "Where am I? What happened?"

"That's easy," Mina said. "You're in a room down the hall from where you were. Sorry about that, but the inn is crowded, what with that group of college students—"

"Stick to the point, Mina," Deirdre said.

"Oh, certainly. And you are back in the modern world." She punctuated her announcement with a quick jerk downward of her chin.

"But I didn't save your brother."

"Well, technically you did prevent the duel, even though you couldn't prevent his death," Deirdre said.

"And he wasn't really our brother," Mina added. "So you succeeded, even if not the way we expected."

"What we know now is that our task wasn't learning a lesson or doing something ourselves. We were merely the tools used to set a few events right that had somehow gone wrong. You helped us do that. Uncle Huxley inherited the title as he should have in the first place. And he was a marvelous guardian."

"But he inherited the title before."

"Yes," Mina interjected. "But this time, because of what he learned about Teddy through your intervention, Uncle Huxley didn't want us to wear mourning for such a brother, so he took us on his world tour. We collected thousands of specimens for his collection. Deirdre and I became quite expert at catching butterflies and moths and had such a wonderful time."

"Did Huxley find his new species?"

"In New Guinea," Deirdre said with a wide grin. "A stunning iridescent blue and green wing with a row of pink spots along the outer edge. The adults measured six to eight inches across. Magnificent. He named it *Papillio huxdeirmin*."

"I'm so happy for him," Eleanor said.

"Extinct now, unfortunately. That's a specimen on that wall," Mina said, nodding toward a framed butterfly that looked like a print.

"You should buy it," Deirdre whispered. "When Uncle died we donated his entire collection to the British Museum, except for a few we kept for sentimental reasons. That silly female who runs this place has a price tag on it of forty-five pounds. It was worth thousands when we were alive."

"And we want you to have it," Mina said. "To remember us by."

"As if I could forget you."

Deirdre stood. "We just wanted you to know how much we appreciate your help. Now we really should go. Our husbands have been quite patiently waiting for us."

"Wait! Did you marry brothers? I worried that since I prevented you from meeting—"

"We did marry brothers," Mina said. "Magnificent, brilliant, kind, handsome Dutchmen we met on a butterfly hunting safari into central Africa."

"They didn't speak a word of English, and we didn't speak any Dutch."

"Oh, but what fun we all had learning."

"Mina," Deirdre said, her tone an admonishment.

"I'm glad," Eleanor said. She wanted to ask them about Shermont, yet she debated whether to do it. She wanted him to have had a happy, fulfilled life and to have found love. Did she really want to know the details?

The ghosts said their good-byes, but as they faded, Eleanor heard them arguing yet again.

"We should have told her," Mina said.

"She'll find out soon enough," Deirdre said.

"Wait! Come back! Tell me what?" Eleanor jumped out of bed and ran to where they had been. "That's not fair," she said to the ceiling. She spun around in a circle and wanted to yell and scream. "Damn it." She stomped her foot, but it didn't provide the same satisfaction as when she was wearing shoes. "Come back. Please."

A long silence was her answer.

She sank into one of the chairs and dropped her head into her hands. Now she would never know about Shermont.

"The reason I was so hesitant," Deirdre began.

Eleanor looked up to find the ghosts seated in the window seat. "You came back."

"Obviously. Although materializing and dematerializing is quite draining."

"Just tell her," Mina said.

"Yes, well, the reason I was so hesitant when Mina first suggested taking you back in time to stop the duel is because we had already taken someone back earlier. That had ended with disastrous results. When we brought you to the present, we had to bring the other time traveler back as well."

Eleanor connected the explanation to Patience's disappearance into thin air. No wonder it was a disaster. She couldn't think of a worse person to take back.

"Because of the necessity of bringing two of you back together and the limits of our available energy, we have returned you to a point two years in the past, if you measure from when you left. You are at the point when you visited the inn the first time. That's why you're in a different room. It's the one you stayed in then. As far as anyone here knows, you arrived last night."

"We're quite pleased it worked out so well," Mina said.

"Wait a sec." Eleanor was a bit confused and plenty worried. "Won't returning to an earlier time create a time paradox? An anomaly? Am I going to explode upon meeting myself?"

The ghosts giggled in response. "Good heavens, no."

"Each individual is unique," Deirdre explained, "and cannot exist in duplicate form. When you came back in time, you replaced the previous Eleanor completely. Quite simple, really. Elegant. As are most big truths of the universe."

"But I remember everything that happened."

"Yes. Your experiences during those two years and what you learned on your trip to the Regency made you stronger. Therefore, you, as the more powerful force, replaced your younger, weaker self. You are still you. The one and only you."

Eleanor was still uncertain, but she had to accept it as truth. She hadn't believed time travel was possible... until it happened. Still, if she met herself in the hallway, she was going to run in the other direction.

"Are you happy now?" Deirdre asked Mina as they started to fade.

"Wait! Please."

The ghosts rematerialized.

"Please," Eleanor said. "Tell me about Shermont. Did he have a good life? Did he marry and have children?" Her voice caught in her throat. "Did he find love?"

The ghosts looked at each other.

"We can't say," Deirdre said.

"Does that mean you don't know or that you just won't tell me?" Eleanor managed to keep her tone even despite her frustration.

"We did leave England just a few weeks after Teddy's death and didn't return for nearly twelve years," Mina said. "After Uncle Huxley died we buried him at sea off Madagascar in the glorious Viking funeral he always wanted, and we continued his work. Until we decided the children needed to go to school. Such a handful they were. Climbing in the rigging, swearing like sailors, vowing to become pirates—even the girls. But they turned out—"

"Enough," Deirdre said. She turned to Eleanor. "We've brought you our journals." She motioned to the stack of more than a dozen slim leather-bound books on the table, some well-worn, some new looking. "We hid them so no one would ever find them. We fetched them earlier this morning."

"While you were still sleeping."

"Please consider them a thank you present. If you want, you can read all about our lives. You can probably auction the books off for enough money to put your business venture on solid footing. Now, it's time for us to go."

"Wait. You do know what happened to him? Lord Shermont?"

"Yes, we—"

"Mina!" Deirdre's sharp tone was more than a warning.

"Why won't you tell me? You told me all about your lives."

"We have limitations. His story is not ours to tell," Deirdre explained.

"What if I ask you to take me back? What if I want to stay there permanently?"

Deirdre shook her head. "I'm sorry. That was never an option. You are where you are supposed to be."

"You have been given the chance to relive two years of your life. A great gift," Mina said.

"Use it wisely," Deirdre added.

As they faded, Eleanor called, "Will I ever see you again?"

They didn't rematerialize, but she distinctly heard their voices.

"Yes, when you—"

"Hush, Mina."

To her surprise, Eleanor was heartened by the prospect.

Seventeen

ELEANOR CLOSED THE BOOK, STOOD, AND STRETCHED. After spending the morning reading the tiny handwriting in the journals, her eyes felt grainy, and her shoulders were cramped. She smiled. The girls had certainly led an exciting life. And she was only a quarter of the way through the stack of journals.

As she picked up the next one, her stomach growled, making her wonder if she should go downstairs and get some brunch before starting another. On the front of the book, rather than the year designation that she expected, was the title *Sense and Sensibility*, and on the flyleaf, *by a Lady*.

"Omigod." A first edition Jane Austen. She gently laid it on the table. The next book in the stack was *Pride and Prejudice* by the Lady who wrote *Sense and Sensibility*. The following four volumes were also first editions. One of each of her novels.

Eleanor sank into the chair. Deirdre had said she could auction off the books for enough money to put her business on solid footing. These slim first editions were worth a fortune.

Inside the last one, published by Jane Austen's

brother after her death, were a number of loose pages. Letters, responses, and thank you notes, all signed by Jane Austen. Deirdre had listened to Eleanor's advice and saved everything.

The provenance of the items might prove a sticking point. She could hardly claim the truth, but she'd deal with that later. She decided, for the time being, to put them in her suitcase, which she found in the closet.

Hanging in the closet was the outfit she'd planned to wear on that day, which seemed like two years ago. She had to smile at the navy blue pinstriped interview suit with the tailored white shirt and sensible shoes. She'd been so eager to get the job. It had turned out one of the worst of her career.

Instead, she pulled out a pair of jeans, a top with a vibrant zigzag stripe pattern that made her eyes look emerald green, and a pair of sneakers. As she dressed, she wondered what she would do that afternoon, since she planned to blow off the job interview.

Walking down the hall and stairs, she passed a number of framed watercolors for sale. One in particular caught her eye. The scene showed a Regency picnic at the site of the ruins. She recognized Deirdre and Mina facing the artist and looking at two men. Even though they were drawn from the back, she knew it was Shermont and Teddy. By eliminating the folks in the background and the chaperones seated at a table to the left, she realized Beatrix Holcum must have been the talented artist. Poor Beatrix. No one had thought to tell her gently when Teddy had been shot. Eleanor hoped the girl had found the happiness she never would have experienced with him.

Eleanor noted the price of the picture, and her eyebrows shot up in surprise. A framed obituary hanging next to the watercolor explained the cost. Beatrix had gone on to become a well-respected artist in her own right, married an Earl, and lent her name and support to women's suffrage, anti-child labor, and compulsory education for all children, among other good causes.

"You go, girl," Eleanor whispered.

From the photo taken later in her life, Beatrix was still beautiful. She lived to a ripe old age and was survived by seven children, forty-two grandchildren, one hundred and twenty-nine great-grandchildren, and a great-great-granddaughter born on Beatrix's ninety-third birthday and named in her honor.

With a wide grin Eleanor continued down the stairs. She wondered if she would ever know what had happened to the others—Alanbrooke with his charming smile and sad eyes, sweet Fiona and Hazel, even Parker and Whitby. And Lord Shermont. How could she find out what had happened to him? Above all, she hoped he'd found happiness.

On the landing she picked up a brochure on the Jane Austen House Museum in Chawton to read while she ate.

Halfway down the stairs she almost stumbled and came to a halt. In the entrance hall stood Jason, her former fiancé. When the ghosts had said she'd gone back two years, she hadn't given a single thought to the fact that she'd met him on her first trip to England. He'd asked her to have lunch with him, and she'd learned he worked at the very studio where she had a job interview. So angelic with his curly blond hair and boyish grin. Seeing him again left her... confused.

With the chance to start the relationship over, she could do things differently. Was that what the ghosts had meant by using the time wisely?

Wait a minute. She wasn't the one who had cheated. She wasn't the one who had found someone else. This might be a second chance, but she wasn't Anne Elliot pining for her noble Frederick Wentworth. Jason would always be a taker, looking for the easiest path. And Eleanor had changed during the past two years, especially in the last six months. She was no longer the mousy doormat who would give Jason her designs so he could shine while she toiled in the pit.

She'd also changed over the last few days. Shermont had made her feel beautiful, valuable, worthy of cherishing. She wasn't willing to settle for less.

What would Jane Austen do if she encountered a person unworthy of her regard? She descended the rest of the steps. Jason smiled with an appreciative gleam in his eye, but she saw calculation behind it and knew his angelic looks were deceiving. She gave him a polite but cool, I'm-so-not-interested nod as she passed him. Just like Elizabeth Bennet did upon meeting Mr. Wickham after he'd seduced her younger sister Lydia and then accepted Mr. Darcy's money to prevent a scandal by marrying her.

As she exited the inn, she felt such a sense of lightness that she couldn't help grinning. She paused on the top step and resisted the urge to spread her arms to welcome the sunshine.

When her stomach growled, she remembered she'd

intended to go to the dining room for lunch. She didn't want to return just yet. Jason would assume she'd come back to meet him and he could be insistent when he wanted something. Better to avoid him.

Off to her right she noticed the inn owner had set up a yard sale on the side of the curving drive, hoping to coax tourists into spending more money at the inn rather than in town. She walked over to see what was available, giving Jason time to eat and leave the premises.

While the young male attendant listened to his headset and played a hand-held video game, she wandered among the rejected remnants of life in a huge old house. Three matching oil lamps with one unbroken glass globe shade. A piecrust table with water rings marring the top. Frayed baskets and old canning jars.

A golden butterfly flitted past her face. A clouded yellow, she now knew. With a smile she followed its path. In the back of the odds and ends, she found two metal-bound trunks, one with the initials DC carved into the curved, wooden top and the other with MC. Deirdre and Mina's luggage.

Eleanor opened one, expecting it to smell like an old basement. But it must have been stored in the attic. Although it did smell old, there didn't appear to be any mildew. There were a few articles of old clothing inside, the white muslin aged to ecru, the colors faded. Not museum quality, but she could use them to make patterns.

She cocked her head. Maybe because she was so used to taking measurements, the inside of the trunk seemed less deep than she would have thought from the outside. She measured using the span of her hand that she knew was eight inches from thumb to outstretched forefinger. Either the trunk had a four-inch thick base, or there was a false bottom.

Once she knew it had to exist, she found the release latch camouflaged into the design of the lining paper and opened it. She didn't have to check whose trunk she was looking in because Mina's collection of jewelry gave the identity away. Sadly, much of it was tarnished, the faux jewels cloudy and dull. Lying on a paisley silk scarf was a miniature of Uncle Huxley with a butterfly net in one hand, grinning from ear to ear.

Eleanor closed the partition and then purchased both trunks. They were a bit pricey and would probably cost a ton to crate and ship home. She planned to add the Jane Austen novels and the journals to the stash, and then once home she would invite a few friends, including a lawyer and a reporter, to view her souvenirs. They would discover the false bottom and the books, and thus establish their provenance. Although the former owners of the trunks would probably kick themselves for selling them, she didn't feel guilty about the ruse because the books had been a gift and didn't belong to whoever that was. She insisted the boy write a detailed receipt that said "and contents." He promised to move the trunks to her room.

In addition to the lightness, she now felt a sense of destiny. She was meant to be right where she was and meant to have Deirdre and Mina's legacy. She headed back to the main entrance for something to eat. At the door she was nearly run over by a tall, skinny youth talking on a cell phone.

"Yo, Professor. Oops. Hold on." He looked down at Eleanor. "Sorry."

"No problem," she replied, but she stepped aside to wait for him to go by.

He paused outside the door and returned to his conversation. "The tables are full, and they said at least a half hour wait. No, she didn't have your reservation. Okay, but you'll have to talk to her yourself." He clicked off his phone and put it in his pocket before loping the short distance to the parking lot, where he mounted a motorcycle parked among a dozen others.

She'd heard what the young man said and wondered what she should do. Call a cab to go into the village? She could probably get something to eat there before going to the museum. She pulled the brochure from her purse to see if it mentioned restaurants in the area.

One motorcycle rider separated from the bunch and drove his noisy machine up the driveway to stop in front of the steps. She looked up. The driver's worn black leathers clung to his long muscular arms and legs as if they had been custom-made. She could feel him staring at her through his tinted visor.

Bolstered by her recent triumph, she refused to be intimidated. She crossed her arms and stared back.

He removed his helmet and brushed back his long dark hair. Eleanor caught her breath. Omigod!

Eighteen

IT WAS HIM. SHERMONT.

But it couldn't be. She'd left Lord Shermont nearly two hundred years in the past.

"You don't look like a professor," Eleanor said, dumbfounded by the motorcycle rider's uncanny resemblance to her lost love.

"Haven't we…" He touched his eyebrow. "Sorry," he said, taking off his leather glove and sticking out his hand. "James Wright."

"Mr. Wright," she said, shaking his hand. That familiar warmth spread to her heart. It had to be him, yet it couldn't be. Confusion warred with unreasonable hope.

"And you are?"

"Eleanor Pottinger." She felt a stab of pain. He didn't remember her. She pulled her hand away.

"It's not like me to be illogical, but I have to say this even though it's going to sound like the worst pickup line in the world." He gave a self-deprecating chuckle. "Didn't I meet you in my dreams last night?"

She realized with sudden clarity that James Wright must be the other time traveler the ghosts had told her about. James Wright, a.k.a James Bond, Lord Shermont. In the past, he hadn't remembered the future due to his injuries, and in the present, he didn't remember much of the past they had shared. She crossed her arms, trying to hold the disappointment at bay. "What do you recall of this so-called dream?" she asked.

"All the best parts," he said, and his wicked grin sent a blush to her cheeks. "Not much that makes sense. It's all mixed up with spies and secret codes of the Napoleonic War era, which is logical, because that's the topic of my research. I do remember enough to realize I want to get to know you. Are you free for lunch? Dinner? The rest of your life?"

"What about your friends?" She gestured with her chin toward the parking lot where the other riders waited, quite interested in what was going on in front of the steps.

"Ah, yes. My students."

"Then you really are a professor?"

"University of Chicago. I took on this summer semester abroad in order to do research for my thesis. They attend classes Monday through Thursday during the week, and I shepherd them around to historic sites on the weekends."

Eleanor now understood the ghosts' reasoning in choosing this man to take back the first time. They probably thought his experience dealing with young people would help him provide a strong guiding force for a younger Teddy and might keep him out of trouble. Something must have gone wrong, and they set James down in the wrong place.

"I'm doing research on that period myself," she said, not willing to let him get away just yet. "Specifically the clothes of the Regency period. I'm a costume designer. I'll be working on a movie that will be filmed near here." Which was sort of the truth. If she made it to the interview, she knew she would be offered the job.

"Maybe we can compare notes," he said. "Won't you join me for lunch? Uh… me and my students. I have them until seven o'clock tonight. Then I'll deliver them to a lecture on the architecture of Christopher Wren. That's why we came here to the Twixton Manor Inn. When the sixth Lord Digby renovated the original building in 1702, Wren designed the new façade and parterre. Unfortunately the formal gardens are long gone."

"I heard there used to be a fabulous moonlight garden here," she said, hoping to spark his memory.

He shrugged. "I'm not really into gardens. But I am hungry. Back to the subject of lunch."

"Well, I was on my way into the village to get a bite before checking out the Jane Austen House Museum at Chawton Cottage." She handed him the brochure that contained a small map.

He flipped through the single-page, trifold advertisement. "What do they have? Maybe I'll take the kids there after lunch."

"I'm not sure what else they have. I'm going to check out a necklace on display that belonged to Jane Austen."

"A necklace?" He rubbed the scar on his forehead.

She touched her throat, a useless habit since her necklace was no longer there. "An amber cross."

"How very strange."

"What do you mean?"

He reached into his pocket and pulled out a small brown bag. "In the village this morning I wandered into an antique store and felt a strong compulsion to buy this against all reason. Even though I usually analyze every action to death before doing anything, I purchased it straightaway. And now I know why. I bought it for you." He handed her the package. "Go on. Open it."

Inside the brown paper was a bit of folded tissue paper. She opened that and found an amber cross on a delicate silver chain. Eleanor recognized it immediately. Cassandra's cross. Her necklace was similar to Jane's, but with five larger stones and a different filigree pattern around the edges. "I can't accept this."

"I'm afraid you must. It doesn't go with my outfit."

She smiled. "You should give it to your girlfriend—"

"Don't currently have one." He flashed her that toe-curling grin. "But I'm working on it."

"Okay." She couldn't deny a thrill at his statement. "Your mother or sister then. You should give this to someone special."

"I have."

She shook her head and reluctantly held the necklace out to him. "We're total strangers."

"How soon you forget. I know you rather well… from my dreams."

"Perhaps you should tell me everything you remember."

"Later. Over supper." He still didn't reach out to take the necklace. "In the meantime, would you keep it in exchange for helping me this afternoon? You could teach the students about the fashions of the Regency."

"I'm hardly qualified to lecture—"

"Not a formal class. We'll do it like a conversation. You'll talk fashions, and I'll chime in with whatever seems pertinent about the history of the period."

That didn't sound too bad. Even as she thought about it, her fingers curled around the necklace as if they had a mind of their own.

"Excellent," he said, taking her action as agreement. "Now, let's—" His words were cut off by the sound of the motorcycles pulling up.

Once they'd stopped and relative quiet was restored, a young male called from the crowd, "Hey, Professor Wright, who's the babe?"

"Watch your mouth, Mr. Garner. Miss Pottinger is our guest lecturer for the afternoon."

"I thought we were—"

"You are wrong. After lunch we're going to tour the Jane Austen House Museum. Then Miss Pottinger and I will teach you about the fashions and geopolitical aspects of the Regency."

Several girls in the group cheered and clapped.

"Jane Austen? Didn't she write those chick flicks?"

"I recommend everyone pay attention, and you, Mr. Garner, particularly so. Your assignment for the week is a five-page essay on the subject: Did changing fashion of the day reflect the new political thinking of the time, or did the new fashions influence changes in politics?"

All the students groaned.

"Mr. Tobias, may we borrow the spare helmet you keep in your saddle pack?"

"What? I don't—"

"Give it up, Toby," Garner said, glad to have attention pointed elsewhere. "Everyone knows you carry an extra helmet in case you have a chance to pick up an English chick."

Garner caught Professor Wright's glare and ducked his head. Toby handed over a Barbie-pink helmet with cartoon decals all over it.

"My sister's," Toby mumbled.

James held it out to Eleanor. "The bikes are rentals, but we each brought our own gear. Sorry, it's the best we have."

Eleanor hesitated, but not because of the color of the helmet.

"Or I could wear this one and you could wear mine," he said.

She laughed with everyone else at the thought.

"I mean it. I'll do whatever it takes to have you with me," he added for her ears alone.

She'd never ridden on a motorcycle before, never gone off with a perfect stranger. But he wasn't a stranger, not really. What would Jane Austen... No. What would the new Eleanor Pottinger, modern woman, do? She shoved the necklace and packaging into her pocket and took the helmet.

James Wright remounted the motorcycle and indicated the seat behind him with a negligent wave, a gesture so like Lord Shermont it made her smile as she put the helmet on her head.

The choice of restaurants was a disaster. Even though the food was decent, the small dining room was crowded and the atmosphere noisy, keeping conversation to the minimal please-pass-the-salt variety. At the Jane Austen House Museum the students scattered with their notebooks to gather information.

Eleanor found what she was looking for. She stood in front of the glass case that held Jane's familiar amber cross necklace. She traced the outline of the cross on the glass and remembered the happiness on Jane Austen's face when her necklace had been returned to her—its rightful place.

James came up beside her. "That's like the necklace I bought you," he said, a bit of confusion in his voice. "Not an exact twin, but—"

"A sister," Eleanor finished for him. She fished Cassandra's necklace out of her pocket and put it on. "Let's go find your students and talk about the Regency."

Later, when he took her back to the inn, he lingered on the steps even after he'd thanked her and congratulated her on a job well done. She had maintained their interest enough so that they asked questions, which was saying a lot, and had given them good information.

"We make a good team," he said.

She smiled her agreement. "You'd better go if you want to make it to Oxford before seven o'clock. There could be traffic."

"I'll drop them off and come right back."

"That's a long trip, and I know you hadn't planned to stay here another night."

"Who said so?"

"Toby."

"He just flunked the class."

Eleanor shook her head.

"Just kidding," James said.

"I know. Look. I'm exhausted. Jetlag is catching up to me. Why don't you come back tomorrow?"

"It's a date then. I'll be here bright and early."

"Not too early," she cautioned. "I'm not a morning person. Don't tell me you're one who gets up cheerful and talkative before a decent hour."

"Best part of the day. Although I'm more the cheerfully silent, read-my-paper-and-drink-my-coffee type of morning person."

"This doesn't bode well for—"

"Sure it does. Opposites attract. I'll pick you up at nine—"

"Ten."

"Nine o'clock," he said. "But as compensation I can promise you a good cup of coffee which, believe me, is a rarity around here."

"Agreed. Nine. Coffee."

"After breakfast we're taking the kids to Stonehenge."

"We are?"

"You'll enjoy it. A real life Druid is meeting us to talk about… Druid stuff. And an archeologist will talk about the dig inside the stone circle."

"Sounds fabulous. Count me in."

"Then Monday we'll be alone, and I'll take you anywhere you want to go." It was an offhand remark, and yet there lingered a promise of more than a mere sightseeing trip in his eyes.

She touched her necklace as he drove away.

Even though he didn't consciously remember her, she believed his heart recognized the connection between them. She believed in their future together.

Nineteen

Two years later

ELEANOR SAT AT THE DRESSING TABLE PUTTING THE finishing touches on her makeup.

"This place is fantastic," her friend Kristen said from the window. She turned around. "I can't believe it's really yours."

"Every creaking floorboard and leaky pipe," Eleanor said, her words not hiding the pride in her voice. She'd purchased Twixton Manor with a portion of the proceeds from the sale of the Jane Austen books. Even though they'd been renovating for the past year, there was still much to do. And everything had cost more than estimated. The rest of their ambitious plans would have to be adjusted to match cash flow.

"It's so cool that the two of you met here and now you're getting married here." Kristen sighed. "So romantic."

She smiled her agreement. Funny how the first time around she'd had so many of the elements right, almost as if it was destined to be. The right place. The right time. Just the wrong groom. On the second time two years later, James had been the one to suggest getting married in the garden on the anniversary of the day they met. He'd even agreed to a Regency-themed wedding.

She'd chosen Deirdre and Mina's tower rooms to dress in, for old time's sake. There had been no reports of the ghosts making an appearance. Of course, she'd told James some of what had happened, but since he had never remembered much, she'd couched it in terms of a dream.

A knock sounded on the door.

"I'll get that. You'd better put on your dress." Kristen walked into the sitting room. "Who is it?" she called through the door.

"I need to speak to Eleanor."

"You can't see her now. It's bad luck for the groom to see the bride in her dress before the wedding."

Eleanor heard the edge of agitation in his voice, and since he so rarely got upset about anything, she decided she'd better see what the problem was. She grabbed her robe and shrugged it on while she walked. She entered the sitting room as she tied the sash.

"It's all right," Eleanor said to her friend. "Open the door."

James stepped in, already dressed in his wedding finery, *sans* tall hat. The dove-gray tails, embroidered blue waistcoat, and charcoal gray pants were a perfect foil for his snowy cravat and stormy eyes. He carried a present, about ten inches square, wrapped in shiny white paper and tied with white and silver ribbon.

Kristen stabbed a finger in his direction. "You have five minutes," she said before ducking around him and closing the door behind herself.

"She's rather bossy," he said with a glance over his shoulder.

"She's the perfect choice to run the L.A. shop." Since she and James would be living in England, Eleanor planned to open an overseas branch of her successful costume-making business. "What's that?" she asked with a gesture to the box.

"I thought we agreed to not get each other gifts. The reestablishment of the garden would be our present to each other."

"We did."

He stared at her as if expecting her to say more. She cautioned herself to proceed with care. James could be a bit touchy where money matters were concerned. His pride. Not that he was poor by any means. He had a wonderful job at Oxford that he loved, his doctoral thesis had been published to critical acclaim, and he had even turned his research into three successful historical novels. It was just that he had been shocked and amazed, as had she, at the fortune brought in by the Austen papers and first editions.

"Then why did you leave this on my desk?" James had taken one of the rooms in the north wing near their bedroom suite to use as an office.

"Me? I've never seen that before."

"The other wedding gifts are downstairs in the parlor. Why would this one—"

"Did you read the card?"

"There isn't one."

"Perhaps it's inside."

He gave the present to her.

"It's heavy." She set it down on the table and

unwrapped it. Inside was a silver box. The cloisonné design on top depicted a man and woman in Regency dress in a garden. When she opened it, the tinkle of music filled the air. "How lovely."

He looked over her shoulder. "Is there a card?"

"No. Just an old key."

He reached around her and slowly picked it up. "This… is the key to the safe that I gave Huxley after I put the jewelry back… I… I remember. I remember everything. It wasn't a dream. I remember the ghosts, time travel, getting beat up, Lord Shermont, Digby, and…"

She spun around and hugged him.

He pulled back to look her in the eye. "And I remember you, Eleanor. You were there. You weren't dreaming either."

She nodded and shook her head in turn.

"You might have told me."

"Would you have believed me?"

"With my head? Probably not. With my heart… always. I think I fell in love with you the moment we met. Both times." He kissed her gently and thoroughly.

"I wonder how the key got here," she said.

"You don't suppose the jewels are still hidden in the wall after all these years."

"Let's find out," she said with a grin.

There was a knock on the door. "Hey, you two. We have a wedding to go to," Kristen called through the door.

"I guess it will have to wait until after the reception," Eleanor said.

He smacked his head. "I forgot to tell you. Carol's flight finally made it, and she arrived about an hour ago. I asked Helga to put her in the blue room."

Eleanor nodded. One wing of the house was still as it was when it was an inn, which had come in handy with all the wedding guests. Their small staff had been stretched to the limit, even with the addition of a veritable army of temporary workers. "You aren't going to spend the evening talking to your editor about your next book, are you?"

"No. In fact, she wants to talk to you about Deirdre and Mina's journals that you mentioned last time we were in New York. She's thinking book and docudrama. Simultaneous release. Could be big."

"Oh."

"What's the matter? That's good news."

"I only mentioned them in relation to the Jane Austen memorabilia. Their story isn't mine to tell. I really doubt they would want their journals made public."

"Time's up," Kristen called. "On the count of ten, I'm coming in."

"It's not something you have to decide right now. The only thing you have to decide is whether you still want to marry me."

She smiled. "Absolutely. In about fifteen minutes, if I can get dressed that fast." She turned her face toward him for another kiss and wrapped her arms around his neck.

"If you keep that up," he said, "you'll have to get married in your bathrobe."

"Ready or not," Kristen called, "here I—"

James stepped back and swung the door open. Kristen, hand firmly on the knob, stumbled headlong into the room.

"You ladies should really think about hurrying. The ceremony starts in twelve minutes," he added over his shoulder as he left.

Kristen let out a huff of exasperation.

"Don't worry about it," Eleanor said. "I've always been a fast dresser."

"Take your time," Kristen said. She, of course, had been dressed in her light turquoise maid of honor outfit for at least an hour. "It's not every day you get married, and it's not like they can start without you."

Exactly nine minutes later, Eleanor started down the main stairway. Her cream silk dress was made in the empire style, cut full in the back, even though there wasn't a train. Thin blue satin ribbons were interwoven through the lace edging on her small puffed sleeves. The long veil that she had draped over her arm was designed to pool behind her, thus allowing the butterfly pattern of the lace to be visible against the sunny yellow runner she'd chosen. The only jewelry she wore was her engagement ring, the tiny diamond stud earrings James had given her on the anniversary of their first date, and, of course, her amber cross necklace.

Her father waited below to escort her to the garden and walk her down the aisle. He looked quite handsome and slightly uncomfortable in his Regency attire.

"You are the most beautiful bride I have ever seen," he said. "Your mother would have been so proud of you."

She gave him a hug while she blinked away a tear.

At the arbor that marked the beginning of the garden path, they paused for Kristen to arrange the long veil behind her. The wedding planner handed them their bouquets and started Kristen down the aisle.

While they waited for the bridal march to start, Dad said, "This is the moment every father fears from the moment his daughter is born. I guess I'm supposed to say something wise, but…" He patted her hand and swallowed. "I'll drive the getaway car if you want to ditch this shindig. It's not too late."

"Dad! I love James and want to marry him more than anything else in the world."

"Good. I just wanted you to know you had an option. I support whatever decision you make."

"That's the sweetest, most loving thing you could have said." She kissed his cheek. "You are a wise man."

"Are you ready?"

"Yes." As she said it she suddenly felt nervous, not for what she was doing, but the how. Would she get down the aisle without tripping and falling? Would she get the words out without stuttering or mixing them up?

Then she looked up and saw James. The love that shone from his eyes made her feel as though she could do anything, even fly, if he were by her side.

The chairs had been set up facing a flower-covered arbor on the western boundary, and as they said I do, the sunset painted the sky glorious colors. The guests had been instructed to open their small white boxes as the new Mr. and Mrs. James B. Wright walked up the aisle. A cloud of yellow butterflies, their transformation from caterpillars scientifically timed to the day and hour, took flight and swirled around them.

The reception seemed a bit surreal to Eleanor. The disparate pieces of her life came together. Family, school friends, coworkers from various jobs, and new neighbors mixed with people from James's life, some of whom she'd met and others who were complete strangers.

A great number of the guests had gotten into the spirit of the theme and availed themselves of her veritable warehouse of Regency costumes, many from movie productions. At times it felt as if she'd traveled back in time again. Several times she even thought that she caught a glimpse of Deirdre and Mina out of the corner of her eye.

She endured comments that ranged from her great aunt saying, "We'd just about given up on you ever getting married," to her newest employee's gushing appreciation for the invitation, the paid time off, the trip, and the job. If Kristen hadn't rescued her, the new seamstress would have gone on to name who knew what, the air they breathed? The whole experience of so many people at once was a bit nerve-racking and a little exhausting.

Dinner, served in two tents on the south lawn, was a blur. She just pushed her food around on the plate. She'd opted not to have a huge wedding cake in keeping with her theme. The dessert function was fulfilled by an assortment of sweets and fruits served buffet-style in the dining room. Finally it came time for her first dance with her husband.

He escorted her to the center of the ballroom and bowed formally. She curtsied and stepped into his arms.

"What's the matter?" he whispered as he led her in wide sweeping turns.

"When I wanted everyone to share my happiness, I didn't realize how overwhelming three hundred and fifty guests can be. How do you remain so cool and calm?"

"I've been to balls Prinny gave at the palace with two thousand five hundred guests."

The remark was so Lord Shermont, she had to smile.

"That's better. The sun is shining again."

"It's night. The moon is already out."

"Is it? I can't tell. You are the sun and the moon to me."

"I wonder how the new flowers look in the moonlight?" The garden had been her idea, something she had supervised while he was busy with the architect and contractor.

He raised an eyebrow. "Quite suddenly I find the subject of gardens fascinating. Shall we continue this conversation outside?" He looked over her head at the other couples who had joined them on the dance floor. With deft moves, he swept her across the room and out the door to the terrace. Hand in hand they ran down the steps and up the white shell path to the moonlight garden.

James rolled to his back and cuddled Eleanor to his side. He looked forward to their little chats, something he once would have thought impossible.

She crossed her hands on his chest and propped her chin on her hands. But she was silent.

"I can see the wheels turning," he said, tapping her forehead. "What's on your mind, Mrs. Wright?"

"Mmmm, I like the sound of that." She snuggled closer. "Actually, I was thinking about that key."

He groaned. "I knew it. You want to go check it out, don't you? It's two-thirty in the morning. We really should get some sleep. We're leaving in a few hours on our honeymoon."

"And where are we going, Mr. It's-my-prerogative-to-surprise-you?"

"I've kept you in suspense long enough. I've rented an island, a small island in the Caribbean. We will be totally alone. No students, no employees, no cell phones or email. Just you, me, and a well-stocked bar and refrigerator."

"Sounds lovely. Ah… no restaurant? Then I hope it comes with a cook."

"How can we be alone if… you mean you can't cook?"

"Never learned. My mother died when I was young, and my grandmother pretty much raised me. She was a lousy cook, preferred restaurants, and thought the microwave was among the top ten inventions of all time, right up there with the wheel and sliced bread. She taught me the art of ordering takeout."

"There's an art to it?"

"Sure. There's no second chance for the sweet and

sour sauce or extra Parmesan cheese you forgot to order. No waiter to bring you butter or sour cream for the baked potato. If you order from the same place on a regular basis, say Thai on Tuesday, you're likely to get the same delivery person. If you tip well, you get faster service, and they might throw in an order of buffalo wings or cheese sticks for free."

"Okay. What about in college? First apartment? I couldn't afford takeout then."

"Neither could I, so I picked roommates who could cook."

James chuckled. "Well, you've done it again. I was always the roommate who could cook."

"You?"

"Is that so surprising? My first job was a dishwasher. I hated that, so I worked my way up. I put myself through school working in the kitchens of several restaurants. How do you think I got so good with a knife?"

"There's something sexy about a man with skilled hands."

"You can give me that look all you want." He looked down at himself. "But the body will need time to recuperate."

Only a man who had already made love four times that night could say such a thing with a smile.

She patted his stomach. "In that case, let's try the key." She sat and climbed over him. "Come on. Throw some clothes on."

He didn't move. "You don't really expect to find anything, do you?"

"No. But I won't able to sleep until we look. And

since we're leaving, we won't have another chance for two weeks." She pulled her nightgown over her head.

He swung his legs over the side of the bed with a sigh of resignation. "I suppose I won't get any sleep either until you know there's nothing there."

"Stop being so grumpy. You're as curious as I am." She tied the sash of her robe and waited for him by the door.

"But I can control my inquiring proclivity and simply wonder about the key as I fall asleep." He grabbed a pair of jeans and pulled them on. He snagged a T-shirt as they left the room and yanked it over his head as they walked down the hall.

They descended the stairs in silence.

The old estate office was in a section not yet renovated, and what furniture was left had been draped in dustcovers. Eleanor put the music box on the desktop and opened it. Tinkling music played.

"I don't know why you brought that," he said.

She shrugged. "I went to get the key, and it just seemed right to bring it along."

They went to the appropriate place on the wall. The wainscoting wouldn't budge.

"It appears to have been painted over a number of times," he said. "I should have brought some tools." He turned around, moved the music box to a chair, and pulled the dustcover off the large darkly stained desk. He found a rusty letter opener in the drawer and used it like a knife to score around the molding. Still the wainscoting wouldn't budge.

"I can't wait to see what's inside," she said, practically bouncing with excitement.

"Someone must have noticed it was loose and nailed it down," he said.

"That would have been me," a male voice said.

James and Eleanor spun around with a gasp.

"Hello, my dears," Deirdre said.

Two fully materialized male ghosts stood against the far wall, and Mina and Deirdre sat on chairs in front of them. She introduced the ghost who had spoken as her husband, Karel Van Stille.

Mina presented her husband, Narve Van Stille. "Brothers," she said, as if Eleanor wouldn't have known from the names or the fact that they looked like identical twins, both tall and blond with blue eyes the color of a deep arctic sea. The men bowed formally, clicking their heels.

James responded in kind despite being underdressed for such formal address. Eleanor curtseyed.

"I'm so glad to see you," Eleanor said. "Thank you for everything. We bought the manor house with the proceeds from the—"

"We know, and we couldn't be more thrilled with the way everything has turned out," Deirdre said. "We see you got Uncle Huxley's wedding gift—the music box."

Mina crossed her arms. "We've been waiting here for hours. It took you long enough to figure out where the key—"

"It's their wedding night," Deirdre said in a low voice to her sister.

"Well, it's not like they never—"

"Mina!" Deirdre said with horror and censure in her voice. After clearing her throat, she turned to

James. "Please continue with your task. We're quite as anxious as Eleanor to see what's inside."

"You mean… you don't know?" he asked.

"We were away for twelve years, and since we didn't know where to look…"

"Uncle Huxley gave us the key soon after we sailed," Mina added. "He said when we returned we should have Lord Shermont show us. Well, you know how that turned out. And since we had plenty of our own jewelry…" She looked up at Narve. "Our husbands are very generous."

The men clearly adored their wives and vice versa.

"We did search for the jewelry but never found anything," Deirdre said.

James went to work, using the letter opener to pry away the molding.

"It was a lovely wedding," Deirdre said.

"I thought I saw you," Eleanor said with a smile.

"We quite enjoyed the dancing and the champagne."

"Perhaps a bit too much," Deirdre said, glancing at her sister.

"No such thing as too much champagne," Narve said, patting his wife's shoulder.

"Man, a lot of nails here," James said.

"If a thing is worth doing, it's worth doing right," Karel said.

"He was always building or fixing something," Deirdre explained.

"Why don't you ask them about their journals while I work," James said.

"What about them?" Deirdre looked a bit surprised.

"It's nothing," Eleanor said.

"It can't be *nothing* if James mentioned it," Mina said.

"Just a silly idea James's editor had about publishing them and making a docudrama, but I know how much you two value your privacy so..." Eleanor's voice trailed off when she realized the girls weren't listening anymore. They were in a four-way whispered conversation with their husbands.

They broke apart, and Deirdre nodded to her sister.

"We think that is a fine idea," Mina said.

"You're joking."

"Noooo. The journals tell of our husbands' and Uncle Huxley's scientific accomplishments. The two of us took an active role. Rather remarkable for the time. So we rather like the idea of everyone knowing about our work."

"Except," Deirdre prompted.

"I'm getting to that." Mina shook her head slightly. "Except we would prefer if you edited out the um... shall we call them the risqué parts?"

"And..." Deirdre said.

"You should have just done this yourself," Mina said to her sister before turning back to Eleanor. "And if they make our story into a movie, we don't want anyone plain to play our parts."

Their faces were so serious Eleanor stifled her laughter. "I guess I can manage that."

"I've got it," James cried in triumph, moving the wainscoting aside.

They all clustered around. Eleanor solemnly took the key from the music box and handed it to him. After some initial resistance, the key turned. James pulled on the door, and it opened a crack. He put his weight into it and pulled the door wide open with a loud creak.

They all gasped as one.

"It's there," James said. "Just as when I unloaded the portmanteau and put it all back." He knelt on the floor in front of the cabinet.

Eleanor sat cross-legged beside him. The three-foot metal cube was chock full of flat leather boxes of assorted sizes and colors. He handed her a black one six by ten inches. She opened it.

"My sapphires," Deirdre said, clasping her hands below her chin.

A necklace of linked square sapphires with a drop of one huge pear-shaped stone rested on the black velvet lining with a matching bracelet and earrings. The gold links and bright blue jewels shone as if on display at Tiffany's.

The next box, covered in green velvet, contained Mina's emerald parure. The next... a diamond tiara. A ruby parure with two matching brooches. A necklace of amber beads and another of ebony disks had not fared as well. The beads were fine, but the stings had disintegrated. James kept unloading boxes, and she opened a rainbow of every jewel she knew and some she'd never heard of.

Mina clapped her hands. "It's just like Christmas morning."

"Except this is our wedding gift to Eleanor and James," Deirdre said.

"Oh, we can't accept—"

"You must. What are we going to do with them?"

"Your heirs..."

Deirdre shook her head sadly. "If the jewels will help defray the cost of your restoration and future preservation of our beloved home, we are well satisfied."

"It's time for us to go," Narve said gently.

The four figures floated back toward the far wall and began to fade.

Eleanor jumped up, dumping the jewelry on the floor, and stepped forward. "Wait! Will we ever see you again?"

"No. You have mended the mistakes of the past and set yourself on the right path for the future. We are released and can move on to other activities." Deirdre said. "This is good-bye."

The gentlemen bowed, and Mina, with a sad smile and a tear in her eye, waved. They all faded into mist.

James stepped to Eleanor's side and slipped his arm around her waist.

Suddenly Mina reappeared. "Of course, we will watch over all your children. But it would be sweet if you named at least two girls Mina and Deirdre. Oh, and invite your friend Kristen back soon. She and James's architect friend are perfect—"

"Mina!" Deirdre's disembodied voice crackled with electricity.

"Oops!" With a snap, Mina disappeared.

Eleanor turned into James's embrace, her gentle tears falling unchecked.

"What did she mean by all your children and at least two girls?" he said.

"I'm sure it's nothing," Eleanor said with a sniff.

"There's no way they can see into the future." She smiled into his chest, hugging her secret to her heart just a little longer.

The End
(or The Beginning, depending on your point of view.)

Acknowledgments

Thank you—

To my family, your unfailing faith always conquers my self-doubts. You guys are the best.

To Lucienne Diver, Agent Extraordinaire. Need more be said?

To my editor Deb Werksman, for being right, even if it did mean more work. You made this a better book with your wisdom.

To my talented critique partner Mary Micheff, for everything from brainstorming to proofreading, but most of all, for your friendship.

To my great boss Darly Doyle, for your understanding and encouragement.

—I could not have done it without you all.

And last, but not least, to Jane Austen for providing so many hours of reading pleasure and such wonderful characters. I didn't want her stories to end.

About the Author

Laurie Brown loves sharing stories that follow alpha heroes and spunky heroines on madcap adventures to a happy ending. Plus writing gets her out of housework.

She lives in a Chicago suburb and works at a library, a dream job for a confirmed bookaholic. She loves to hear from readers, especially that they laughed out loud while reading her books.

HUNDREDS OF YEARS TO REFORM A RAKE

BY LAURIE BROWN

HIS TOUCH PULLED HER IRRESISTIBLY ACROSS THE MISTS OF TIME

Deverell Thornton, the ninth Earl of Waite, needs Josie Drummond to come back to his time and foil the plot that would destroy him. Josie is a modern career woman, thrust back in time to the sparkling Regency period, where she must contend with the complex manners and mores of the day, unmask a dangerous charlatan, and in the end, choose between the ghost who captivated her or the man himself—but can she give her heart to a notorious rake?

"A smart, amusing, and fun time travel/Regency tale."
—*All About Romance*

"Extremely well written…A great read from start to finish." —*Revisiting the Moon's Library*

"Blends Regency, contemporary and paranormal romance to a charming and very entertaining effect." —*Book Loons*

978-1-4022-1013-6 • $6.99 U.S./$8.99 CAN

Lady Anne
AND THE
HOWL
IN THE
DARK

by Donna Lea Simpson

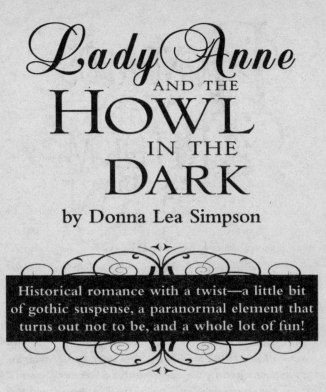

> Historical romance with a twist—a little bit of gothic suspense, a paranormal element that turns out not to be, and a whole lot of fun!

LADY ANNE ADDISON IS A RATIONAL AND COURAGEOUS woman. So when she's summoned by a frightened friend to Yorkshire to prove or disprove the presence in their woods of a menacing wolf—or werewolf—she takes up the challenge.

Lady Anne finds the Marquess of Darkefell to be an infuriatingly unyielding man. Rumors swirl and suspects abound. The Marquess is indeed at the middle of it all, but not in the way that Lady Anne had suspected...and now he's firmly determined to win her in spite of everything.

978-1-4022-1791-3 • $6.99 U.S. / $7.99 CAN

A *Duke* TO *Die For*

BY AMELIA GREY

THE RAKISH FIFTH DUKE OF BLAKEWELL'S UNEXPECTED AND shockingly lovely new ward has just arrived, claiming to carry a curse that has brought each of her previous guardians to an untimely end...

Praise for Amelia Grey's Regency romances:

"This beguiling romance steals your heart, lifts your spirits and lights up the pages with humor and passion." —Romantic Times

"Each new Amelia Grey tale is a diamond. Ms. Grey...is a master storyteller." —Affaire de Coeur

"Readers will be quickly drawn in by the lively pace, the appealing protagonists, and the sexual chemistry that almost visibly shimmers between." —Library Journal

978-1-4022-1767-8 • $6.99 U.S./$7.99 CAN

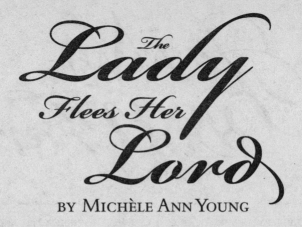

The Lady Flees Her Lord

BY MICHÈLE ANN YOUNG

DESPERATE FOR PEACE AND SAFETY...

Lucinda, Lady Denbigh, is running from a husband who physically and emotionally abused her. Posing as a widow, she seeks refuge in the quiet countryside, where she meets Lord Hugo Wanstead. Returning from the wars with a wound that won't heal, he finds his estate impoverished, his sleep torn by nightmares, and brandy the only solace. When he meets Lucinda, he thinks she just might give him something to live for...

Praise for Michèle Ann Young's *No Regrets*

"Dark heroes, courageous heroines, intrigue, heartbreak, and heaps of sexual tension. Do not miss this fabulous new author." —Molly O'Keefe, *Harlequin Superromance*

"Readers will never want to put her book down!" —Bronwyn Scott, author of *Pickpocket Countess*

978-1-4022-1399-1 • $6.99 U.S. / $7.99 CAN

No Regrets

BY MICHÈLE ANN YOUNG

"A remarkable talent that taps your emotions with each and every page." —Gerry Russel, award winning author of *The Warrior Trainer*

A MOST UNUSUAL HEROINE

Voluptuous and bespectacled, Caroline Torrington feels dowdy and unattractive beside the slim beauties of her day. Little does she know that Lord Lucas Foxhaven thinks her curves are breathtaking, and can barely keep his hands off her.

"The suspense and sexual tension accelerate throughout." —*Romance Reviews Today*

978-1-4022-1016-7 • $6.99 U.S./$8.99 CAN

THE PRINCE OF MIDNIGHT

BY LAURA KINSALE

New York Times bestselling author

"Readers should be enchanted."
—*Publishers Weekly*

INTENT ON REVENGE, ALL SHE WANTS FROM
HIM IS TO LEARN HOW TO KILL

Lady Leigh Strachan has crossed all of France in search of S.T. Maitland, nobleman, highwayman, and legendary swordsman, once known as the Prince of Midnight. Now he's hiding out in a crumbing castle with a tame wolf as his only companion, trying to conceal his deafness and desperation. Leigh is terribly disappointed to find the man behind the legend doesn't meet her expectations. But when they're forced on a quest together, she discovers the dangerous and vital man behind the mask, and he finds a way to touch her ice cold heart.

"No one—repeat, no one—writes historical romance better." —Mary Jo Putney

978-1-4022-1397-7 • $7.99 U.S./$8.99 CAN